Deadly Inception

Martin Dawes

For Ali,

with thanks for everything.

Table of Contents

Prologue *7*

Chapter 1 .... *8*

Chapter 2 .... *13*

Chapter 3 .... *19*

Chapter 4 .... *24*

Chapter 5 .... *31*

Chapter 6 .... *34*

Chapter 7 .... *42*

Chapter 8 .... *49*

Chapter 9 .... *53*

Chapter 10 .... *60*

Chapter 11 .... *63*

Chapter 12 .... *70*

Chapter 13 .... *75*

Chapter 14 .... *79*

Chapter 15 .... *89*

Chapter 16 .... *96*

Chapter 17 .... *100*

Chapter 18 110

Chapter 19 115

Chapter 20 122

Chapter 21 126

Chapter 22 135

Chapter 23 139

Chapter 24 146

Chapter 25 152

Chapter 26 161

Chapter 27 167

Chapter 28 176

Chapter 29 184

Chapter 30 190

Chapter 31 194

Chapter 32 198

Chapter 33 204

Chapter 34 210

Thorswick Hall 210

Chapter 35 218

Chapter 36 225

Chapter 37 231

Chapter 38 237

Chapter 39	241
Chapter 40	246
Chapter 41	252
Chapter 42	257
The Author	265

Prologue

This had to be the end. Of me. And the inheritance. Ending here. Amidst explosions. Scything metal and staccato hammering. Rotors coming closer. Blasting khaki dust. Too late for me though. I'll go in their tornado. The burning in the back fading. Shouting. A face close up. Sweaty and bearded. Much loved. Saying something. Shaking my shoulder. I know what he wants. The words shaping through black whiskers. 'Hold on. You don't do this'.

What can he mean? He doesn't understand. This end is right. My blood feeding this ground. Some legacies age badly. Generations of mine have passed here. Some with the flag. Others disguised. Always with promises. Drunk the tea. Played the politics. Took the drugs. Lived with the mountain. And women. Sometimes the men. Time for it all to stop. The world is far from what it was. No longer a place for what they did. Nor me. The inheritor.

The hammering is slowing. Deep chirping now. From the helicopters. Delivering death streams from the sky. The face has gone. Others are lifting. Thumping in my head. The back an agony. I thought it got more peaceful at the end. Just my luck.

Chapter 1

Thorswick Village, Oxfordshire.

Victory hung on the last ball of the post siesta session. Not a soul stirred on the crowded veranda of the thatched pavilion, or under the deep shade of the old oaks around the church. In the humid October heat sweated palms gripped amber glasses of beer and cider. Tension transfixed them all.

'I can't watch,' breathed young Jimmy Robinson. He did though, of course. On the pitch an unprecedented drama was reaching its climax. In the fetid heat, tiny Thorswick was one ball and four runs away from claiming the county village cricket championship. Nothing less than a boundary from a single strike would do it. Never had Thorswick cricket achieved anything like this, and they were doing it against Hathleigh, a side whose name was engraved on the waiting trophy with impressive regularity.

The bowler was ready for the final effort. He had muttered with his captain. Then flicked his arm right and left to send the rest of the team to the edges of the pitch. Turning now, rubbing the ball down the front of his trousers, his feet began the shuffle that would turn into a thundering run. But he was forced to stop. At the far end the batsman had moved off the wicket and imperiously held up his gloved hand.

The escape of breath from the spectators was audible. They all stared at the batsman as he looked around the field placings, and seemed to take in the church, stately home and village as if seeing it for the first time.

The spectators wondered what might have distracted him. There was nothing moving behind the bowler's arm. No cat or stray dog wandering onto the boundary. Not a single plastic cup or discarded napkin twitched on the crisped, brown grass of the outfield. After coming in at a lowly number seven the player had treated them to a virtuoso performance, lifting hopes and leading many to wonder why his obvious talent had not been revealed before. He was usually a steady, unflashy type. Today he was displaying a level of skill and intensity usually seen only in first class matches. His pause now, after a brutally effective performance, was like the breaking of a spell.

Despite the baleful stare of the bowler, and the inquiring eyebrow of the umpire, the man they knew as Ash still seemed reluctant to pat down his bat and receive the last ball. It might have been assumed he was savouring the moment, or suffering from a momentary attack of nerves. In fact he was seriously conflicted.

Ashley Moxon had seriously dropped his guard. He was a man who needed to live in shadows. Now, by his own hand, he was about to become a local hero. A person talked about and, chillingly, remembered. He could not have it.

Something about the heat and nostalgia for other games on dusty pitches far, far away had led him astray. Setting his mood also was the increasing tempo of an action coming to fruition in the lands he still considered home. It was something that would finally bring retribution for souls he loved. Even closure. Today's play, so innocent in comparison, was a welcome distraction while he could do nothing but wait. But now he must throw the game, disappoint the village and return himself to being a nearly man.

Taking two steps down the wicket he looked fixedly at the ground for the moment and gave it a couple of prods with the end of his bat, before crouching in front of the wicket for the final ball.

From his vantage point down the wicket, umpire Walter "Well" Able, watched as he set, and didn't like the look of him one little bit. 'C'mon on boy,' he muttered. 'Only one more to go. You can do it.'

"Well" Able was a Thorswick man, born and raised. He made it his business to know what was going on. However, Ash was still something of a mystery. His playing talent was obvious, but he seemed adept at never revealing much about himself. There was something else too. He tried to describe it one night to Maureen, who ran the bar.

'He seems to take everything in. What do you call that?

'Absorbent?' Maureen also did the cleaning.

'Sort of, but more than that.'

Maureen liked a puzzle though. 'Instinct?', she hazarded.

Walter Able rolled the word around for a moment, before his face gave the slightest glimmer of a light bulb moment. 'Got it. He's intuitive. Or,' he hesitated. 'Empathetic. That's what he is. And I've never seen anything like it.'

Crouching over the wicket "Well" Able heard the bowler running in behind him. The man was more than competent, and might even be described as talented. Right now he was putting everything into a final, lung busting effort to smash the wicket of a batsman whose shoulders had suddenly slumped. With an explosive grunt the ball was unleashed in a cartwheel of legs and arms. Riding the heated air, with polished surface uppermost and stitching at an angle, "Well" Able saw it curve, cut viciously into the ground before heading with the speed of a striking snake for off stump.

It deserved to succeed. At the moment of release however, there was a change. Ash squared, rising on the bat. In a blink he was perfectly placed to take that last precious effort midway through the final stage of its destructive flight. The sweet spot in fashioned willow connected, the bat following through as the red spot travelled upwards in a sky flecked with gossamer clouds. It was a six from the moment of connection. Two more runs than was actually needed.

'Over', said Umpire "Well" Able. 'And match', he added unnecessarily to the bowler, who was still watching the fate of his last effort.

The dot was falling beyond the small road that skirted the cricket pitch, impacting unseen to the sound of breaking glass around the small row of aged cottages. From the pavilion there arose a wild whoop and cheers, mixed with the thumping of feet beating a tattoo on the floorboards. 'You could at least have hit your own bloody house,' said Able.

Behind the deep peak of the claret and yellow cap, the grey eyes flickered. 'My aim was off. It hit the blue one next door.' He really should not have done it. But the man had fallen for his lure. He had bowled to hit the perfectly good piece of ground Ash had patted with his bat. Ash was not a superstitious person. He could not afford to be. Even so, as soon as the ball left the man's hand, he knew his final mind game of the match had worked. It would be churlish not to accept the omen.

There was no time for more self-examination. Ash was engulfed by a rush of players from the pavilion, and even some from Hathleigh. "Well" Able noticed a grimace of real pain as Ash received a particularly enthusiastic back slap before he was hoisted onto shoulders for the triumphant procession to the pavilion.

Able let them go. There would be plenty of time before the presentation and the party would be long. In the meantime he savoured the moment. It was certainly one for the annals. He looked around. Taking in the bucolic familiarity of his village and the milling throng below the low thatch roof of the pavilion. Never mind that the oaks were dying, the square towered church was falling down and best sellers were being written by computer code. As long as men and women hit balls without a bloody machine being involved, all was right in the world.

A thought occurred. He would need that ball. At least the blue cottage was empty, and had been for nearly a year. Someone would have to go and search around. A presentation case in the pavilion could be made and the ball taken out for special club occasions. The annual dinner for example. That's how traditions are made. You simply couldn't have enough of them.

He pulled the wickets to the sound of loud clapping and whistling from the clubhouse. Ash was being applauded up the wooden steps where he turned, briefly touched the brim of his cap and, with a sweep of his arm, indicated the open door. It was time to party. Not that Ash stepped through. He caught the eye of young Jimmy, who slipped through the press and handed over a mobile. It was an expensive one.

With nods, smiles and a few 'I'll be there in a sec.', Ash edged along the veranda pressing buttons as he went. His phone was alive with messages. In a secure chat room was the information he badly wanted to hear. 'The bride is about to arrive. Principal guests will be travelling within the day.'

Ash checked the timing. He had less than twenty four hours. A tremor passed through him as his heart picked up pace. Pause, he thought. No need to rush. He had known for weeks what he would do at this moment. Briefly he sent a message into the room. 'We're on. I'll fix the bouquet.'

'Ash!' It was Jimmy, eyes shining, his own mobile readied. 'I need a picture of you for the league and our drumbeat account. All I've got so far is lots of your cap!'

His efforts were forestalled by the pavilion door being swung back with a loud bang as Thorswick's Captain and Jimmy's father heaved his way through beer in hand. 'You,' he boomed. 'In here. We've taken a vote and we decided you still have to wear the newbie blazer, you poor sap, but you don't need to buy a drink. Hurry up, it's like Hamlet without whatsisname in there.'

Ash went, slipping his mobile into pocket of his whites. Face smiling, and cap still pulled low over his face as he passed Jimmy, he shrugged into the proffered, stained blazer, his mind calculating. He knew all too well it was one thing to bait a trap, quite another to make sure nothing happened in the next few hours to spook the prey. There was also a lot to be done to get everything in a row. He needed to calm down. Successful closure was still a long way off. Before him people were cheering again. Raising their glasses. The noise was incredible. He was going to have to spend time here. Minutes he could ill afford. It would be too odd just to disappear.

Ash smiled. Nodding around. Thanks. He would have a bitter shandy, heavy on the lemonade. No definitely. Just for the moment. He was dehydrated and didn't want to add to whatever was down his blazer. Laughter.

Chapter 2

Walter "Well" Able eased his bulk through the crush to his stool at the side of the bar. With a beam and wink that gave full benefit of her green eye shadow, Maureen pushed over the waiting pint of mild before addressing the counter in general.

'One at a time bless you. I'm all on my lonesome. Now which of you lovely fellas is first?'

The aged pavilion was suited to clubbable conviviality. Military badges and gaudy sporting pennants jostled gold lettered honour boards bearing the names of Presidents, Honourable Secretaries and Captains. Amidst the memorabilia were faded pictures of beneficiaries, the Clarey name from the big house being prominent amongst the pointed beards, mutton chops and moustaches. The latest portrait though, was not of that breed. It depicted a man in a red tie smiling through full lips and cheeks, his blue eyes hard in a hairless head. Amidst all was a large electronic screen showing a montage of images from the cricket game. Young Jimmy had been busy.

From his roost "Well" Able caught the eye of one of the elderly Thorswick players, who shambled to the summons. 'Sorry about the dropped catch,' mumbled Ben Whistledown. 'Had it right there. Easy as pie. Don't even want to blame the sun. Just slipped through.'

It should have been a certainty. The batsman was already walking to the pavilion. Instead the entire field watched Ben Whistledown shout 'Mine', as if the point was ever in contention, put himself into a squat, rise up and drop it. 'Well,' said Able, 'at least we got him next ball.'

Ben scratched through his thick beard as he looked across at the visiting team. 'I think they're still arguing about that.'

'Nonsense. One of my easier decisions. Trapped right in front of wicket.'

'Robinson didn't even bother to appeal it. He thought it was well off.'

'Yes, he's young. He'll learn.' Able took a slurp of his mild. He did not think much of Whistledown. He was not really a club man, and apparently made a living as some kind of aid worker while being all too apparent around Thorswick. Often he was in a Pakistani shalmar kameez or, in winter, a plate like woollen hat from Afghanistan. Carrying on like Mahatma Ghandi might have been alright for the youngest of the last Clarey resident at the Hall, but "Well" Able felt such affectations were best left to aristocrats. On this occasion though, Able was prepared to overlook the rubbish fielding, because he wanted a favour.

'Get over to blue cottage will you, and have a search around? I want that ball.'

Whistledown scratched his beard. 'Well I'd have to ask the owner first, obviously, and from the noise it made it sounded like something got busted. So they might be annoyed.'

Able was surprised. The house had been empty for months and not even on the market. The former owner was taken away to die in an old peoples' home having come to Thorswick late in life. His evaporation was so far in the past that speculation about the house had long since dried. 'I didn't know it was sold,' Able said testily, 'when did that happen?'

'A van came, when was it? Must have been about three weeks ago. It was just after the Saudi Airforce bombed that hospital in Yemen, and I was already up to my eyeballs with villages getting swept away by a mudslide in Afghanistan. I thought I could get a call into the Taliban to get aid moving faster there, and wanted to tip off a few websites about the origins of the bomb. Anyway, in the midst of all that, a van arrived and a couple of blokes started unloading stuff.'

It was always like this. Any conversation with Ben Whistledown involved a swim in an ocean of disaster. Able had no idea why a bunch of foreigners in the Middle East were destroying hospitals, or why it mattered. He gave Whistledown a brutal glare.

'And an owner?'

Whistledown looked glum. 'The removal chaps didn't know much about all that. They'd picked up in Lincolnshire and were told to put everything where they thought best. Today I saw some curtains twitching, so I guess the owner is in.'

Able nodded a dismissal. 'Looks like it's your round,' he added maliciously. A dropped catch of that magnitude required amends.

'It was made in Britain', said Whistledown as he turned to the bar. 'The bomb in Yemen. Took the place apart.'

Able shook his head. Ben really was a bizarre man. He seemed to take pleasure in finding out matters of no consequence, and his idea of what makes for conversation in a clubhouse left a lot to be desired. At least he was wise enough to get him a treble, which was just at his lips when the door of the pavilion opened. Framed by the bursting orange rays of the October sun was a tall young woman, with a cricket ball clasped in her fist.

Silence fell. Maggie Johnson would have preferred a far less dramatic introduction to her new neighbours. Something that did not involve starring, sweaty blokes and a cricket ball taking out several panes of her cottage. Also, as she feared in a place like this, her arrival raised significantly the percentage of people of colour. 'Yours?', she managed self-consciously. 'I presume.' And then felt more like an idiot.

The ball was taken by Dunstan, the home team's gully specialist, a silver fox with a lean hungry look, honed by the need to fund two divorces. With his other arm and a low bow, he swept her over the threshold with a cheery, 'and what's yours?'

Someone new to Thorswick was always going to be a source of curiosity. Having gained a Pino Grigio, Maggie informed listeners that Blue Cottage was indeed hers. It was all a bit of a surprise. A bequest from an old family contact, which came 'out of the blue', and, with a smile, 'no pun intended'. It was especially surprising as she had never met him, even as a child.

With a look that could have encompassed the entire bar she asked if anyone in the village knew much about him? She would be interested to know more.

'This guy lives next door,' said Dunstan indicating Ash. 'He might know something, and he's the one that hit your place.'

Maggie turned to the person indicated, taking in the public health hazard he was wearing and his swiftly supressed annoyance. Ash was using the distraction of Maggie's arrival to make for the door. Like a cartoon character he froze guiltily mid move. He was now going to have to make polite conversation, while his heart jolted along with each new mobile message.

'Sorry,' he shrugged, 'and I heard you speaking about the owner of Blue Cottage. He moved to a care home before I arrived, but I can tell you he was extremely well thought of. It sounds as though he was a thoroughly nice gentleman.'

'Thanks,' she said, and meant it. Then, 'the jacket?' she asked, doing a small wave with her wine glass to suggest an understanding that there must be some deeper meaning, rather than taste.

Dunstan butted in. Keen to engage her again. 'It's the newbie coat. Its worn by the latest recruit.' He smiled at her in a winning way. 'We like our traditions around here. If someone were to get you in the club, you'd have to wear it.'

A momentary silence after this was broken by Ash. 'I suppose it's as good a way as any to make sure the newbie works hard to get someone else to join', he said smoothly. 'And yes, tradition and all these emblems of ships and regiments long gone. The snare of history's tentacles, and empire in particular.'

Maggie blinked. For the briefest of moments, she thought about saying something about them both being, uniquely in the current company, colonial legacies.

'Looks like it's time for the presentation,' said Ash, indicating movement around the portraits and a table being set up. 'You see what I mean about tradition? They're proud to stand in front of aristocrats whose ancestors made money from slaves and sugar before coming to the countryside to rule over more peasants.'

It was a strange conversational tack, not least because he seemed distracted even as the words came in an even, considered way. She dismissed the thought that he was trying to impress her. That had happened countless times, and she could usually spot the drift before words were even uttered. At least he was proving interesting. She nodded her head toward the front. 'Is the picture up there that Ellroy man?', she asked.

'The same. Norman. Carrying on the tradition of making a fortune at the expense of billions.' Ash paused. 'Global entrepreneur, current owner of Thorswick Hall with all its titles and Honorary President of Thorswick Cricket Club. It's said he farms data from ninety five percent of the world's population and gets the remainder if ever a canoe goes up a jungle tributary in South America. A man who saw early the potential for data enhanced weapons.'

'I knew some of that, but not that he lived here.'

'He doesn't, most of the time. But he likes to wear tweeds'

'He basically runs our government, if you believe what's reported'

'You should be more careful about what you read,' said Ash lightly. 'As we are often reminded by the party, we are a democracy.'

Dunstan was giving him a disapproving look. Perhaps he heard, or maybe it was because "Well" Able was speaking, his pink head glistening as he rocked backwards and forwards. 'Before we get onto the presentation of the Summer Challenge Cup to the captain of the winning team,' he paused and gave a massive wink, 'and that's Thorswick, by the way, some news just in about our generous supporter Norman Ellroy.'

The big screen on the wall changed to show a live stream from a horse race meeting. Norman Ellroy, in a dark morning suit, stood with a woman in a silken yellow ensemble holding out a cup. A horse tossed its head, flecking them both. The caption running at the bottom read; Buzkashi owner Norman Ellroy receiving the King William Cup from Georgina Vavascour-Rhodes, wife of Minister, the Right Honourable Carrick Vavasour-Rhodes, MP. That was Ash's minister. The one who chaired the Intelligence Committee and oversaw the growing number of agencies charged with spying and counter intelligence.

'Buzkashi', Ash thought as he watched the niceties of the photo opportunity. Interesting. Buzkashi was a Central Asian passion, involving a wild melee of horsemen, riding their wild-eyed mounts as they competed for a goat carcass. It was more than a game. It was a bonding experience and, historically, a training for the hordes that rode from the steppes to challenge Empires. In so many ways it was war by other means. And then he stiffened. A woman in a large pink hat craned forward to get a better view, briefly exposing a face before it turned swiftly away.

Bearded and dark. Sharp. An individual with no right to be there at all. A killer. Transplanted. Hobnobbing with His Majesty's Secretary of State for Security and one of the most powerful billionaire's in the world. Years of training prevented Ash from giving any sign of the shock he felt. Even so, his armpits prickled beneath that hideous jacket.

'As I say. A big day!' "Well" Able was back on song. He gestured Young Jimmy forward with his mobile. 'Before we go any further I just want the man who gave us such a thrilling batting display this afternoon to come and take a bow.'

The bar erupted in cheers. Feet again thumped the wooden flooring as the entire gathering swung around. But the man they sought was not there. Looking back at them was Maggie and Dunstan, while hanging on a shield bearing the Clarey coat of arms was a stained blazer.

Chapter 3

Ash left through a side door to the changing rooms, pausing momentarily to make sure he was not followed. He then headed for the trees. Amongst their struggling boughs it was quiet, and he needed that.

'Safedeen Khan' Whispering the name, while registering how the sound seem to rhyme with the rustling leaves. He said it again. This time, adding a bemused 'well, well', and taking an appropriate sigh. Ash did not believe in coincidence. After months of planning he was about to close a trap with the aim of killing two of Khan's blood soaked allies. Him appearing on the TV screen, in that company, at this moment, was therefore not just a shock. In normal circumstances it would call for a reappraisal of the operation he was masterminding thousands of miles away.

It was definitely him. Even from the briefest glimpse caught on camera there was no mistake. They had been born within two days trek of each other. Both into families embedded in espionage amidst the countries, mountains and frontiers of the Hindu Kush.

Their first meeting was at St. Dunstan's in Darjeeling. 'The Harrow of the Himalayas' was recognised as neutral ground. Amongst the quad and spires the sons of sworn enemies and, latterly, even daughters, could mix, even if the six year olds in khaki shorts and shirts were known by the legacies of their fathers, grandfathers and kinsman. The first time Ash and Safedeen saw each other was in the melee of tearful mothers, stiff lipped fathers, drivers and directing teachers as the venerable establishment swallowed another intake. For the briefest moment the eyes of the two boys locked. Passed between them in a micro second was the fear and curiosity of two children who knew that anyone they met now would progress with them into the blue shorts and shirts of intermediate before the grey flannel of seniority. Behind him a tall man with a beard matching the black of his turban and waistcoat looked over. His knowing eyes taking in Ash's family.

Amongst the vehicles of the Indus elite the rust red Toyota jeep of Ash's family tea estate stood out like a shaven weightlifter in a beauty contest. His mother stepped out of it, managing not to sully her electric blue Sari on the mud spattered wing, while his father swung out in shorts and shirt that looked as old and crumpled as the car. At the sight of the Khans Ash remembered how his father's blue eyes had crinkled in a not unfriendly way, while giving a nod suggesting respect for a fellow professional.

The tall man inclined in a similar way, and then put both his hands on his son's shoulders, fixing him in the direction of Ash's family before bending and saying something in his ear. They were from the strategic Swat Valley in Pakistan, Ash's father explained as they went over to Raleigh House, and were traditional leaders. You could tell from the silver ring. His region was a place of apple and peach blossom, where ancient Buddhists carved huge statutes in rocky outcrops and, as in all the tribal lands of Pakistan, 'outsiders are wise to tread lightly and with respect'. Ash remembered vividly how his father gave that bit special emphasis.

Over the next twelve years Ash and Safedeen traversed their school lives, sometimes in the same classes, always in the same cricket team, scrapping at times and sharing friends. They sat around camp fires and sang songs on tiger safaris and heaved backpacks up mountain trails. Their rivalry on the school Go Karting circuit was legendary. As they go older they both went on birthday bashes as it became quite the thing for the richer contingent to hire circuits to race super cars. They would laugh at the same things, give high fives after a sporting victory and be within the orbit of shared groups, but there was always a restraint. Often Ash wondered what exactly was said behind the cupped hand into the listening ear on that very first day, and what seeds were sown.

From the meadows beyond the cottages a white blur released and came skimming across to long grass by the roadside ditch. A barn owl. Lifting in flight it came to a hover at height above an unsuspecting prey before swooping down, it's stoop delivering a back breaking blow. He watched it fly off with something limp in its's talons. A successful kill.

Still watching to see if there was anyone else about, Ash started for the cottage he could not yet call home. Sometime after school Safedeen appeared on Ash's radar working for the Pakistani Intelligence Service. Through a particularly bloody period in Afghanistan Safedeen seemed always close when enemies of regimes were assassinated. Up until Ash was caught in the ambush he was detecting something different in the pattern however. Safedeen seemed to have become semi-detached from his Pakistani mentors, and was as likely to pop up in Shanghai, Dubai or even Tehran. A constant throughout his career however was how two Afghan warlords and power brokers, Amanullah Tarzi and Mahmoud Ali, were ever loyal. And it was those two men that Ash was aiming to kill that night.

In many ways Ash and Safedeen were all too similar. Sometimes they pursued similar goals, but more usually it was as fierce opponents twisting and turning in a dangerous, complex web of clashing interests. Often it felt to Ash that this murderous alter ego was never more than a breath away, even if they hadn't met face to face since handing over their prefect badges.

Grimly Ash stooped for the knife hidden by his gate, his back rewarding him with a spasm and pull on the old injuries. He held it in a fist, the broad blade down ready for an upward slash, as he looked for the tells. They were intact. The peanuts under the mat uncrunched and hairs still trapped in the front door. He had been reaching the point of thinking such precautions were pointless in Thorswick. Nagging away was the diagnosis of hypervigilance, that so interested the service psychologist and her suggestion that he needed counselling.

In Ash's world you watched for when threat entered the outer and inner circles, assessed the risk and took action accordingly. Safedeen being in the UK counted as a big fat entry into the outer circle. Count that as strike One. Hobnobbing in the Royal Enclosure with the owner of Thorswick Manor and his Minister were strikes Two and Three. Either one of those would have merited alarm and an alert to HQ. Such a spectre popping up just when a long laid ambush was being set for two of his shadowy mates would demand a service backed counter operation. The trouble was, HQ knew nothing about what Ash was planning. On this he was freelancing, working with a network of trusted individuals driven by a personal loyalty to him and a desire for revenge.

Gripping the knife Ash moved inside. Quietly shutting the door behind him he felt the darkness of the cottage, every nerve taut. His breathing shallow. For all he knew, he was now being hunted. Here, in the place he was required to call home. A chocolate box cottage that might now be as dangerous as a blind alley in Karachi.

@@@@@@@@@@@@@@@@@@@@@@@@

Firing rippled the sky as soon as the Land Cruiser swung around the corner and entered the mountain village. On the cream leather back seat the two young women knew what to expect. Both were dressed in round necked, bright, Salwar Kameez, their heads loosely framed by shawls that also enveloped their shoulders.

'Happy shooting,' said Jannat. And so there should be. This village in her home area was going to do very well out the wedding festivities over the next few days. Her companion Shameeza Noorzani eyed a youth of about twelve waving a Kalashnikov in salute as they passed, and hoped he knew what he was doing. While both did the obligatory visits as they were growing up, she and Jannat were more at home in London or Dubai. The next few days in the mud walled houses was going to be a trial.

'Chill karoo,' said Jannat as they readied to get out of the car. Take a chill pill. That and 'CK' was what they agreed between them to say, or mouth when asked for the umpteenth time why they were not already married at their advanced age. The truth, that Jannat was a stellar star in the business world and

Shameeza was her right hand, would not cut much ice here. They would have to look downcast as if this was their sad fate. More firing of rifles and ululating from woman erupted as they stepped out.

Jannat and Shameeza smiled at each other before turning to accept the greetings of the bearded elders. Around them the houses were decked with multi coloured strips of cloth while most of the space in the village centre was filled by marque. It looked the perfect setting for the deal.

Chapter 4

Thorswick

Having searched the cottage Ash went to the spare bedroom and the computers. Once into the systems he ignored the messages and went straight to the heavily encrypted chat rooms. He had set up four, creating a virtual cell structure where contacts were unknown to each other. There were nuggets and snippets in all.

The marriage of Jannat Gadhi was always going to draw attention. A graduate of the London School of Economics, with an expensive house London close enough to make Harrods the corner store, she featured regularly in the South Asia business coverage. What particularly interested Ash was her family connections to his targets, and why a remote village close to the border in mountainous Balochistan was chosen for her wedding to the playboy son of the Pakistani Minerals Minister.

Having Amanullah Tarzi and Mahmoud Ali on the guest list, even if they were related, was a risk for someone as image conscious as Jannat. They were not just warlords and chieftains holding sway over provinces. They were murderous shape shifters whose allegiance at any time was likely to be sinuous. Ash knew them well. Their bearded faces, etched into his brain. When they spoke the Afghan government and religious leaders listened. In the fastness of their fiefdoms they were protected by three constants. Sizable armed retinues, the drug traffickers who paid them off and the Pakistani Intelligence Service. At various times both had crossed over lines that would have brought down others.

'The yanks want them badly,' said Adrian Holesworthy, Ash's boss. How long ago had he said that? It must have been eighteen months at least. 'This comes from the top. The White House is being knocked about for not taking down these two, and there is an election coming. The mother of one of the aid workers killed is making life especially difficult and keeps quoting the claim from the one who said they were shot while trying to escape.'

'Amanullah Tarzi.'

'That's the fella. And the other who put a bomb into their embassy annex.'

'Killing the American agents working on the heroin trade?'

'They were diplomats. Anyway, we've said you'll go there as your networks and information are streets ahead of anything they have on the ground or in the dataverse. They want them dead or alive. No expense spared on this one.'

And Ash had gone. Stalking two men whose own networks were more than a match for his own. Twice he missed assassination. A safe house was blown up when a contact went ahead to get the tea going, and a car he was supposed to be in was raked by gunfire. Looking back, it was London that got greedy.

'Tarzi wants a deal. He's got some kind of kidney problem and needs to get out for treatment. We've checked it out with a consultant his people have been sending test results to. To ensure safe passage to a clinic in Abu Dhabi he's prepared to set up Mahmoud Ali.' Holesworthy sounded excited and impatient with Ash's objections.

'It's a good chance, you know. We've had our best people here go over it. Done the data thing to verify the documents and his genetic disposition to have such a condition. It was more than eighty per cent likely. One his sons is already at the clinic under a false Iranian passport talking to doctors and arranging a secure room. We've also tapped into the systems of some suppliers of relevant drugs. They're sending to a known address in Pakistan used by the intelligence service. It all fits.'

He did not believe a word of it.

'We need you to get eyes on Mahmoud Ali and call it in. The Americans will do the rest. They have an entire carrier group waiting, drones in the air and all sorts of whatnots. But they want someone they trust to do the eyeballing, so that's you.'

It was another trap of course. More elaborate than the others, which, in this world, was a compliment. The ambush was text book, the convoy being sprayed with bullets miles away from where Mahmoud Ali was supposed to be. Ash could easily have died there but for his best friend from St. Dunstan's, now the army chief for that troubled province. The idea of the those two turning against each other was possible, explained Ibrahim. But not this way. Tarzi, he said, would not want to be seen to be hiding behind the Americans. Altogether, the idea stank.

Without telling Ash he had helicopters on standby. When their cars came under attack it was Ibrahim who whistled them up. Ash heard later he had lied, saying they were dealing with some kind of rebel activity otherwise his chiefs would never have allowed the aircraft to fly against the two warlords. When they arrived overhead their belt fed guns stripped the blossom off the almond trees creating fearful destruction. Not that Ash knew much about all that. Pulled from the car badly wounded by Ibrahim he was evacuated and flown to a military hospital in Wiltshire. Coming out of the medical coma he heard Ibrahim Afridi was dead. Killed as he led his men. Dead also was Ash's father and mother. Both shot in their home. Being retired was apparently no protection.

'You over reached yourself,' said Holesworthy with an apologetic air and a bunch of flowers. That judgement still stung.

'You'll never be able to go back. For you that war is over. We don't conduct personal vendettas.'

Ash heard the words. Keeping them warm in his head for the months he lay in the hospital and the additional year he was kept in the rehabilitation centre somewhere remote in the Scottish highlands. During that time the world went through another pandemic spasm, economies tanked further and the UK government changed to become even uglier. It was not a climate that bred tolerance. Throughout Ash nursed his hatred.

There was a lot of chat room information to absorb. The setting for the wedding in Balochistan, he realised, was neutral ground for the two men. This was necessary if those two were going to put themselves in the same room. When Ash took to the cricket field for Thorswick it was still not certain if either of the warlords would attend, but the confirmed arrival of Jannat Gadhi and Shameeza Noorzani seemed to have kicked off activity.

Crucially it appeared that several disposable burner phones on a watch list he had drawn up weeks ago had suddenly gone quiet. All were numbers his network of informers had managed to associate with close retainers of the two warlords. The burners were changed regularly, but there were enough people in the forces and family of Ibrahim Afridi thirsting for revenge. When the phones were changed it was not long before the replacements were known, circulated and flagged.

Ash knew that while the leaders themselves would not use mobiles, the goffers, drivers, couriers and henchmen would. The latest list of active phones showed that a similar number amongst known associates of Tarzi and Mahmoud had gone dark. Five each within an hour of each other. Five on each side. It suggested a negotiated agreement on the number attending a meeting. It had to be. The wedding would be the ideal place where hospitality and protection could be offered. Ash still did not know what they were speaking about, and why Jannat Gadhi was involved. Nor did he care. The bottom line was that Amanullah Tarzi and Mahmoud Ali were breaking cover in a known location.

Ash let out a breath and got writing. Carefully he drafted an urgent. Kicking off the message was a line reminding how the two leaders were pre-identified as legitimate targets with particular American interest. Then came the intelligence garnered from contacts built up by himself and his family. The mobiles in use, the timing of the switch off. The location of the meeting in a village just fifteen kilometres over the border in Balochistan. The most likely route was that used by their drug smuggling associates. It went through the Nimruz desert and into the mountains where they would need to be guided up the single track mountain road. How there were likely to be six travellers, if the now silent phones were anything to go by, and that could mean at least two cars. Those two were unlikely to travel together anyway. The vehicles would almost certainly be loaded with extra tyres, fuel cannisters, food and medical kits. These he suggested, might help identify them.

His finger hovered, eyes scanning the page. There was not a hint of any personal interest. That was essential. He also wanted the message to sound as if this had only just come up. Satisfied on that score, Ash pressed send.

He breathed. He had done his best. Idly he went back to the main screen. On the news feeds there was a report from a baggage handler contact that a top Chinese delegation had passed through the VIP lounge of Karachi Airport in Pakistan. A Minister and officials. Not so unusual these days. They were buildings roads there and coal power stations, and then there was their extension to the Turkmenistan, Afghanistan Pakistan, India natural gas pipeline, a Soviet era project the Chinese wanted to take on and expand. It was routine and he was tired. Even so there was always someone who wanted to know what the Chinese were doing. He flagged it quickly under different headlines and sent it off.

It was a quarter past two. He badly needed some air. He went soundlessly down the stairs into the front garden, and was surprised to hear activity from next door. Maggie Johnson was reaching into the back of her car.

'Leaving so soon?'

She jumped and looked cross before carefully closing the tailgate. 'It was only a flying visit. You know, to see the place and make sure the removal men hadn't smashed anything.'

'Sorry, I didn't mean to startle you. And you have to travel now? Its late.'

'I would have gone before now but for this.' Maggie offered him a printed paper. 'Could you get to this to whoever in the cricket club can pay me?' It was a receipt from a window replacement company. 'Please,' she added as an afterthought.

'Sure.' Ash pocketed it, still curious. 'When are you likely to be back?' he asked.

Maggie's eyes looked beyond him to where the cricket pavilion lay invisible in the darkness. 'Not sure really. I wondered if this could be a place for a bit of rest and relaxation. You know, respite from the daily grind. But not sure if,' and she hesitated before finishing quietly, 'if it's what I'm looking for.'

'Or whether you'd fit in?'

She looked at him evenly. 'Yes, I suppose that's exactly what I mean.'

Ash did not answer. He looked away from her and Maggie got the impression he too would rather be living somewhere else.

'I have to go,' she said. 'Early shift. Even on a Sunday.' She opened the driver's door. 'Tell me,' she said. 'What the hell is that noise?'

The sound was of a deep throated car being driven at speed and was coming from somewhere beyond the parkland of Thorwick Hall. A growl of power switching into highly tuned whines he now seldom noticed.

'Sounds like one of the Ferraris,' said Ash. 'Stay here for any length of time and you'll get good at identifying what kind of super car is being taken for a spin.'

'You've got to be kidding. At this time of night?' Maggie was poised with a leg on the sill of her car, listening now even more intently.

'It's not that unusual when Norman Ellroy is here. Especially when he has something like the horse race to celebrate.'

'And he can do that?'

'Ellroy likes to be the benevolent squire. How else do think a place like this has a cricket club, and the village still has a pub?'

'That's so feudal.' Maggie looked as if this was another reason for not returning to Thorwick. 'Where's all this happening?'

'There's an old wartime airstrip he's brought into the park and converted into a racing circuit. He uses that. I've walked it a few times and its quite a set up. Not that he's much of a driver apparently. Just goes up and down at nowhere near the capability of the cars he's got. Sometimes he lets house guests have a go. It sounds like this one knows what he is doing.' And who, Ash wondered, might that person be?

'How very strange.' Maggie smiled, very briefly, and he picked up something of a sadness about her. He stood watching her drive off and wondered vaguely about what might make her happy. He breathed night air and surveyed the village. There was a good moon tonight. A hunter's moon. It held the cricket pitch and now deserted pavilion in its blue light.

He was too restless to go to bed. Perhaps he should go over the walls of the Manor and see if it really was Safedeen beasting the Ferrari. Then at least he would know he was finished here. His cover and assumed name blown sky high. Known to a killer. The enemy in the Royal enclosure.

He shook himself. That was emphatically not what he needed to do right now. There had been quite enough grandstanding today. His priority must be the strike. Whoever took responsibility for action would want the source to be a grey, analytical, anonymous professional. Not someone pinging off mobiles for snagging the security systems at the home of the superbly connected Norman Ellroy.

Heading back inside he stopped. It sounded as if the Ferrari had finally come to halt, the idling barely audible before it was gunned into a scream. Once, twice, three times in a kind of fuel injected roar of challenge from deep in the jungle that echoed over Thorswick. And Ash knew.

Chapter 5

Balochistan

Shameeza shut the door with relief, Jannat having staggered past and fallen backwards onto her bed. They were stuffed.

'We'll be on a regime when all this is over.'

Jannat groaned and smoothed her hands over her belly. 'Maybe I should arrange a throwup.'

'Don't start that again.' Shameeza tone was sharp, before softening. 'We knew it would be like this.' She sat down away from the bed. Someone had been in to light candles. 'We just have to roll with it.'

Wedding custom dictated certain formalities, and the limited time available meant these were being concertinaed. Immediately on arrival they had gone to the house set aside for the Minister to receive the gold jewellery and lavish gifts Shameeza had already arranged and paid for. His Excellency beamed at the approval voiced by the elders for his generosity, while profusely apologising for the absence of his son.

'Chicken shit coward,' Jannat muttered to Shameeza, although the lack of a bridegroom would not matter a jot.

'Passport difficulties,' stated the Minister, his eyes sliding briefly over the two women. 'But nothing need derail the wedding. I can stand in to make the promises for him.'

The corpulent Minister for Minerals had lost whatever bearing he had in the military, and could not believe his good fortune. The son, whose antics and nature was a political time bomb, was being thrown a marital screen by someone with wealth and clout. And with it came another deal that would hand him a big fat fee, and much needed kudus in the political bear pit of Islamabad.

After the welcomes, the food. Sajji lamb crisped on an open fire with Kurnoo wheat rotis as smooth and round as tennis balls. Alongside it was a spicy lamb stew, dahl and bahjis, all followed for desert by jelly and kheer served with raw onions. After refusing a third glass of sweet tea they moved onto the next stage. This involved going with every woman who could walk, and some who needed help, to each of the houses to give the formal invitation. The whole village was ready, and were not going to pass up the chance to press more food and sweets on the two mysterious women suddenly in their midst.

Only once was there a discordant note. An elderly woman somewhere around the mid stage placed her lassi firmly down with a clunk and demanded 'Where's the bridegroom?' She was lent across by two of the other woman, using their head scarves to shield whatever it was they were whispering, but there still came a very audible 'can't be a proper wedding without a man to get between the legs later,' as she was taken out.

'That bloody crone,' breathed Jannat as she looked up at the freshly whitewashed mud of the bedroom ceiling. That set them off. Sniggers at first and then the releasing tension had them lapsing into smothered laughter.

'We need to be careful,' sighed Shameeza eventually, wiping tears with her scarf.

Jannat shrugged into the mattress. 'At least the nasties are on the way, and one way or another we'll be able to get on.'

'Do you think they'll actually get here and agree something?' The candles were guttering in the draughts from the doors and wooden shutters, lifting soot and shadows around the room.

'You know what I think. My very, very distant relatives are time expired as far as I am concerned. Between them their areas hold riches others want, and the government can't agree licenses without their agreement. And they will keep fucking everything up. This whole charade is the last chance saloon for them, as far as I am concerned. If they settle and let in our friends, then they might see their grandchildren grow up and we get a share. But, if something happens you won't find me grieving. They're just too damn slippery.'

It was not a new argument, and they had both worked over different outcomes repeatedly. 'And if you really want to make sure I don't throw up, perhaps you had better stay and keep an eye on me.'

Shameeza stood slowly her eyes never leaving the form on the bed as Jannat moved onto her side toward her. 'This may be a smuggling village,' she said softly, 'and they will turn a blind eye to a lot.' The words took her to the door of her room, 'but it's far from home and there are limits.'

Chapter 6

Thorswick

The mobile rang after four, but well before five. Ash was slumped at his computer. He had been working through systems, checking Home Office data, all airports, the police central computer and that of his own service for Safedeen Khan. The man was on a high priority watch list.

There were no image matches through ports of entry, and that included the few private airstrips licensed for the foreign flights of the rich. In the deeper reaches of the security service though, he struck gold. A report, from the Australians, of a confirmed sighting a week ago, and a follow up positive DNA confirmation from a hair brush collected by a hotel cleaner in Dili, the capital of East Timor. The covering report speculated he was spying for the former power, Indonesia. It was a slam dunk. Incontrovertible.

Whoever he saw, it must have been someone similar, even with the coincidence of some clown gunning a super car around Ellroy's estate. Before his eyes closed he remembered how the tame shrink at that place in the Scottish Highlands had warned his hyper-vigilance was likely to make him read too much into innocent events.

'Hi Albert.' This after a pause. Albert being the name that came up on the screen of his mobile. Albert being the duty office. Sometimes Albert was a woman. In which case the ID name changed. The end to end encryption was automatic, which meant no fumbling around with codes while a tired mind tried to remember which one worked this month. A relief. There were still some formalities however.

'Hi, sorry to bother you. How are you doing?' A reasonable attempt at sincerity and a chance to confirm he was free to talk. This would allow him to use 'dusty', 'holistic' or 'indigestion', these being his code words for the next two months to let HQ know if he were speaking with a gun to his head. Ash was opened eyed now, mind alert.

'Have you got anything else on the cars your two Uglies are using, I've been told to ask.'

'They're not mine.'

'Figure of speech.'

'What more is needed on the cars?'

'Oh, well you know. Registration. Where they are now. Colour would be helpful.' The tone was weary. It sounded as if Albert was at the end of a very long shift and wanted his bacon and eggs.

'I'm sorry, I am not there.'

'I've no idea where you are mate. Was just told to ask that's all, as you seem to be the source.'

'I gave the likely routes, approximate timing and vehicle types.'

'They always want more.'

'Try the Americans. They've spent a lot of money putting face and DNA recognition on most border points. They like to think no one moves without their image bouncing off the CIA,' although Ash knew that wasn't true. Not out there.

'I don't think that's going to happen. There seems to be a lot of excitement around here at the moment. I think the idea is to bring this dish to the American table ready cooked as it were. A little gift to remind them just how useful we are.' Albert terminated without bothering to say goodbye.

Ash leaned back on his chair. He should be euphoric. Such a call meant the strike was on. Someone was ticking boxes, making sure all possible information was gathered to show how diligent they were. Despite the hour, Ash felt an overwhelming exhaustion. He had no illusions about what it would mean. After the drone strike there would be a witch hunt amongst the followers and network of the two Afghan targets as they searched for the information leak. He would have his work cut out protecting his contacts. He also realised the termination of those two men would be a big full stop for him personally. His determination to settle that very big score meant a barren, stale future. A future that was laid out for him and a few other foreign based agents at a meeting in London when he was finally signed off from the rest cure in Scotland.

'For you, the foreign life is over'. Saying things like 'for you, its over,' seemed to be a favoured turn of phrase for Adrian Holesworthy. Since he had loomed through his morphine induced haze the man had gone from 'Head of People' at the service to the top chair. Not bad for someone considered as little more than a bag man for the chiefs, and who had never operated abroad. He was a paunchy man with a mop of grey hair and an unfashionable Zapata moustache, who seemed to be saying words only recently learnt.

'There has been a significant re-organisation in-house,' Holesworthy explained. 'The real cash now is going to integrating information and data from innumerable sources, or dumb systems eavesdropping and extracting data dumps. It is also being argued that facial recognition on every street corner and choke points such as airports, plus the ability of artificial intelligence to cross reference data sources, DNA and locations, make it impossible for spies to work as they have done for generations. Put simply, if you are not already exposed where you are, you soon will be. The consequences for you and yours could be terminal.'

His eyes flicked over to Ash, who was trying not to fidget. The injuries to his back were still too painful for him to lean back and go to full slouch. But all in the room knew it was not just about data. The world was enduring another pandemic. That along with conflicts around Russia were conspiring with maverick climate events to corrode economic, political and cultural life at every level. There was not a nation or community untouched by food shortages. Not only had poverty increased everywhere, but in most corners of the globe governments were assuming more powers over their populations.

'The dynamics we face mean we need new ways of operating. Everything is changing, and we who are charged with our country's security have to do the same. There's also a question about bangs for the bucks, and whether the old ways are the best.'

He had their attention. All were professionally young, but old enough to have the expectation of a career for which they had sacrificed normality. They were in a room of wire mesh built within the former lingerie section of a prestigious London department store, a consumer mecca that closed its doors after repeated economic tsunamis. Incongruous bra adverts still adorned the walls, some torn and flapping in the air from the newly installed ceiling fans.

'The Americans, as some of you may know,' and here Holesworthy could not resist a look at Bunty Cavender who was wearing a face mask bearing the stars and stripes, 'are about to launch version five of their Joint All Domain Command and Control system, which already employs hundreds and which will need a new nuclear power station to run it. From the successes of the previous versions, and our own very similar and highly successful developments in that area, we know warfare, espionage and counter measures are undergoing revolutionary change.'

He paused to allow Bunty Cavender, who had flown back still thinking she was the liaison with the American CIA, get over a bout of coughing. As she wiped under the mask the room was left in no doubt about her difficulty with the idea that the U.K. could come anywhere close to matching the Americans, in that field at least. Holesworthy looked as if he might have wanted to say something to her, but Bunty was not easily contained. Before her more diplomatic posting she worked undercover as an academic studying the Russian Orthodox church while establishing networks amongst priests, before one of them confessed all to his patriarch.

Contenting himself to a stare, Holesworthy resumed as soon as her mask was back in place. 'We are talking about their taking Exascale supercomputing to another level. They already search for data and information from every imaginable source, correlating with what is already known, and all at eye watering speed.'

He sucked his moustache, perhaps realising there was still food there. 'Such systems have already reset the game. They have widgets going over social media, getting across chat rooms, dumb listening devices in areas of conflict, linking up with satellites, sucking juice up with drones and cracking data from just about anything out there. Mobile operated entry systems, vehicle movements and city traffic systems. You name it they'll use it. It means they are the best informed about targets, threats and emerging hazards. With Version Five they are about to take it all to another level. Everybody is going to struggle to keep up. Even us, for that matter.'

He eyed the room. A sure sign that the nasty bit was coming. ''We are also well advanced in this field of course. But we will also need to step up. And we will do this despite the cost, we are being told. The problem is this latest advance by the yanks is likely to make anything we have to put on the table superfluous. Because by the time we've told them they will either already know from their own analysis, or because they're right up our arseholes having hacked us to buggery.'

Ash filled Holesworthy's next pause with a quick look around the group. None of these he reckoned would be naïve, or simply silly enough, to mention the special relationship.

'And don't any of you for fuck's sake waste a gnat's breath on 'the special relationship.' Holesworthy went on. 'Any special relationship with them died a few days after they dropped their atomic bombs on Japan and they pulled the loans. It's just that it took a few generations to realise. And some of our leaders still haven't got it.'

This was a rare example of pub talk coming to a briefing. Ash realised Holesworthy was struggling. The life, and perhaps even the service he had known, was coming to an end. Even as Ash grasped the insight, Holsworthy stretched his scrawny neck and looked up at the skylight. For all the world he was like a reimagined dinosaur image in a documentary with eyes catching the flash of the asteroid strike heralding destruction.

Holesworthy collected himself and continued. He was coming to the meat about what this select group of foreign agents were now going to do. It was, experimental. And their part was very left field. They were to put their shoulders to the wheel so their experience, insights and knowledge of culture could be used to enhance the application of Artificial Intelligence. They would be doing this from separate locations, isolated from central offices to prevent cross contamination. 'We want you feeding into whatever the data delivers while operating your networks and contacts as if you are still out there as the primary analyst,' he said. 'What data delivers is all very well, but we want to have judgement. And judgement based on solid experience.'

A hand came up and Holesworthy stopped. 'My limited understanding of things Adrian, is that there are systems mapping the shape and composition of billions of proteins, and others that are working out the gaseous,' and here the Scottish accent seemed to infuse the word 'gaseous' with a separate emphasis, 'composition of billions of planets. For all I know these systems, along with those trawling through the entire back catalogue of medical research to siphon out new drug uses, are also playing chess around the world with millions while composing a play about someone's cat in the style of William Shakespeare. And yet,' a big pause here, 'and yet, this is where you want to place us, and suggest that we'll be able to add value?'

The speaker was Robert Stevens, a noted linguist with a beard and face of an ascetic. From an island only marginally controlled by the Philippine government, he conducted a ruthless war against the intelligence operatives infiltrated into Chinese student associations across Asia, while recruiting sources from amongst the Filipino scientists and software engineers going to work in China. 'And even,' he resumed, 'if it were possible to add value to the data crunching, can't we do this from where we are currently, or here, together, where at least we could bounce ideas off each other?'

His question drew a bleak smile. 'It's all about veracity, verification and avoiding group think. Separation is key. There will be times when scenarios are delivered to you thanks to the data. You will be asked to rate likely outcomes from one to five, based on your on the ground knowledge. At other times you will be working as you know best, while remembering at all times that anything to do with this country is off limits because you are not allowed to work here. In fact if you are found to be doing anything regarding the work I am describing, then this office will deny that you ever worked for it. If that line becomes impossible to hold, then we will simply say that you are some kind of maverick and hold the coats for those who undertake your defenestration.'

A legal nicety, clearly articulated. They had no legal cover. Having delivered Holesworthy headed out of the cage. Before pulling on the door handle, he turned suddenly and looked back. 'It could be worse you know. Those of us who wanted to save you really believe this is worth a shot. You know how it smells out there, we want you to be the tendency spotters within the chaos, because that is something no bloody machine can give us.'

He may have meant it, but a duller reality soon emerged. Banished to a cottage in the Cotswolds, Ash soon discovered that much of his work was mundane. Marking scenarios by ticking boxes numbered one to ten. Stalking Tarzi and Ali, on the other hand, was old school. The tips coming through connections, assessing the varied motives, weighing the rumours and planning a strike with the lightest of steps.

He stood up from the computer, stretched and lifted the slats of the blinds. It was still dark outside, but there was enough light from the moon and stars to show a dog fox crossing a field toward the woods. It cannot have heard the shutters, and there was no light in the room, but it must have sensed a change. It stopped and turned, the white fur down its chest showing well as it stared directly back at Ash's cottage. The pose was held, stock still for nearly a minute, before it turned and lopped away.

Ash needed to get to bed. By the time he woke all would be done. Just one more thing. He rebooted his computer. A final check. The shrink would not approve. He could hear the tutting. Ash went onto a video site and searched out the moment when Norman Ellroy was presented with his winner's cup. He watched intently at the crowd behind the smiling ensemble and saw again the woman in the large pink hat dip sideways to show the face of the man behind. And this time it was nothing like Safedeen Khan.

Chapter 7

RAF Bincton, Lincolnshire, UK

'Well done. Nice of you to make it.'

Great, thought Maggie. A sarcastic policeman.

'We wouldn't want the Prime Minister to miss your contribution to the war effort, would we?' A very long pause, broken just before it became insubordinate. 'Ma'am.'

Behind the white capped RAF policeman a World War Two Lancaster bomber stood on a trimmed lawn, its nose pointing up to the horizon. Visitors and passers-by could be left in no doubt. This was a place for exporting death. Where tradition and sacrifice was honoured.

Maggie did not rise. Taking a strip off service police was not advisable. There were just too many ways they could get back at you, even as an officer. Usually when such things happened she made a flip remark of the kind which went with service life. With this one however, there was barely concealed malevolence. Like many in that line of work he had the peak pulled down so his eyes were barely a glint in the cave. Under his hooded stare Maggie was suddenly more conscious of the tightness of her black T shirt and jeans. He held a look for a moment too long before signalling to the armed sentries in the impressive guardhouse to raise the barrier and check her car for bombs. 'The war starts in 10 minutes,' he said. Another pause. 'Ma'am.'

Of course, she was aware of that. Which is why she could have done without the delay having her windows fixed. Driving in she how uncomfortable he made her feel. Perhaps he did that with any woman. Or perhaps it was worse. The thing she was dreading more and more with each passing day. Being the subject of gossip. Talk which would be well founded in her case.

In the dawn light, amongst the regimented lawns, bleak offices and grey hangers, all set on a ruler flat landscape, preparations were well advanced for yet another real time exercise. At various places squads of men and women in camouflage were forming at their stations like algae blooms. She doubted she would ever feel at home in such places. At the same time she remembered the cricket club atmosphere at Thorswick and gave an involuntary sigh. That would not work either. Pulling into the last parking space in front of the newest hangar she saw the base padre give a welcoming wave that caused the cross emblem on his collar to glint in the sunlight. Judging by the vaping, it looked as if he had been hanging around waiting for her.

'Greetings Maggie', he called, 'welcome to the war.'

As he spoke a tannoy sounded from the hanger. 'Incursions in sector nine.'

'It's all going so well', said Reverend 'Call Me' Chris Ridgewell. 'Still a few minutes to go before the conflict kicks off properly and they're already set to shoot the local civilians.'

He cocked an eye at Maggie. Far down the perimeter road an aged Landrover with blue lights flashing was heading in their direction followed by a pickup.

'I've seen the scenario,' Ridgewell said. 'There are no things hidden from God. For the next three days ourselves and our assorted allies are battling the forces of darkness. We have had indications for sometime that there was trouble at mill. After a series of misunderstandings followed by a number of aggressions, only by the other side naturally, the forces of Red have massed and are finally preparing to take out a number of allies down the Baltic. Amongst other things, as the clock ticks down to open warfare, alarmed peace protestors try to invade our beautiful amphitheatre to prevent us gladiators doing to the others what they will be trying to do to us. Obviously therefore the citizens have to be dealt with. Cue our brave boys heading for the barbed wire.'

The military police vehicle sped past them. In the pickup were a number of men in helmets clasping pick axe handles between their knees.

'The ridiculous thing is,' continued Ridgewell as he breathed out another apple scented cloud, 'they keep running these exercises and assume civil insurrection will happen. But there is no one within miles unaware that stepping over the wire stands a very good chance of having their stupid head blown off.'

It was true. As the main base in the country for air intelligence gathering RAF Bincton was heavily protected. It was also the British home for the drones that flew from bases far away. Unusually, there were also aged Eurofighter Typhoons preparing to take off, as their own airfield was being resurfaced. Two of the jets, looking at this distance like spiky, dangerous toys, were trundling fast toward the runway. Without a pause they turned, throttles opening with a roar. Together they swept like arrow heads into the blue sky. The war was on. 'Bang on schedule, said the Chaplain.

They watched them disappear, their ears still reverberating. The pilots of those aircraft were at the apex of the air force culture. Everyone else, no matter what they did, was a long way behind.

'They get all the kudos those boys,' said Ridgewell. 'Everyone understands their role. They inherited the Battle of Britain thing. The few against the many. The saviours of the nation when it's back was against the wall. So whether it's Afghanistan, Syria, Iraq, or other places we are not allowed to mention, they get medals for what they do. You and your colleagues however, well this man's Airforce can't decide whether you are technicians or computer operators, and are not given much glory for your type of conflict.'

He paused and Maggie declined to fill the gap.

'So are you in because you are a 'my country right or wrong' type, or was it necessity?

A lot asked that, eventually, as if they sensed she was never quite at ease. She had an answer off pat. 'I was a pandemic variant nine student who didn't have the wit to use AI cheats to push my grades. Family circumstances meant I was a soft touch for recruitment when I shouldered my student debt onto the job market. I was working in a pub at the time and got in. Thousands didn't, and I know I should be grateful. '

'You look like you could have been a model,' and Chris, and he blushed.

'Yeah a porn star maybe or a gangster's girl, d'you think? You know, or one of those skinny girls on a rap video? No Thanks. I know a few who've gone down that road.'

'Sorry.' The padre turned pink. 'That came out wrong, but still a gender crime. Or worse.'

Maggie toyed with the idea of digging him in deeper but relented. 'It's not like I didn't think about it. But the RAF gave me an interview, I did the physicals, the medicals, and all the conundrum tests after which they said I had aptitude and the right psychology. And then of course they take you for training in the States, which was a temptation to a poor girl with debts and not much future. It turns out, after all is said and done, they decided I was most suited to being a drone jockey.' She paused for a moment. 'When all I really wanted to do, if I were going to be a pilot in this lot, was that.' Maggie nodded her head over to where another two fighter jets were warming up. 'I even learned Russian in my spare time.'

Over in Sector 9, with no peaceniks to club, the soldiers were practising on each other. The wooden handles clacked above their heads. At this distance it looked like a folk dance by Morris Men. Jingle jingle, round we go, in and out, sticks crossing and hitting far too close to knuckles. She was sure it would end in tears.

'For what it is worth,' said Ridgewell, 'I think you have a far harder job in a way. It's the mental thing.' Maggie shot him a look.

'I do my job,' she said. 'I'm well trained, and don't feel the need to talk much about it.'

'Of course. But what I am saying is that you are asked to exist in a different universe. Your aircraft isn't even here to coo over. It takes off from the Gulf and you fly it from a console here. You do the job, and if that involves sending a missile down someone's throat you do that, log off from your shift and are in a supermarket within an hour trying to decide between a Chinese or

Indian ready meal. It's not like that for those glamour pusses in the Typhoon's who may get into a fight where its dog eat dog. Someone in your position looks at the image and does it cold. That, I think, sets up all sorts of emotional complications.'

'I'm part of a team Chris. We back each other and most of the time we are just watching. If we do have to do something, as you well know, there are all sorts of checks. We're not Americans. We shoot when we know it is at bad boys and back off if there are others around who might get hurt.'

'That doesn't answer my point exactly. I just think that kind of situation may cause you to,' and here the padre paused in emphasis, 'do things you might not usually do.'

And there it was. The reason why this man was sucking in apple smoke and finding it difficult to look her in the eye. He was always one of the first to hear any rumours. Behind them came an electronic bleeping and the sound of something heavy beginning to trundle. The big doors of the hangar were on the move. With a sharp crack of static, the aged public address system came back to life.

'Attention, Attention. All personnel. Enemy missiles are being readied. All aircraft are to go to survival scramble. I repeat - survival scramble. Personnel to shelters. Nuclear and bacterial suits must now be worn. This base is now a target.'

Without another word Maggie turned and ran for the hangar. Once in she headed in a fast jog trot for the nearest of the concrete staircases that led to the underground complex of offices and flight rooms. As she worked her way down the different levels she came across increasing numbers of people moving to their stations as thick doors were secured into place.

'Saw you coming on the vids Ma'am,' said Flight Sergeant Hayman as he pressed a button and sent the last door moved into its slot. 'It was like something out of that classic flic 'Raiders of the Lost Ark' with you running and those things chasing you as it were. You were going so well we thought we wouldn't slam the jobby in your face.'

'Too kind Flight.' Not that she had any idea of what film he was talking about. Breathless she went to the locker room where she stripped in record time and got into her flight suit with the pilot's wings picked out in blue that signified her as a pilot of an Unmanned Aerial Vehicle. Her crew was already in the briefing room. There was barely a chance for a hello and get seated before the door opened and their commander came through the door. As they scrambled to their feet Maggie felt surprise, and shame. Surprise because Squadron Leader Richard Pickett would not usually attend routine briefings. Shame because of their affair, and the weakness on her part. It was something that should never have happened. Not only was he, apparently, happily married, but also because he was a man boy wanting to take risks. At least she had broken it off before her flight away to Oxfordshire.

'Thank you. Take your seats please.' He nodded as he took in her and Jack Stevens, a newly promoted Flying Officer who would be running the systems and Mike Thompson, another flight lieutenant her age, who was in charge of intelligence. When the Squadron Leader was sure she was looking he made a movement, pointing a finger upwards after drawing it discreetly from eye to ear. The meaning was clear. For some reason, others were listening in.

A familiar view came onto the screen as the lights dimmed. Iraq and a circle. 'Our Protector unmanned vehicle is already in flight,' said Thompson. He tapped the circle. 'It's here.' How many times had she flown over there, Maggie wondered. Brown hills, the Tigris and Euphrates, Babylon, Baghdad, incursion routes and massacre sites. Places from the Arabian Nights and archaeology. There and Syria. Afghanistan less frequently these days. Her working life involved prowling over vast territories and cities. Looking down on brown walled villages and square compounds. Gathering intelligence, identifying targets, collecting electronic data strands. Watching demonstrations organised by ISIS, or fighters massing. Spotting those who were laying ambushes, or wayside bombs. Illuminating a sniper nestling into position. Getting the clearance. Pressing a button on the control stick to send a Hellfire down to where she held the crosshairs.

A new map was on the screen, and it was not somewhere she had ever been before.

Thompson stepped forward. 'Balochistan', he said.

Chapter 8

Thorswick

Ash sat at the dark screen for a very long time after seeing the image at the race course. The video was not from some viral ridden social media outlet. It was the sports pages of the BBC. Admittedly this was an institution way past it's best, and seriously politically compromised, but even so.

Worse, far worse, were the reassuringly authoritative intelligence reports placing of Safedeen Khan thousands of miles away in East Timor. Someone able to create a new reality was going to a lot of trouble to put Safedeen anywhere but in the UK, and in the Royal Enclosure. And that person had to be his companion, the billionaire and owner of Thorswick Manor, Norman Ellroy. Those circles. They were now tight enough to be throttling. In his world, Ash knew what that meant. He was blown. By rights he should be on his toes, getting away from Thorswick and pleading for understanding and protection from his service.

Sitting in the dark he remembered the conversation after the spies were told by Adrian Holesworthy that their futures lay in Kettering rather than Kuala Lumpur. Eight of the most experienced went to a city hostelry where they set about breaking all sorts of rules by holding their own debrief in an unswept building having been reunited with their mobiles. The aged medieval pub, sited under Roman wall remnants, had beams and low ceilings that seemed to invite the sharing of shady secrets in dark alcoves.

Uneaten before them was a Scotch Egg to conform to yet another government order that groups in the pandemic could only meet if it involved a meal.

Robert Stevens, spoke for them all. 'So, it seems we're joining middle ranking lawyers, accountants and novelists as the latest profession heading for the junk yard thanks to AI. Because, I for one, did not believe a word about being needed to mark the homework of quantum computers. I give us six months before we receive our cards'

The group collectively took a pull of their drinks at that.

'Dissonance. Cognitive dissonance. That was what was happening there'. Bunty set down her Negroni. 'He was saying things he did not believe. Or he did not expect us to believe. For one thing that stuff about verification. How can we do that when our useful experience will wither, the computers are learning all the time and are quite capable of creating a new history and, for all we know, embedding it our archives, within nano seconds.'

'But without people on the ground you can never be sure of anything,' protested Stevens. 'Then there's all the other stuff. Getting someone with a woman, or a boy, and making sure the image is all across social media. Or, loading their account with unexplained wealth and making sure the leak is in the right ear at the right time. It's going to be very difficult to spot the inception moment from Basildon.'

'But these days everyone will say the image of the double backed beast was machine created, and prove it by producing another machine created picture of them being all lovey dovey with a suitable body outside the Taj Mahal.' Bunty took another large swallow to all but finish her cocktail. 'And you know why we are being brought back and all split up into carefully managed little nodes, don't you?'

Nobody did.

'It's so they can keep an eye on us. So they can retire us when we are no longer of use to them, or anyone else. And it's being done in such a way that it would be difficult for anyone to use us to plant information in their systems. Which by the way have been hopelessly compromised anyway. The Americans know the Chinese, and even some non-state types, started stalking those corridors in the last upgrade but one. And yes, the Americans. When they look at the lingerie department they are not impressed at all. If anything they are embarrassed for us. But our bosses are desperate to keep something of a relationship.'

She sighed. 'And if you want to know how I know this, then never underestimate the lust of a certain kind of American for English posh totty. Yes, folks I did that for my country.'

She gave a small bow of her head as if acknowledging applause. 'And that's why I'm with you now. Apparently they didn't like me spying on them, so I got bounced after they admitted I was rather good at it.'

Ash had been careful ever since that drink in the Merry Monarch about what he put into the service systems. To organise the strike on Tarzi and Mahmoud though, he had been forced to step more into the light than he would have wished. And with him, inevitably, came the network he had built so carefully from those with good reason to hate the two men. Even disguised and unnamed in that single message he was not naïve about what could happen if a super computer crunched his messages, cross referenced his entire back story and soaked the data from all mobile contacts since the first mast was erected. Everyone would be exposed. It was only a matter of time.

Ash wearily got up and went to one of the unpacked boxes labelled Srinagar. He used to have house boat on the lake there. It had been a refuge. Digging around he came out with an old school photograph. There they all were, standing, sitting or squatting in front of the Edwardian buildings of the senior school, the skyline dominated by the snowy peaks of the eastern Himalayas and Kangchenjunga. Within days of the picture being taken they would disperse to whatever the world was prepared to offer. In the middle row, a few seats in on the left, was Safedeen, already with the look of his father. On the back row was Ali, his arm around the shoulder of Ibrahim Afridi.

Ash breathed deeply. His eyes alternating between Safedeen and Ibrahim. What he should do was to get onto the chat rooms and warn everyone. To tell them to find safety. Some of them he had never met, but others were not like that. He knew their faces. Even their families. They might still have time, if he did it now. After the strike, inevitably, the window would become very narrow. Ash knew though a warning now would send off all sorts of signals to anyone who was already suspicious, and might blow the planned killing of Tarzi and Mahmoud. Putting away the school picture in the box with other memories, he knew he would not do that. It was all too far down the road. Everyone was going to have to take their chances. In the meantime he badly needed a gun.

Chapter 9

RAF Bincton, Lincolnshire.

Maggie rolled her neck. Then brought an arm over her head, pulling the side of her head to the right before bringing the other arm over to give a stretch on the left. Throughout she kept a light touch on the control stick, her eyes never leaving the set of screens around her. Beside her Flying Officer Jack Stevens was taking a break. He was standing in tree pose, his left foot firmly in his crotch, eyes closed and hands together above his head in tree pose. It was a very long flight.

She sensed him coming back to earth and looked up briefly as he resumed his seat at his own console. 'That's better,' he said. 'We're ought to be heading back soon, shouldn't we?'

'Yes, by the time we put the bird down we'll have done nearly the full range.'

Jack nodded. Their drone was doing figure of eights at maximum altitude above the Sulaiman Mountain range, a place of dramatic and forbidding scenery. To Maggie it seemed as if the rocks were reaching for the sky, their upward strata a witness to the violence of crashing continental plates. In this land of deep, rocky gorges and closed valleys Pakistan had hidden its burgeoning nuclear weapons development. A place designed by nature for secrets.

The cameras of their warplane never left a village in a tight gorge near the Bolan Pass, one of the few passable routes to the more affluent plains of India. A gaily coloured marquee was utilising most of the flat land available. They watched as coaches covered in whirls of bright paint wheezed and puffed their way up the road and disgorged woman laden with baskets and children, who ran around before disappearing under white awnings rigged between flat roofed, brown houses. The covers made it impossible to see who was walking around underneath. It was something they were used to seeing in places where people have reason to fear eyes in the sky.

'Hold Up,' it was Maggie, pulling into close focus a white pickup of uncertain age which was swinging out of the village.

'Let's follow it.' Mike Thompson from his post in the gallery.

The driver seemed confident. The vehicle was bucketing down the mountain road.

'Maybe they've run out of Cola', said Jack dispassionately.

If that were the case then the driver was prepared to take some risks to slake the thirst of the guests. 'He's shifting like he's got a bee up his ass,' said Thompson before they all let out a 'Wow!'. The pickup so nearly went into a smoke belching coach coming round a blind corner. It slewed as the brakes bit and took a side swipe into the rock wall. And yet it did not stop or slow.

'Me thinks,' said Thompson, 'we may be about to get lucky. Stay on him.'

In a final cloud of dust, the vehicle left the mountain road and turned left and slotted into traffic on the highway. It did not need to go far, apparently. After a few kilometres it turned into a truck stop, and drove slowly past ranks of ranks of parked juggernauts. Near a clump of trees and tables full of men drinking tea it parked. Maggie, Jack and Mike were all leaning forward toward their monitors. But, as far as they could tell, no one got out of the car.

'Odd that,' said Mike. 'I thought everyone around here would always take a tea when they had the chance.'

The drone stayed focussed. 'Don't have too long left.' Jack was right to sound a warning.

'Let me try something,' said Maggie. She pulled back to show a wider view. A solitary man was momentarily between a line of lorries. There was no obvious place where he could have come from. He certainly had not left the tea shop. They watched him disappear into a canyon of eight axel vehicles. Maggie zoomed in but the man seemed to have disappeared. It was very dark between the lorries and several had tarpaulins pulled between to create shade. Frustrated she pulled out to get a wider view.

'Bingo'. This from Mike because out of the lorry canyon a beige brown Toyota Landcruiser emerged, its paintwork mud splattered and dusty. A blue Nissan patrol followed, its paintwork in a similar state. They were more or less exactly what they had been told to look for. The pickup left its parking place and raced toward the entrance, the other two falling in behind

Briefly Maggie took her eyes of the screens and looked up at the darkened gallery. Squadron Leader Richard Pickett was leaning forward, his right hand extended as he pressed the talk button.

'Prepare. Targets confirmed,' said Mike.

From then on the cross hairs never left the cars. As they sped up toward the road for the village the watchers selected close up and medium views, peering through the mud smeared windows, took shots of the illegible number plates and captured every human detail they could. A beard, a knotted leather bangle on a wrist, how the driver in blue Toyota always seemed to be slow on the brakes. It was, thought Maggie, as if he wanted to force the pace, push along the Land Cruiser and get out of the open as soon as possible.

A good view of a face. A driver, grim and focussed. There was too much mud on the back windows on both to get any view of people in the back. She remembered the pre-flight briefing and the orders that the targets were to be taken out 'at any cost'. In theory that could mean immediately, even if it resulted in other victims such as other drivers on the road, or even, and she did not like the thought at all, at the wedding party. She had raised her hand and asked for clarity about that. It was Richard who answered.

'Thank you for raising that very important question.' And he paused as to show just important he really did consider it. 'Such an approach is exceptional, and even unprecedented. In this case the standard rules of engagement to avoid any additional casualties might have to be suspended. The justification was the high profile nature of the targets, and the fact they very rarely emerged into the open. You should be assured this approach has been agreed at the highest level.'

It goes without saying', he went on smoothly, 'that everyone hopes and intends that a worse case will not happen. We should all direct the flight with the intention that only the best possible result is achieved. The terrorists we are targeting have claimed hundreds of lives, included those of many British personnel. Our task is to make sure they will not kill any more while showing others you cannot kill our people and not expect justice.'

'Thank you, sir. When you said that the approach has been cleared at the highest level. Does that include the highest legal circles?'

'Of course.'

During the drone's endless figures of eight over the village Maggie had studied the mountain road looking for the best possible place to hit any potential targets. She obsessively took in the smallest detail, the mountain, the rocks and any huts that might be providing shade for people.

On their screens the cars swung off the highway and started the climb. They would soon be at the ideal location where they could be hit without any danger to anyone else. It was a hairpin bend that elbowed sharply against the mountain contours. Get the timing right and positioning right, she calculated, and they could both be destroyed in a solitary strike

The vehicles were approaching the bend, and slowing. In anticipation she had dropped the drone to seven thousand feet and got behind them. Maggie moved the cross hairs so it would hit the blue vehicle, sending the blast barrelling forward to engulf the brown. There was little, she thought, that would survive from the explosion. There was also the very real possibility that both wrecks would be blown into the ravine.

'Targets acquired,' she said.

There was no answer.

'Both targets as acquired as identified in the briefing', she added, by way of a hint. The ideal moment was passing.

'Permission to fire.' Her thumb was over the button, her body leaning forward. The first target was eating the diesel fumes of the vanished pickup.

'Hold. Do not launch.' Mike Thompson was speaking clearly. Stamping out each word.

Maggie and Jack looked across their equipment and both raised their eyebrows. The perfect place to launch was passing them by. As she watched the blue Nissan slipped around the corner leaving a haze of dust and blue diesel fumes.

'Maintain observation.'

She lifted her warplane up to gain height, and moved it around the mountain. The long view showed them picking up a bit of speed as they headed toward the village with its suspicious canvas. While they had been away another coach had arrived. There were four parked around the edges.

'Last chance,' said Maggie watching their targets. It was a more difficult hit. The cars were speeding and the tail end Charlie Nissan was lagging behind. Still she could get the Toyota easily, as it sped on a straight line like something from a fairground rifle range along the rock face. She calculated that a missile would be best for the first and, if the Nissan was intact and did not fall off the edge, then the laser guided bomb could do the follow up.

She illuminated the Toyota and sent a silent request for the order to fire. She badly wanted it to come. It would be very quickly be at the village, and she was beginning to wonder if this is where the strike was meant to happen, and if this was something aimed at assessing her willingness to do whatever was asked. There were persistent rumours within the service that parameters for their new type of warfare were being reset all the time, and that this required regular testing of those with their fingers on the fire button.

Despite the air conditioning, Maggie was beginning to feel hot and suddenly nauseous. Her breath was shallow. Surely, she thought, they can't be actually wanting to send a missile into that village. She didn't want to think about what that would mean on the ground, the carnage.

For the first time ever, in a short career with a number of attacks, she was wondering whether she could do what might now be asked. Not asked, actually. Ordered. Above the firing button her thumb was beginning to twitch as if the tendons and ligaments were themselves becoming agitated and alarmed. The cars were nearly at the village, a grey, brown dust plume behind them. They passed the man in long robe and scarf that seemed joined to his turban, sitting on his haunches nursing a rifle with a curved magazine.

She was breathing hard. The cars dived into cover like rabbits into a burrow. Maggie's finger was still twitching over the button. She dreaded the next words she felt were coming.

'OK, time to go home.'

'That's it?' She blinked, not quite believing.

'A late change apparently,' this time the voice in the headphones was Richard Pickett. 'Well done everybody. They also serve who watch and offer choices to the powers that be.'

As Maggie breathed out the air came in a series of shudders. Leaning back she realised rivulets must have been running down her spine. Overwhelming she felt a huge sense of relief. So, home it is, she thought. Good job, and within a couple of hours a gin and tonic, although probably not in the mess.

A small movement on the control stick put the drone into a slow turn. The sun was past its best in that part of the world which meant the mountains and gorges were showing dramatic colours and shadows. It was a welcome exchange from the sights Maggie has thought she might be delivering. On the railway line built through the pass by the British a train was moving slowly through the picture. Geology and the grey looking river had created the gorge as a narrow cut in the earth. The railway ran close to the main road and just for old times' sake, Maggie shifted sideways a little to take a last look at the truck stop.

'Who are they?' she asked sharply.

The close up ground view was showing another group of vehicles, again discreetly parked, but this time with people out in the open. She counted. Five. They seemed to be stretching their legs after a long drive before huddling together in a group for selfies, mobiles raised above their heads. She stayed the drone to watch. There was laughter and some of the group seemed to want a repeat picture, this time with the train going past. A famous pass, high mountains in lovely evening light and a train. Why not? Well, they were not the only one taking pictures. The drone was recording. They were all men, she noted and looked Chinese. No, there was possibly a woman? A slighter frame, but also dressed in a suit. Slightly more tailored. None in the group were wearing clothes you would normally expect to see in such terrain. They were all dressed as if they had only come with dark suits.

'What are you doing?' Mike Thompson sounded querulous. There was always a tension about who was actually in charge on flights like this.

'Just checking them out.'

'No much fuel.' This from Jack.

'Got that.' He was right to warn her.

'We obviously want to avoid landing the bird in the Gulf.' Jack again.

'I know.'

'The waters of the Gulf I mean.'

'I get it.'

'Nothing to see here.' Intelligence speaking. But as he spoke another white pickup swung toward the group. High above them the drone recorded the meeting. Someone, somewhere, thought Maggie, as she turned to nurse her bird home, might find something useful there. Altogether it was a lovely night for a flight.

Chapter 10

Balochistan

There was no happy shooting when the two cars swept into the village. The elders had been clear about that. The spreading canvas awnings and marque erected overnight made happy firing skywards impractical anyway, but Shameeza got the impression also that the villagers were nervous. Coachloads of rent a crowd set about welcoming the two Afghan leaders as their vehicles halted under the shade, the men putting hands to foreheads and the scores of women giving high pitched ululations. Even so, she sensed anxiety amidst the curiosity. The welcoming clump of elders had fidgeted nervously, soothing their beards or clicking prayer beads through their fingers while occasionally looking sideways at each other.

'You don't seem happy.' Jannat and Shameeza were standing alone, well covered in dark robes and headscarves, leaving the men to do the formal welcomes.

'I'm fine,' whispered Shameeza. For some reason she felt it was better not to move her mouth. She coughed. Dust from the arrivals caught at her throat. 'We have so much riding on this. And these men...', she faltered. 'Are so dangerous.'

Jannat nodded. She wrapped the flowing material around her lower face as if against the flying dirt. 'They're tigers,' she muttered. 'The people here depend on their drug smuggling and goodwill. But you don't need to worry. As long as I'm here that is.'

Men were now getting out of the cars, the doors opening as if synchronised with legs in voluminous leggings, arms and assault rifles leading the way. Each carload formed around a central figure and, to Shameeza, it was striking how alike they looked. Both were tall, well bearded and might have once been commanding, but that effect was diminished by full bodies pushing against clothing that would have flowed around thinner frames. It also seemed to her that Amanullah Tarzi and Mahmoud

Ali, even here, could not take their security for granted. Just then her mobile vibrated. She pulled it out, an action that had Mahmoud Ali turning as fast as a cobra to stare at her. He said something and one of his gunmen started in her direction, waving a hand.

Jannat stepped between them, nodding her head briefly at Ali. 'This is my assistant Shameeza Norzani. She needs her mobile to coordinate our meeting. When we are all together, all mobiles will be switched off and their chips taken out. I assure you cousin.'

Tarzi was already with the elders, but it was obvious that huddle was frozen mid formalities at what was happening behind them. Shameeza kept her eyes down, her face nearly entirely covered as she looked at the screen. 'Our other guests are at the foot of the gorge and waiting,' she said quietly and then held out her mobile, pulled the back off and took out the chip and battery.

Slowly Ali advanced, giving a perfunctory nod to Jannat before placing himself in front of Shameeza. 'I apologise sister,' he said as he took the whole lot out of her hands and sank them somewhere in his robes. She stood stock still aware that he was staring at the top of her head as she looked fixedly at his toes and sandals, her breath coming quick and shallow.

Jannat clapped her hands. 'We have a lot to do and our guests will want feeding.'

The men moved off, Jannat with them. Shameeza followed well behind. She was not in the least bothered by the mobile. She had two others. If all went according to her plan they would all be leaving soon with a deal to mine the considerable Lithium reserves for a world hungry for more batteries and storage systems. Afghanistan was also rich in other valuable minerals such as cobalt. Get the lithium deal she reasoned and a cornucopia of opportunity would open. The dream was long standing. Six months ago she had gone to Jannat with a plan, and been almost laughed at.

'Do you know for how long outsiders have been eyeing all that? It's not going to happen. Every time someone dips their toe something happens to make them go away. There's a shooting, or even a stoning. One of those clowns gets greedy and puts the squeeze on some local manager who runs home to mummy. It's an impossible place to work. Trust me. There's easier ways to make money.'

She had talked her round, even got her to sign up to fake marriage idea to cover their visit. Now the principles were going to meet. Shameeza let out a long breath as she reached the tented area under the awning where the talks would take place. Ever since she got Jannat to focus she had been working covertly to bring all this about. Her share was going to be enormous, even with Jannat insisting on a sixty forty split for bringing the deal home. The real money would be made by her one per cent share of future profits.

The men and Jannat were having tea in the house of one of the elders. Shameeza looked around the multi coloured tent. It was a large space, with cushions around the side and low tables they could all sit crossed leg at for tea. She had been told that conventional chairs and tables would not be expected by their guests. She took that as a signal of agreement and they were coming to sign. That, and the nature of the delegation. People like that did not waste their time.

The sound of engines outside, crunching gravel and fresh ululating told her the final party was arriving. Time for her to be out there to meet and greet.

Chapter 11

Thorswick

The bulletin pierced Ash's sleep. World news. An unremarkable saunter through a litany of mankind's latest sadness. There was nothing about a drone strike. No reason why there should be, he thought. They were common enough. Listening to something about beheadings by insurgents in Mali he ticked off who would need protection. What he could do for some. But not all. Who would have to ride out the risk. This was going to be his last hurrah. Time to resign. And get a life.

His mobile buzzed. Now the fun starts he thought, as he readied to get through security. There was no need. Directly on the line was Adrian Holesworthy, sounding flat. So flat in fact that Ash felt the need to ask the question.

'It didn't happen,' said Holesworthy. 'It was stopped. By the Minister. He heard about it late, and was furious. Said that anything like that should be cleared by him. And what the hell did we think we were doing attacking a marriage party.'

'I thought the plan was to get them on the road.'

'He said that wasn't the point. They were all part of the wedding. It would be an incredible affront when we are trying to get on terms with leaders out there.'

'Which we have been failing to do for years. And what does he mean by affront? I think the Americans feel pretty affronted by what those guys did to their citizens.'

'The Minister says we're not here to do the American's dirty business.'

'Really? When did that start?' Ash needed to think. He got up and started to wander.

'This is serious, Ash'. Adrian Holesworth hesitated. Either because of the unfamiliar name, or because of something else. His voice sounded tight. 'He wants you suspended. He says you're conducting a vendetta and you would say anything to get those ghastly fuckers killed. Altogether he reckons your judgement's off.'

There was a very long pause. 'Untrustworthy was the word used.'

"Untrustworthy" hung there between them. It was an adjective that could have you terminated in their world. One way or another. Despite himself, Ash was shocked. It was one thing for him to think about leaving and flouncing off into the sunset. It was quite another to be told you were unreliable. Inevitably such a suspicion meant process, with suspension being the first stage. In his experience, those pushing for process usually had one end in view. While it might all be done by the service handbook, with interviews and committees, the circle of trust was breached. Somebody, somewhere had called you out, and things were never likely to be the same again. They both knew that.

'This concern about the wedding,' said Ash eventually. 'I got a call early and it sounded as if the drone strike was on. Nobody in the chain seemed worried about offending anyone.'

'The Minister was taking some down time. His deputy had a headache and says she wasn't fully briefed. Otherwise, she says, she would most certainly have prevented it. It was a very fast bit of arse covering on her part. As it was, Carrick-Rhodes came to it late. When he called in and asked for details he killed it dead. Said such a thing would never have got past first base had he been asked, and that's why we have politicians in charge.'

'So he called it sometime last night then.'

'What? Oh, yes I think so.'

Ash thought about the timing. Carrick-Rhodes had called in the aftermath of watching horse racing and sipping champagne in the Royal Box with Norman Ellroy and Safedeen Khan. 'Lucky he called in then. I expect he does that when he knows a major intervention is about to go off.'

'Not usually no. Communication might be compromised as he was out and about, so we followed protocol by keeping it in house with his deputy. She may have tipped him, I suppose, although she seemed on board, whatever she says now. In fact she was preoccupied with watching wrestling on a North Korean channel.'

Ash hoped Holesworthy would pick up the obvious question about how the Minister got to hear about a secret mission while watching horses. If Holesworthy did have that in mind, he was not about to start a discussion. 'The fact remains Ash. You're suspended while there is an investigation by Ethics and Legal.'

It was a moment. One of those when there is a line to be crossed. A button to be pressed, or a word to be said, that is irrevocable. 'Don't worry. I quit.'

Holesworthy barely missed a beat. 'The Minister called me at sparrows. He said if you expressed a desire to leave the service, then we should not stand in your way. So you might want to think about what you're saying.'

Ash took a deep breath. 'I'm out.'

A dismissive sniff came down the line. 'As you wish. It goes without saying that's wholly your decision. I understand you'll get three month's pay and must quit the cottage.'

Dammit thought Ash, he was prepared. 'What about a new identity?'

'Why on earth do you need another one?' Ash imagined Holesworthy now, his curiosity thoroughly roused. 'Are you blown?'

Possibly, thought Ash. That admission would involve saying an assassin and long term opponent was in the neighbourhood having been mixing in the Royal Enclosure with their Minister and, by the way, the records of the Service had been hacked. That was quite a rich cake to bake just now. Nor was it a good time to ask for a Glock handgun as a farewell present. 'No', he managed.

'Good. If you were in that particular difficulty it might make us wonder what you've been doing.'

A sniff again before Holesworthy resumed, as if speaking from a script. 'You leaving the service is effective immediately. You will be required to leave your mobile connected to the system so that sensitive apps and service systems can be stripped. I am sending you now a copy of the latest version of the Official Secrets Act. You don't need to sign it because you will be crucified anyway if you so much as think about stepping over lines.'

'Is that it?'

'What? Oh yes. Thank you for your service.'

The line went dead. As if on cue the computer screens came alive with an instruction to connect his mobile. He did, and watched for a minute as the systems mated and screwed over the hard drives. Ash left them to it and went back to the bedroom. He was in a daze. The suddenness of the dismissal was brutal, leaving him unsure about what to do next. Going back to bed was even an option. Before him was a day, a week, even a life without purpose, and it scared him. Loss was not a new feeling, but without any warning he was in a void, without any idea of a future in a country he found profoundly foreign.

He looked out of the window. He should get out before it got too hot. Take a run and beast himself up the hills and set off some feel good endorphins. Follow the fox. Resist the urge to get back into bed and howl. Or take some of the morphine he had squirrelled away while being treated. He was tempted. More than that he got out the packet. There had been times when drugs were used without the excuse of having being shot in the back. He blinked at the memory. Of the nightmare days locked in a room, sweating, and disorientated. Unable to sleep and not awake.

Running, would be better. Slowly he pulled on a running shirt and shorts. At the top of the stairs he heard it. A distinctive sound of a thoroughbred super car, coming down the village road. It was not travelling at speed. If anything it was crawling, and in a low gear making the it purr rather than growl. Ash stood at the stairs, his head on one side. Tracking it. How likely was it that it was something to do with him, he wondered. And if it were, would Khan be driving? He doubted it. In their time busting around circuits in someone else's cars they got to know each other's driving style. The Safedeen he knew was fast and controlled, not blipping the engine like this. Outside the car came to a stop, the engine faltering to silence. No big finish.

Ash waited. Whatever this was, he did not need to rush. A car door opened, and then the other. And then a single set of steps to the door and a knock. Knuckles on wood, not the tinny thing on the letter box. If his mobile was not being gutted and defanged remotely by the service he could have used it to see who was there through the hidden camera. As it was he was blind, but not in the mood to play safe. Striding down the stairs he flung open the door. There, preparing to knock again, was Norman Ellroy. Behind him on the road was a sleek Ferrari with a young woman in a short skirt whose scarlet lips matched the car perfectly.

'You're in!,' exclaimed Ellroy. 'I am delighted. You are Ash, I presume? I really have heard so much about you. And that result in the cricket. Absolutely incredible. Top banana.'

He paused, and stepped back. Ash was at a loss to know what to say. For the briefest moment he tore away from Ellroy's pale blue eyes to look at the woman, who hoisted a smile of flashing intensity at him.

'It's seems strange it's taken so long for us to meet. You've been here, what six months roughly?'

Ash nodded.

'Thought so. I can't always be here much myself. But as President of the Club I wanted to thank you in person.'

He shifted back again. Right down the road under some trees was a black four by four with tinted windows, backed into a passing place. Anyone in the back seat on the passenger side would have a very good view of Ash's front door, particularly now that Norman Ellroy had moved out of the way.

'As a token of my appreciation, I thought you might like to have a play with this.' The non-specific arm wave encompassed both the Ferrari and the woman. 'You can take it for a beating up on my track at the back of the Hall.'

The woman's eyes were now appraising, with an amused challenge. A hand went to her hip.

'That's very kind of you.'

'I don't know what you think, Ash. May I call you Ash?' There was an emphasis in the way he said the name that suggested there was knowledge behind the request. As if he knew he was playing along with an alias.

Ash nodded politely and his eyes went back, briefly, as if he was taking in a pleasant view, to the luxury four by four. It was one of the new Rolls Royce ones, made in China. He imagined Safedeen Khan sitting there, his thin face forward, eyes staring at him.

'You have probably heard I intend to build something here for these beauties.' Again, with anyone else if may have been unclear from his arm movement, which of the beauties he was talking about. 'It will be more of a homage really. For me petrol super cars were the apotheosis of western art incorporating the most sensual lines, with the promise of unrivalled pleasure and sensation of power. I think you are a man who would appreciate that.'

'I had heard you are building a circuit.'

'Oh, it will be so much more than that. It is a travesty, to my mind, that cars like this are not created any more. There will soon be very few knights who can ride them properly, who know how to use them to their best potential.'

Certainly not you thought Ash, who was struck by the man's curious phrasing. As if careering around a race circuit in aged cars was something noble.

'I let a few friends use them when they come down.' The key fob was being offered. 'Please.' Dumbly Ash took it.

'And I hope perhaps we can do some work together. I am always in the market for people with the right contacts and talents.' This time there was no mistaking Ellroy's meaning. The blue eyes bored into him intently, and in that moment Ash saw the drive of the man. The look was fierce and acquisitive. 'Let me know if you are available.'

Ash smiled and assured him he would.

'And perhaps you could do with some company.' A statement and the eyes never leaving his face as it was searched.

Behind Ellroy the woman, hearing that her time had come, lifted herself off the bodywork and took a step forward.

'Just the car thanks.'

'Sure? No matter. And do think about the other offer. With me you could be very rich. I am sure you have heard all sorts of things about what I do.' A pause which Ash did not fill. 'But these are changing times, and the few like me who ride that wave, are the future. Around us, nations are falling, climate is driving millions from their homes and populists manipulate to drive people apart. The one truth in the world is data. Those who own it, and know how to use information, are in charge.' Ellroy tapped the side of his nose and then pointed the finger at Ash. 'I would include you in that category.'

After another searching look he turned and caught up with the woman, imperiously waving her back. For a time Ash stayed in the doorway watching their progress up the road before softly closing the front door and then racing up the stairs to watch. A chauffeur for someone like Ellroy, he thought, would usually spark into life as soon as he saw him move. The black car though stayed put, removing the possibility of a glimpse of whoever was inside.

Ellroy had not bothered with subtlety or pretence. His knowledge of Ash was as up to date as the dismissal five minutes ago. The strike being stopped and job offer, showed he was stuffed and peppered liked a festive turkey. For all he knew he may have been prey for weeks, if not months. His every move played on a chess board against an opponent harnessing awesome computing power. Ash fingered the key fob of the Ferrari. The sweetener. Join me and all this new world has will be yours. An offer that was not possible to refuse. Ellroy had not needed to spell out consequences. No one in their right mind would turn it down, especially if they knew the capability of the watcher sitting in the leather luxury of the Rolls.

Chapter 12

North of the Taiwan Straits, South China Sea.

It was a beating burst that lasted for the briefest of moments. It was heart stopping though for Lieutenant Eiji Sato. He was officer of the watch for the dark hours before dawn on board the Japanese Akizuki class destroyer Sakaki. Designed as a ship protector it was riding point some distance ahead of the multi-national fleet progressing into the South China sea. The Sakaki's whole hull was a listening device, and from the cacophony of the ocean it sifted for sounds that could only be machine made.

This was an area of work where computers had all but replaced human audio experience, but Lieutenant Sato was a dutiful officer. He listened twice before ordering the destroyer to alert. Signallers put the sound on the fleet's network, allowing shipboard and land based systems to start crunching. Everybody knew what it meant. Somewhere below them was a potential threat. The 'Freedom of the Seas' exercise was going ahead despite vociferous opposition from China, and that sound came from well within the exclusion zone. A zone designed to prevent deadly misunderstandings between anything above and below the water line.

The ocean floor they were traversing was scarified by the crashing of tectonic plates. Ridged and rippled with deep set canyons, the broken formations were ideal cover for any submerged intruder and hard for hunters. As Eiji issued his orders he was clear. The priority was detection. Securing a fix that would allow other warships to bring their systems to bear. Identification would be a bonus. Yes, it was a hunt. But it was not to be killed. Unless it went hostile.

Across a wide underwater arc the search was on. As the first to get a trace The Sakaki took the lead. Very soon after the klaxons sounded the warship's commander, Yumiko Tanaka, made the bridge as Lieutenant Sato was ordering the launch of the towed array. A forty year old who passed top of her class at the academy, she presented a trim, disciplined figure in the beige uniform shirt and trousers. Her head under the peaked blue cap nodded her approval at the decision to deploy the sonars, and he was pleased she seemed willing at this stage to take a back seat. In the year since Eiji joined the Sakaki he had learned to respect her coolness and authority. He had seen other officers being given room to exercise their own judgement, with Commander Tanaka, managing with nods, an encouraging word and only the occasional raised eyebrow of interrogation. Now it seemed, it was his turn. Just to be sure, he drew himself to attention and gave a quick bow from the waist.

'Carry on Lieutenant. Let's land that fish.'

The hydrophones splashed over the stern into the churning wake and went out more than half a kilometre, listening for a repeat that would allow a precise fix, and perhaps even identification as to the type of beast they were dealing with. The operators in the darkened sensor room adjusted the fins so the devices rose and dived as they probed under the various thermal layers, while across the fleet other specialists listened in. They were treated to various sounds. A pod of sperm whales complained loudly amongst themselves about the passing of so much manmade noise, while a keening pygmy blue whale, as identified on the computers, drew a 'nice one!' from underwater warfare specialist Abby Dayton on board the British aircraft carrier HMS Queen Elizabeth. The rare species completed her private whale bingo game, and she ticked her pad while never taking her eyes off monitors that traversed the seas around her ship. Her systems though, like all the others across the fleet, remained blank as far as any man made device was concerned. There was nothing.

On The Sakaki, Eiji moved around the various operators conducting the search. But with each passing hour he knew the chances of finding any trace was vanishingly small. Any submariner worth his salt would be using the fractured seabed, deep channels and multiple layers to sit tight and quiet. A look at the Commander made him realise she was leaving it to him to call it off. She gave the smallest of nods.

'Reel them in. Stand down'. He was bitterly disappointed. The first light was on the horizon, and not for the first time he felt the hopelessness of the vast ocean.

'You could not have done anything more, Lieutenant'.

Eiji gave the smallest shake of his head. 'We did not find it Commander. I am most truly sorry.'

'But we did, at first. And you reacted very fast. There can be no doubt you made it run scared. Whatever it was.' Commander Tanaka would soon be leaving The Sakaki to take command of one of Japan's five escort flotillas. The slim, youthful looking officer was set to be only the second woman to be given such a commission. 'If there was anything else to be done, I would have suggested it. As it is, the most interesting question is what could it have been, and why was it so difficult to detect.'

Around them in the gloom of the bridge new bodies were replacing the outgoing watch, and a signaller presented a slip of paper to Tanaka. After quickly looking at it, she read it in English to the Lieutenant. It was from American Admiral in the US carrier, a colossus that dwarfed every other ship in the fleet. 'We can expect our defences to be tested many times over the coming days', she said slowly. 'Thanks are due to our colleagues aboard the destroyer Sakaki for their vigilance and swift action. Tonight we sent the message. You cannot go unseen or unheard.'

Commander Tanaka folded the paper thoughtfully. It was unnecessary for either her or Eiji to voice the shared thought that the detection was fleetingly brief, and for all they knew their unwanted visitor was still amongst them. She turned to go and then stopped. 'I have been invited to a reception at the end of the exercise on board the British aircraft carrier Queen Elizabeth. Perhaps you would accompany me? I am sure they would like to hear as much as possible about what happened tonight.' Commander Tanaka smiled briefly.

Eiji was stunned. A reply was not necessary, and the slim figure was already stepping through the blast doors on her way out. While others, in different cultures might have leapt to some kind of conclusion about such an invitation, he knew from the way he had been addressed that this was a formal reward from a superior to a junior.

A steward handed him a steaming cup of coffee. As he sipped he studied the emerging shapes of the other warships. With the hydrophones deployed The Sakaki had run at restricted speed, and the rest of the fleet was catching up. Amongst them were the flags of India, the Philippines, Thailand and Australia, the ensigns flapping above the keen, grey hulls. Also present in numbers were ships and submarines from America and Britain.

Eiji put down his coffee and raised his binoculars as one ship in particular came into view. The ten times magnification brought detail to HMS Queen Elizabeth, even if it were still at such a distance that the whole ship was visible. Tiny aircraft on a flight deck the size of three football pitches were being readied.

The aircraft carrier was turning slightly toward him, a vision of majestic power on a sea being lightened from grey to azure by the morning sun. Eiji checked the pennants on The Sakaki and realised the carrier was coming into wind. He would stay to see the Super Eagles launched. As long, as they did it quickly. His stomach was telling him it was due to be fed, and there was still the matter of some sleep before his next watch. By then the Exercise should be in full swing. The stiffening of the bridge crew let him know that the warship's second in command was approaching to take over. He raised his binoculars for a last look at the pride of the British navy. The aircraft were ready but then he saw something strange. Around the ship the sea was changing colour. It was darker as if the carrier was floating on a spreading flower of a deeper blue. As he watched the shape changed and became white as foaming water rose in great plumes from the sea. Nestled in the middle the carrier rose and twisted into the folds, displaying its deck and tipping aircraft over its side. Coming down like a breaching whale it sent its own watery ruffles up and around, leaving the massive ship wallowing and settling. Eiji leapt across the bridge, almost colliding with the second as he slammed his palm onto the alarm. Reaching for the public address microphone he breathed once, and then spoke.

'General Quarters. General Quarters.' He paused and took a breath. They had been warned, both by Tokyo and the fleet commander, that, in these waters, a careless order could ignite a war. But with something like awe, Eiji said the words no officer hoped to say in anger.

'Battle stations.'

The second gaped at him. Eiji pointed through the window.

'They've hit the British carrier,' he said urgently. He thrust the binoculars at his superior before again pressing the microphone button. All around the klaxon was sounding, while steel doors were slamming and feet pounded through corridors.

'Officer of the Watch,' announced Eiji. 'This is not a drill. I repeat. This isn't a drill.'

Chapter 13

Oxford

Ash's body was being swept, teased and lashed by salon smooth blond hair. The strands fizzing over his skin, as she moved. Bowing her head to let it brush, dance and circle whatever she chose, her lips following through. Sometimes she would sit up giving him a view of her enhanced breasts, the nipples sharply defined and, almost as a concession, allowing his hands around them while she gathered breath before moving back down. Anything else would happen when she was good and ready. Ash understood her need for being in charge. It was several months since he had cut her off without a word.

'You bastard,' Charlotte Dayton said when he called her.

'I know.' He had expected little else. At this stage at least.

'You fucking loser. I hate you.'

'I made a mistake.' They had met by chance at one of the retro style Fish and Chip shops that were becoming popular. It was not somewhere he had ever been before, having come across it in a bohemian part of Oxford while he was wandering as an aimless sightseer. She was two ahead of him in the queue. If she were a tail, or intending to hook up with him, she could not have placed herself there. They quickly became lovers. She was sharp, and a good people watcher. Which meant it was never going anywhere. His scars and her observations about his habits, especially the dropping of things to check underneath his car, provoked too many questions. Curiosity became a fast spreading weed in the carefully segregated pleasure park. The ending came through ignored calls on his side, and him not making any.

'Get the hell off my mobile. Do what you're good at and lose the number.

'Let me make it up to you. Come for a drive. And wear a hoodie.'

'A hoodie?'

'One without logos.'

He was banking on her usual curiosity and was rewarded when Charlotte Dayton walked out of the terrace house she could not afford, her head well hidden. He was at the corner of her street and hung back.

'Bear with me,' he said cheerfully. 'I've left the car in that housing estate where the police go in fours with dogs.'

'That's brave of you.' Her voice was muffled by the grey hood.

They walked to the estate, him staying a few feet behind, something she accepted. He had always explained that it might be good for her if they were not seen that often together, or captured on cameras which automatically fed into face recognition systems. With the government they had, staying off camera and minimising virtual presence was a political statement for many younger people now anyway. Even so, it was one of the habits that had got her asking too many questions. 'What exactly is the problem?' she had asked. 'Are you activist, terrorist, drug dealer, policeman, or all of the above'? His response "social marketeer" caused a rise in her perfectly shaped eyebrows.

As they turned into the estate he brought the Ferrari to life.

'Is this with you?' Charlotte asked as if it were a child or dog, but he could hear the delight. Ash knew the car would have all sorts of tracking devices and bugs inside. It was why he had parked it some way from her house.

'Hop in.'

'There's scratches all down the sides.'

It was true, someone had taken a key or knife along both sides exposing shiny lines of metal. Ash briefly took in the blank windows of the housing estate and a bunch of kids at a corner. He shrugged and popped the driver's door. 'Not really my problem.'

She looked at him oddly, and then mimicked his shrug in a mocking way and dropped into the passenger seat. In their brief liaison Ash had picked up on a deep streak of resentment and rebellion in Charlotte. She was adept at selling houses to very rich people, but was trapped in a job with bosses who reneged on her deal to get a percentage. While she might be considered to be doing quite well despite that, like so many she was angry. For now, she was a perfect foil for his own. And as far as sex was concerned, it had been a long time between drinks.

He drove straight for the old wartime airfield from which Norman Ellroy had carved his race track. Once the Ferrari gained the old concrete strip he got out and moved around to the passenger side. 'Let's see how fast you can go. Just on the straights'

Charlotte tried, and with coaching achieved a creditable 130 miles an hour before easing up with plenty of room to spare. Then it was his turn. Turning onto the circuit at the Hall proper he took it slowly at first, passing the house and noting the newly built pit lanes and gantry lights. No one stopped them, but he knew there would be many eyes watching. Perhaps Ellroy and Khan. After a couple of laps that would not have disgraced a driver of reasonable ability he got going, taking corners with screeching tyres setting speeds in excess of two hundred on the straights. Charlotte was a mute observer, staying quiet but for gasps on turns that would have caused many to scream. By the fourth circuit fuel was getting low, and the rough housing of the tyres and frame risked him breaking down, something he did not want to do there.

At the top of the track he went back onto the runway, where he spun the car into a pivot, raced up to a hundred and fifty, turned on a hard circle raced back to where they had started and spun it again before slowing right down and heading off for the lane.

'What have you just done?, asked Charlotte.

'I was just drawing something for a man who sees this type of car as an art form.' His shoulders were aching and the paintwork was pitted and pebble dashed. There was no going back now.

Charlotte's head was singing but her eyes shone. 'Let me see, you had us spinning around, roared up the runaway and then back again. I suppose if someone looked at that from above it might look like two balls and a prick.' They had reached the lane and her hand slipped between his legs. This time he returned to Oxford on the motorway, tripping every camera as they went and burning off two police cars.

Back in the bedroom his mobile pinged.

'Leave it,' she ordered. He did. By now the cops would have got hold of the registered owner. They may even have found the Ferrari in the housing estate

A light slap hit his face. 'You are still with me?'

He looked down and smiled. 'Evidently.'

Charlotte rose slightly. 'Better use while I've got it.' Which, with another move, she did. By the time they finished, his phone was vibrating repeatedly. With a theatrical raising of the eyes Charlotte got off and made for the door, 'I'll get some more wine,' she said archly. 'I'm sure you want to be alone with that thing.'

There were a whole load of messages. Prominent amongst them was 'Get back to work', followed by a 'Where the hell are you?' There was also a message from the Service IT department instructing him to reconnect his mobile to the secure computer so systems could be reinstalled. Gazing at the screen Ash wondered what could have caused such a sudden recall. He had been in trouble before, but usually it took a few days, if not a couple of weeks, before being told he was very naughty and they needed something from him.

Downstairs he heard Charlotte opening the fridge, the clunk of a bottle being pulled out and some media coming into life. Suddenly she gave a cry of shock. His legs were swinging off the bed when he heard her bare feet slapping the flooring, and then up the stairs to the bedroom. She was still completely naked, a computer tablet in her hand, her face stricken. 'My sister', she moaned and gulped. 'She's on that boat.'

He looked at her blankly. She choked, held out the screen, and gave a sob before collapsing into him. 'Look,' she managed.

Chapter 14

RAF Bincton, Lincolnshire.

After her flight Maggie went to the gym. She was tired, but knew sleep would be easier if she stretched and mulled a few decisions while working up a sweat. Another reason was the expectation she would have the place to herself. The rest of the base was still at war even if, according to the plan, it was a smoking pile of glow in the dark debris. Pushing open the swing doors she stood for a moment in the corridor. Not a sound came from the officer's gym at the end. When she stepped into the locker room the towels were untouched and piled in a neat square. The room clear of steam. Perfect.

Going into the gym she switched on the lights and the main switch for the machines and screens. These were old fashioned, and still operated with remote controls. Having voice activated devices were not considered a good idea on a base primarily concerned with listening and spying. They were too easily hacked. Down the room screens flicked on with some kind of music show with automaton hosts. Fortunately the sound was on mute.

As always she started on a mat. Pulling herself up, arms stretched above her head before lowering them down slowly to her toes. With her head between her knees she wondered again at her stupidity over the affair. There would be trouble of some sort, that was certain. She gave a long breath out as she came up. At least it was over. By her. Taking control. Going down again she was relieved. The pull on her hamstrings was needed. It had been a long time seated. And it took two to mess up. Yes, she should have walked.

Sitting down she stretched out her right leg and brought up her left knee. Carefully twisting, she hooked her elbow over. If it came to any fallout though she was sure, even though he was senior, she would get the blame. She held the pose. He had hinted at that throughout. The blame thing. The pose calmed her.

Time to get on the cross trainer. To build up some sweat. She had to think of what to do with the blue cottage. It really was not for her. Too much of a dream. Nothing in her life equipped her for what was on offer there. It was not just a question of Labradors and tweeds. It went deeper than that. The problem was if it were the right thing to do when there were so many unanswered questions about the man who left it to her.

She knew a little. In the way that family mysteries are often hinted at, or vaguely referenced, she surmised the former owner was the man her church going Grandmother had an affair with shortly after she arrived in Britain. This was backed up by the family bible, a volume to which a lie could never be laid. Written there in copper plate was Granny's only wedding. It was to a man from her native Barbados, who soon disappeared off the scene. Also inscribed was the birth of Maggie's mother, six months after the nuptials.

Questioning the matriarch was not possible. With time her religious enthusiasm increased, along with the repeated statement, 'As the Bible says. God helps those who help themselves.' Along with the mistaken reference, 'Romans.'

Yet, as Maggie grew she noticed there was often some other help coming to the high rise council flat. She was frequently lodged there when her mother 'went away', which she did frequently. With a child's perception she soon worked out that if things got tight, a cash injection somehow could be summoned. New school uniforms were purchased without recourse to the second hand stall at the start of each term. Television sets were upgraded with reasonable frequency. An abusive 'friend' of her mother suddenly disappeared from their life after putting her in hospital. It was Granny who vetoed the desperate option of going to the police.

'I know someone,' she said. And this someone was obviously not the vicar, because they never had anything like that trouble again. In addition, on the estate the daily harassment from hooligans and racists seemed to have been switched off. Even when Granny visited Trinidad to bury a last surviving relative and her right of residence in the United Kingdom was suddenly questioned, it was resolved within a day. Waiting for her at her flat on her return was a letter of apology from the Home Office, an event unheard of in their community.

First Maggie's mother died. Shortly afterwards, Granny. There was nothing in any of the sparse paperwork or photos left behind to give a clue about a benefactor. A slim book from a dresser in the council house held a number of telephone numbers and some addresses. Maggie baulked at the idea of ringing complete strangers, but she did send a card notification on the passing of her Grandmother to those with an obviously residential address. She got two 'in sympathy' replies from former nursing colleagues, and an equal number of return to senders. Two years later the letter from the solicitor arrived informing her of a bequest of a small amount of money and a house in Thorswick, a place that did not feature in the address book. It arrived like an arrow. No forwarding and no ambivalence. It knew where she could be found.

In the place where the water bottle should be her mobile illuminated. Without breaking her stride she picked it up. An image. It was what was known as a CCC, or 'camouflaged covered crutch' shot. With it came a message. 'How is our love nest? Can't wait to christen it.' Before her eyes both the message and picture dissolved and disappeared. There would be nothing to find.

Irritated she shoved the mobile back. 'Bloody man,' she thought. Grasping the handles of the machine and pressing down with her feet she powered into a faster pace.

Ping. Another message. Despite herself she picked up the mobile. 'I love the way your ass moves on that thing.'

She swung around, the machine now in charge, moving her legs and arms as it slowed. Pickett was half way into the room, smiling sardonically at her, his own mobile being waved in greeting. 'Pleased to see me?', he asked.

There was something about the way he said it that made her look toward the door. Richard Pickett had a charm and the kind of looks, her grandmother would have said, that could sink a battleship. The last time though he had hurt her and seemed to know, and enjoy, what he was doing. She wondered afterwards if their previous, rather prosaic encounters, were him warming her up for a very different experience. It hadn't been a pleasant thought.

'Don't worry. We won't be disturbed.' His other hand reached into the voluminous pocket of his camouflage and jangled something. 'I have the keys.'

Slowly Maggie stepped down from the machine and thought again how tall he looked. He was a man who liked to look after himself too. He was often down the other end of the gym working his way through the weights. 'It's over,' she said simply. She could have added, it should never have started and you know it.

'I thought it interesting how you raised all those things about Rules of Engagement in the briefing,' Pickett said. He was speaking quietly and moving slowly toward her. 'All the time I was thinking of the Rules on our Engagement.'

He smiled, the charmer trying. Somehow though the effect was not pleasant. Maggie wanted to step back but the machine was in her way.

'And those don't allow you to say "it's over". It'll be over when I say.'

'Don't Richard…..'

But he already had her by the neck, forcing her back on to the guard rail of the cross trainer while pressing himself against her, his face against her head, his feet forcing a passage between hers. 'I going to fuck you,' he hissed. 'Right here. It may be the last time, or not. It's all up to me.'

There it was. The lick of venom. This time in his voice, and not just in the grip. Her head was being forced upwards, the throat gagging under the pressure. She twisted, but he knew what he was doing. Holding her hard, a hand scrambling. Onto her breasts and then down before pulling at the waist band of her leggings. Thank God for Lycra. It wasn't proving easy. She thumped hard at his side, but that just caused his grip to tighten. She jerked and suddenly went limp. He almost laughed. 'Not good enough I'm afraid.'

Maggie felt powerless. The ceiling was being covered in slow moving coloured dots, his pressing body preventing leverage into muscles. Her throat unable to scream. His other hand now between her legs. His hair, she thought, pull it out. Yet something else was holding her back. This man was her boss, her superior, and, right now, the only thing that would stop him was to inflict real damage, even if she could.

One more go she thought as she heaved against him. He was very close to getting what he wanted, his excitement coming in violent, pleasured grunts. It was useless.

It was the siren that stopped him. A loud alarm. Nothing to do with her. From all around the base. It was one they had never heard before, but both knew what it meant, and it was enough to override even his moment. Simultaneously their mobiles pinged with messages.

'This isn't over,' was all he said. And he was gone. Not that Maggie saw. Her eyes were closed. As she heard the doors close she turned onto the arms of the machine, sagging over the them gulping in more air. The sobs came from somewhere very deep, and were as big as the first intakes of breaths. Tears dropped onto her arms, and the pedal of the cross trainer. But for the rails she might have been on the floor. From the pain she knew there were going to be bruises. Her breasts for one and definitely her neck. Those at least could be hidden by her zipped up flight suit. She wasn't going to wipe up the tear marks from the machine. Sod it and sod them.

Slowly she straightened, and pulled up the waistband of her leggings. The screens around the gym were showing a map of the South China sea with a red cross on it. Maggie looked around for a TV controller. She found one by the weight machines and turned up the sound. The voice was speaking about some kind of accident or disaster. At the bottom of the picture was a stream of words racing across the bottom. Something had happened to the arrier, Queen Elizabeth. It had suffered an explosion while on an exercise.

Maggie looked at her phone. The text was from the Ministry of Defence in London. All personnel were to stand by for an important message.

The map disappeared to be replaced by two men at a desk in a newsroom type setting. One of the men was reading something while the other presenter listened intently, his face a grave mask.

'There's no word of casualties yet. No idea of cause. A ship that many of the British public, and indeed others who had seen it during its visits across the world, had grown to love. A ship that was designed to project British power. And indeed a deep commitment to international peace, the laws of the sea and solidarity with all sorts of people.'

Very quickly a retired Admiral was put on air, speaking down into his computer with an incongruous set of flying plaster pigs on the wall behind him, and nostrils that should have been plucked.

Indeed, if there were a flagship of today's Royal Navy, this was it. And then a hasty correction. I am sorry I mean is it. A very powerful weapon and expression that Britain still has a place at the top table. Far too early to speculate. Things can go wrong on a ship. Accidents can happen. Not that today's Navy does not operate at the highest level of safety. No. No. One should not speculate at all. Well there could always be something like an old wartime mine. One in a million chance of course. Very unfortunate. Difficult to know what could have caused an event of this size, however.

And back to the studio. As the Lord Whatsit High Admiral just said, very important not to draw early conclusions. But the carrier was entering seas that are considered the most dangerous in the world thanks to the rivalry with China and that country's expansionist ambitions. But also worth mentioning that strategic channels were also heavily mined during the Second World War and although they obviously have been cleared and are some of the busiest lanes in the world for globalised trade, old mines can lose their anchorage and drift. There was no word from the Ministry of Defence in London on casualties, and obviously there will be many families now very concerned. MOD was simply saying they was an incident affecting HMS Queen Elizabeth.

Maggie listened transfixed up to the point when the repetitions got too familiar. She wanted to be back in her own apartment. Scooping up her clothes from the locker she jogged back, for all the world like a woman who had lifted clothes from a laundrette. Getting into the service flat she dropped her bundle and switched on the little used television. There were now pictures. Taken at some distances from another ship, and bearing the insignia of the Thai navy in the top left of the screen, the images showed the carrier with a flight deck tilted into the morning sun. Above it were helicopters, swooping up and down. Helpfully the Thai language script scrolling along the bottom had one word in English. 'Mayday'.

Back to the studio. What are we to make of that? And uneasily, well it doesn't look as if the ship is in a good position at the moment, but as the Admiral said, safety in depth was built in from the very beginning, and the Ministry of Defence has not given us any reason as yet to have real concerns about either the ship or the crew.

We are getting more pictures. This from the Spanish news agency, who received them from their Navy Ministry as they have a ship there. Here they come now.

A deck. In bright sunlight. By the look of it a fairly large warship. Big enough for stretchers to be lowered from the air. There were six, with another arriving from above into vision. Around each of the stretchers were medical looking staff, with masks and flame hoods. It froze after about thirty seconds. Blank screen, and cut to the studio with the presenter and the reporter, both looking unsure about how they were going to handle this one.

'So, it looks as if there have been casualties.'

'Yes, that's correct. A disturbing piece of video there, but as I say no official word from the Ministry of Defence.'

Maggie got up to put the kettle on as the TV coverage went to a report by someone using archive footage of the Queen Elizabeth from launching to its various missions, while running through what it carried in terms of aircraft and crew numbers. When she returned with a mug there was a new statement from the Ministry.

The presenter read it at first sight, holding a piece of paper portentously in front of him, while obviously being torn between a desire for the dramatic and finding a suitably sombre tone. 'The Ministry statement, which we have here, has confirmed that there have been casualties in the incident affecting HMS Queen Elizabeth in the South China Sea. A number is being provided for relatives and those concerned. Oh, I am told the number is now available on the screen now. The Ministry adds there is no evidence at this stage of the cause.'

'Can I interrupt you there, Peter? Washington says that the British navy carrier Queen Elizabeth was attacked. The White House is expressing anger, and says there will consequences for those responsible. The United States Navy Department says its ships are offering rescue and hospital care for multiple casualties.'

'Well thanks Seb,' said the presenter eyeing his own bit of paper balefully for the briefest of moments before coming to himself and redirecting the look at the correspondent. 'Although I think we do have to give weight to what the Ministry here is saying.'

Seb suddenly cottoned on. 'Of course. Washington may have jumped to an early conclusion. I think our own people would know best what is happening.'

'Could not agree more, Seb. It would not be the first time our friends on the other side of the pond had got things wrong.' The two men looked at one another as if trying to remember such a previous occasion, and failing. 'Or exaggerated.'

'Yes, indeed Peter,' managed Seb eventually.

Both men then involuntarily touched their ear pieces. 'We're hearing that the Prime Minister will be speaking in Downing Street within the next hour.'

'Yes, and the House of Commons has cleared all business this afternoon.'

Maggie's tea was getting cold. She picked the mug up her mind whirling. They were repeating the video, while others were now being added. The massive ship looked as if it was somehow flattened. The effect Maggie guessed, of it being lower in the water. With each succeeding video it seemed that the activity around the carrier was increasing as if she were a Queen Bee and all the workers in the hive were dancing around her. There were helicopters, launches and other warships close to, some unmistakeably, in a sentinel role. Some of the pictures coming out broke away from the ghastly image of the stricken ship to show missile systems and guns swivelling through arcs, threatening the sky. She turned down the sound and went onto the web. Clearly she was going to get much more useful information from Washington.

Her mobile pinged. It was a message in three parts. The Ministry of Defence is ordering all UK armed forces personnel to their bases. All leave is cancelled. The third part was from the Commanding Officer of the base. They were now in a lockdown. The Exercise in pretend war was terminated. The security state was set at critical.

Maggie took a swig of the cold tea. Anyone hearing the news, or the tens of thousands in uniform who received the text messages, would remember what they were doing at that moment. For ever more the attack on the Queen Elizabeth would be linked to her near rape by her commander. The mixture of her disgust and violation mixed with the moment when men and women were dying and her job might be to avenge. To obey orders while wrestling with the loathing for him and herself for not fighting back. Because, surely, there must have been something she could have done.

The shots now were of the injured. For all she knew there would now be a war. She wore the uniform. That meant she would do have to do whatever was asked. Whoever asked. And whatever she thought. That was her job.

Chapter 15

Oxford and Thorswick

It was an effort to get out of Charlotte's house. Instinctively she knew he might be able to help. Her twin sister was 'something to do with the listening things'. Abby, she remembered, was always talking about hearing whales and other sounds from the deepest depths.

'I really need you to stay,' Charlotte implored, her face smudged with mascara. 'With me.' He could not. Nor could he explain. The messages were recalling him as if his exit had never happened. And, while knowing himself to be a fool, he welcomed the return. He did make tea, the steaming mug being received without a word, and left under her angry, distraught stare as she huddled in a dressing gown, her mobile on speaker, the large screen in the corner on one channel while her fingers hopped on a tablet. As he looked back a voice on the mobile said her call was number 76 and someone from the Ministry of Defence care team would be with her shortly. Stay on. Your call is important to us.

Ash walked away rapidly, glad the road was badly lit. The darkness fitted his mood. Charlotte, and shame, were acknowledged, admitted, and left where people once put out milk bottles. Being back in the fold of the Service meant he would have to get on the network as quickly as possible. His thoughts tumbled, the options being assessed and filed. There would soon be a time when he should come clean about his identity being blown and known to a potential assassin. He must also tell them about Ellroy's offer, and how its rejection made him vulnerable. Given what was happening in the South China Sea he knew it would be impossible to get anyone to focus on his local difficulties for some considerable time, let alone take him under their wing.

Before he even got to the corner, the reflected flash of blue lights bouncing off the road and buildings spoke of trouble on the housing estate. Rounding the bend he saw a number of police vehicles and vans drawn up in front of a crowd of stone throwing youths. Facing them lines of cops in helmets, sheltering behind riot shields. The Ferrari was midway between the two sides, a fridge having caved in its roof. A flaming bottle arched toward it, and crashed near enough to have flames licking a back tyre. A cheer went up as a second flamer landed on the fridge, the flames quickly spreading down.

In the street opposite were taxis, their drivers clustered around the open door of a car as they listened to the radio and took in the riot. They did not seem too bothered. Ash watched them and saw one in particular with a sallow face on the edge of the group. A man not being included. He was thin, with a black T shirt loose around heavily tattooed arms, the shapes bagging from the lack of tone. The skin suggesting illness and drugs.

'Looks like you've lost a car.' It was difficult to know which of the men had spoken. He gave a small shrug.

'Easy come, easy go.' He was very aware of their reaction to his words. Indifference to such a loss was for elites, and that opened up a yawning gulf that was wider than the road between them. 'You'll do'. A jerk of his head picked out the man on the fringe in a "come on, let's get on with it fast" kind of way.

Ash could tell the other drivers did not like his choice, while the man himself seemed surprised. He chucked away a slimy brown sliver of roll up and leapt toward a beige saloon three cars down. Without a word Ash joined him. Bucked by being chosen the man was effusive and wanting to please. He was soon delivering on what was happening in the South China Sea, fuelled by an undercurrent of speech from a radio station usually given over to rock.

'One bloke was saying it was probably a second world war mine, one of those hedgehog ones. Bet it was a Jap one. Ironic if it were one of ours. Says there's been that whatsyermercallit? That big load of rain they have down there?'

'Monsoon'.

'That's it. Thinks one could have been released in that. Seemed a clever bloke. After all this time, but it's got to be a

90

possibility hasn't it? You have to think of all those films about what happened out there. Was all over those islands. War and stuff. Must have left things behind. Should have dropped the bomb on them earlier, if you ask me. Can't believe anyone would do it deliberately because they know what they'd get.'

Taking advantage of a red light the man smacked his fist against the steering wheel. 'We'd hit them. Bang. Like that. Eye for an eye. That's what I say. And what's the point of having nuclear things if we don't use them? Yup.' His watery eyes flicked into the mirror for confirmation. On his wrist, another insignia that looked as if it were inked by biro. An early version of the ruling party's logo.

The Russians, droned the radio, were saying there should be no hasty assignment of blame. The announcer then floundered around saying they were going somewhere. Oh yes, the Ministry. In London. Of Defence that is. Because someone was going to be speaking there. Obviously they were going to be speaking about what had happened to that ship. That very large ship about which we are all so concerned. Let's hope there's some good news!

'Turn it up will you,?' With a grating electronic crash they moved listeners into the live press conference, just as a someone was drawing breath.

'Good. Morning. I am the Chief Information Officer and I shall not be taking questions. The Secretary of State will be making his first comment to the House of Commons, which, as you know, the Prime Minister has recalled.' A fastidious tone, each word separated without inflexion as if by a robot. He sounded to like a man who judged by grammar, and damned for a misplaced gerund.

The statement rolled out. 'The Ministry of Defence is dealing with an incident affecting the aircraft carrier, HMS Queen Elizabeth. The ship has been damaged, but not,' long pause. 'Repeat, not, sinking'. Another long pause and Ash imagined the man looking around the room, perhaps over the top of glasses, to give everyone a chance to make a careful note.

'There have been,' he resumed, 'a limited number of casualties, and unfortunately some fatalities. We shall wait until next of kin and relatives have been contacted before releasing further details'. A pause for some water, judging by the sipping noise in a silent room.

'There remains the possibility of discrepancies as some casualties were taken to other ships taking part in the exercise, and communication with the ship has been compromised.'

Ash pounced on the word 'compromised'. That should never have happened. Front line assets were built with layers of independent communication systems to prevent a blackout. He wondered if that was a ploy, slipped into the statement to give the Navy time.

The metronomic robot was reading out a telephone number for relatives to call, before wrapping up. 'Contrary to some reports, there is no immediate threat of HMS Queen Elizabeth sinking. There is no confirmation, at this stage, that the incident was the result of a hostile act. The aircraft carrier will be escorted by other ships from the 'Freedom of the Seas' exercise to dry dock in Singapore for an assessment. It is, of course, a place where the Royal Navy has many links. The Exercise has been postponed. We are grateful for the assistance being given by our allies, and volunteered by others.'

'And others', thought Ash. That would be the Chinese. They were offering to send nearby warships to the scene, and 'help with any investigation.' No mention of an investigation, Ash noted, from the Ministry of Defence, and there was no way that such help would be accepted.

'Fucking arseholes,' said the taximan. He switched off the radio, glancing again in the mirror. 'Big mistake to park a flash car like that there, if I may say so.'

'I was there to find something.'

A rheumy eye was cocked back at him. 'Something like what? Someone like you doesn't need to go to a place like that for drugs.'

'An automatic pistol. With ammo.'

A long pause. 'For hire?'

'To buy. Not a printed one and preferably clean. If it's on police records for something I'm not interested, and I will know.'

'A virgin like that would be expensive.'

'So was the Ferrari.'

They had left the outskirts of Oxford and were in the country. 'I know a man,' said the taxi driver. 'I can get you a piece.'

'Tomorrow?'

'I will need payment up front.'

His license said he was Robert Collier. The picture was recent, suggesting he was new to the business.

'How long have you been out?' Ash asked.

The eyes were back on him. 'What's it to you?'

No denial. 'I need to know if you are still in need of favours from the police.'

'I owe them nothing.' The man was not an actor. His vitriol was genuine.

'Good enough. Pull in.' They were in the wooden hills on the outskirts of Thorswick by a crossroad with routes to three villages. Across two fields was the back of Ash's cottage, not that Collier needed to know that. He got out of the car and indicated for the driver to follow. 'Bring the dash cam with you.'

He did, the equipment trailing wires which Ash took from him before pulling out two Gold Sovereigns. He turned them so they caught what light was around. Ash never left home without at least two. It was not a habit, more a basic component of an ingrained survival strategy. Gold was currency anywhere. The 22 carat ounce in each coin could be exchanged in places that did not demand paperwork and, unlike crypto-currency, did not need computers.

'There's two full sovereigns for you now. That's more than enough to cover your costs for what I want. You'll get two more on delivery. Three if I am very happy and you get extra bullets.'

The taxi driver started and might even have thought about making a grab for them. Ash's fist closed. 'Two now, possibly three later on delivery.'

'And where will that be? At your house?' A bad attempt at a joke.

'Tomorrow morning at eight. You see that lane? Go down there a hundred yards to a tree stump. On it tomorrow will be an old shoe. You will have the gun in a box. Leave it there and go away. Come back in half an hour and the money will be in the shoe. Don't try to come back earlier.'

Collier nodded. 'That it?'

'Almost.' Ash smiled in the darkness. 'If you try to turn me over Rob, you will find so much child porn on your computer that the remainder of your life will be spent trying not to be slashed to ribbons in prison.'

He sensed the fear and guessed he had hit several marks. It was a risk. Trackers on the Ferrari would mean any hunter could easily pick up his trail. Taxi drivers at the estate were an obvious first check. He had to hope the gun sale would make Collier lie low for a while. Even so, Ash knew that he might have placed a noose around his head. It would only be a matter of time before someone persuaded the other drivers to say who got the fare from the bloke who didn't care about his super car becoming a bonfire. Collier himself was a caricature of a washed up, not too bright criminal and it would be the work of minutes to open him like a can.

Ash watched for a long time after Collier had driven away. Only when he was sure the taxi really had gone did he climb the gate into the fields and start jogging down the hill towards Thorswick. The next few days were going to be incredibly dangerous. Those circles of threat were closing in. His inability to raise the alarm meant he was trapped. Even armed, what were his chances? Nearing the pub he felt like a tethered goat in a tiger shoot. Trembling as the predator got nearer and near. It's scent filling nostrils. Triggering every flight sense. The whole point though was to get the tiger. Didn't help the goat much. A sacrifice. Stop. He drew breath. Now within sight of his own back door.

'It isn't positive you know,' the shrink had said. 'This over thinking thing you do. Coming up with a false analogy. Do you know when you seem to do that most?

Ash had not answered.

'It's usually when you're really quite fucked,' she said.

Chapter 16

Thorswick

Ash knew immediately someone had been in the cottage. The hair across the bottom of the door was broken. Moving quietly, he went into the hall and felt under the worn carpet runner. The peanut on the fourth stair was crushed. He listened for a moment in the darkness. Not a sound. Quietly he went further up the stairs. Nothing.

He should be on line. Steeling himself he flicked switches in the computer room. There was always a chance of a booby trap, but the computer began its usual start up. One of the first things he needed to do was to hook up his mobile to reinstall the service software and security. The house camera for one.

The computer flashed up two messages. One specific and one general. As a matter of urgency, underlined and in bold, he was to find out all he could about the Chinese delegation he had highlighted after their arrival in Pakistan. Copies of the passports used, if possible. Ash breathed for a moment, the cursor moving over the words. Such delegations came and went all the time these days. It was so routine he remembered wondering if he should even have flagged it.

The second message on his computer announced a briefing with the Chief of Defence Intelligence, a man reputed to have once spoken to the Prime Minister as if he were a wine waiter who refused to acknowledge the claret was corked. A briefing from such a warrior was going to be interesting, and time was short.

So short in fact that he disconnected the mobile. If he was going to get the details needed about the Chinese without a delay between sending and receiving he was going to have to call a contact directly. And that meant without the benefit of ironclad security. This would bring an immediate risk to whoever he called. On his mobile there was a commercial system for calls and messages which promised end to end encryption. A ludicrous claim. There were always back doors. This particular one had holes drilled into it by the United States at least, almost certainly the Chinese. At least by placing the call through another app. the number would be shown as having come from within Afghanistan. Even so, he was hesitant.

Another message pinged on the computer. It required acknowledgement of the urgent information. Yes, he tapped out. It's in hand.

'Abu Bakir,' he announced when the call was answered.

'Who?' This in Urdu.

'Abu Bakir, from the Immigration Ministry in Kabul. We met at a regional conference last year'. Ash was focused. Feeling the familiar language and cherishing it on his tongue.

'Now I remember. How are you my friend?'

'I am doing well, and thanks be, so is my country.'

'I am relieved to hear it. We over here tend to catch a cold when there are sneezes in Kabul!' A laugh came down the line. Ash was relieved to hear it. It was open and confident, devoid of the nervousness the individual had every right to feel.

'My Minister wants to see if it is possible to extend an invitation to a Chinese trade mission which he thinks is in Karachi. He has a real bee in his head about the famous pipeline and clutches at any chance to advocate for it. I have no idea about whom he speaks, but he is on my case and wants to get to them while they are around. He would come over to your side if there is a chance of a window. My brother, as I am in the dark, know nothing about what he speaks, and would dearly like to keep my job, could you send me all their details so I can help set things up?

'I can't see that this would be a problem. We are always keen to help trading links across the region and help a fellow toiler in the machine!' Another laugh and the call ended.

Ask breathed and sat back in his chair. His mind several thousand miles away. Not in the mountains, but in a faded apartment in Karachi and with Hassan, the immigration official he had just spoken to. He was more than a contact. A rarity amongst the network, he was a friend who knew Ash's real name having been recruited years ago by his father. Despite energetically pursuing a life of diverse pleasures Hassan was devoted to his second wife, a lecturer at the University of Cumbria in northern England. The man's desire to spend his last years with her had long ago overtaken money as a lever.

Ash returned his mobile to the system to continue its security upgrade as a ping on his computer told him new documents had dropped into the virtual safe depository system. There were copies of five passports. Four men and a woman. They were accompanied by a note. It said that the first of the passports, the one for the leader of the delegation, was official, issued by the Beijing government, but fake in that the individual was known to be 'incognito' and travelling under a pseudonym. It was not known why.

The picture showed a well fed man, with clipped hair one notch above a buzz cut, who eyed the camera in a confident, if not arrogant, way. Ash checked the date of birth. Sixty three, although that might also be false. After all, if you are going to get false papers, why not lie about age? Especially if travelling with a woman as young and as polished as the sole female. Two of the other men looked like the products of the New China. Young scions of the Party hierarchy and rich with it. Types who were used to cutting a deal, wearing the latest designer clothing and a lifestyle in which revolution was a night club. The fifth was more homespun. Skin sunken over cheek bones suggesting a life of some hardship, or a career that hardened. That would be the security guy thought Ash, but would leave speculation to the analysists.

Pausing only to put the note from the source into his own words, stripping it of any possible identifiers, he set the priority as High, and pressed send. It went as his screen illuminated for the briefing with the Chief of Defence Intelligence.

Standing at a podium was the man who headed all the different intelligence gathering divisions within the armed forces. When the heads of the foreign, domestic and listening services met he would be expected to bring knowledge gleaned from military sources. Fortunately, given the nature of the emergency, he was a navy man. He was also in a hurry.

'Ready?', he asked and then started without bothering to wait for a reply, or anyone attempting to stop him. Even in his rumpled, white shirt with rolled up sleeves and no tie, he looked like a man unused to having his authority questioned

'Good evening. This is a briefing for those who need to know, and it may differ significantly from some other statements you hear. Just disregard those. Disregard particularly any horse shit about this having been done by some old mine. Disregard also political efforts to suggest this was accident.'

The grizzled grey head dipped for a moment before the sharp eyes, as cold and grey as a winter wave in the Atlantic, rose to the camera. 'HMS Queen Elizabeth is in dire straits. If it makes Singapore, it will be a tribute to the men and women aboard. Our analysis suggests the following. The sophistication of what happened puts it beyond doubt that we have suffered a State on State attack. We think we know how it was done, and the smoking gun leads to only one likely aggressor. And, the politicians are telling us, there's bugger all in the military sense we can do about it.'

Chapter 17

The Online Briefing

The Director nodded and a video came on screen without introduction. It did not need one. All too obviously it was from the bridge of the stricken aircraft carrier, the four rings on the torn uniform shirt denoted a Captain. A rough, white sling matched the ski mask like flash hood. His words were muffled but carried despite that, even if some were lost amidst the shouting electronic bleeps and regular klaxons.

'It's as if the shock of the punch has messed up every system and opened up even the seams,' Ash made out. He leant in, straining toward the screen, as he took in what he could from the man's eyes. In them he saw exhaustion, shock, and a tremor of fear that competed with desperation. 'It was like the sea just rose around us and in the middle was an iron fist. It threw us up, dived us down and left us pitching. Real hand of God stuff. Out of nowhere. We lost two choppers amongst jets that were being prepared on the flight deck. And their crew. Nobody was prepared. Braced I mean. I doubt there is anyone without some kind of injury. There were a lot of falls and heads being bashed against metal. Some other things, like broken collar bones.' He shrugged his sling slightly, and despite the veil like face covering, there was an obvious swallow.

'So far its twenty six dead. Or missing, presumed overboard. We have a number of serious injuries. Head wounds and broken backs as people were pitched down stairwells. Oh, and burns galore in the galley. As far as the ship is concerned,' and here he paused and looked around as if those haunted eyes were looking for something positive to say. 'we are keeping afloat a sieve operating on the barest minimum of power, being driven by one prop. Our orders are to get to Singapore at all costs and save the ship. That means no delays, even for medi-vacs. We started getting a few off, but with these new orders we are sending any undamaged aircraft onto other ships or land bases. We have to keep moving. Quite literally I am afraid that if we stop, we may not get going again, and are not in a position to receive flights. This means we will have people dying who might otherwise be treated'.

Someone off camera caught his attention and he beckoned them in so the back of a mask came into view as something was said. It did not look as if it were good news. The Captain nodded, said something and waved him away as he resumed. 'Amongst the fifteen we are most concerned about is one of our sonar specialists. She had stood up for a stretch and was thrown across the room and into the head up display. She seemed alright after dusting herself down and volunteered for the work parties throwing supplies, damaged aircraft and equipment over the side. She then collapsed. It's a subdural hematoma.'

Ash blinked at that, and wondered. What are the chances of him hearing about two separate women sonar operators on the Queen Elizabeth within the space of a couple of hours? Almost certainly it was Charlotte's sister, and he was hearing about a fight for life that was more textured than the others. It added to a sense of unreality, as if a character in a film had reached beyond the screen and made a personal connection.

'Was there any indication, Captain, of anything beforehand?' It was the Director asking.

'Nothing from our sonar and listening side at all. The fleet was aware of activity of some sort in the area and we were all watching. But nothing. Absolutely nothing beforehand. Whatever did this blind-sided us completely.'

A message from Ash's personal email system popped up. It was from Charlotte. 'Can't get through to the number they're giving out for relatives. Desperate. Feel something is wrong.'

'And will you make Singapore?', on screen the Director asked the question very quietly as if he already knew the answer. The flash mask billowed slightly as the Captain expelled.

'I am telling the crew we shall do it. And I had a call from on high, and I mean political 'on high', saying that national prestige requires us to get this baby berthed in a place that is where we have historic links. And I get that. We don't want to fail the old Queen, and we shall do whatever we can. But it is now a journey that is at the mercy of the sea. Subic Bay in the Philippines is nearer but that would leave her still close to the people who have done this and, frankly, we are in full retreat. Unable to fight and counting each minute we are above the waves as a blessing. Make no mistake though. The extended crawl to friendlier waters will be measured in lives lost on board, quite apart from the limbs and injuries going without proper treatment.' A roar of an aircraft stopped him for a moment.

'That's the last of our planes off to the US carrier. All our choppers are damaged and will be tipped over the side, along with everything else we don't need.'

'We'll let you go.'

'Before I do, I am told I am speaking to the people most likely to fuck over the people who did this,' and here the eyes above the flash hood looked like shards of flint as the Captain stared into the camera. 'If this is so, please do what you can to avenge this and return our pain in spades.'

'Good Luck Captain.' Given what they heard, Ash thought, that was one of the most inadequate signoffs he had ever heard. At least he knew now why he and others like him were on the call. They were to send retribution wherever it was demanded. Another message popped up from Charlotte. 'Any ideas? Need a word. Feeling desperate'.

A picture of a very different ship was on the screen. 'A brief bit of history.' A click and another picture showed what could have been half of the boat being suspended from a gigantic ship board crane. 'This is the stern of the 'Cheonan', a corvette of the South Korean navy. It broke in half and sank after an explosion during a naval exercise with the United States in March 2010 in waters contested by the two Koreas. Forty six of the hundred off crew died in the incident, and right from the start it was thought the most likely explanation was that it was struck by a torpedo. Satellite images caught a flotilla of North Korean mini subs with a support ship setting out from their base some days before the exercise began. However, when the stern was lifted and looked at by international experts they found no trace of a direct hit. Instead they saw pressure marks on the hull, which you may see in the picture.'

The Director paused. 'Such marks, along with traces of the explosive RDX as well as the remains of torpedo of a type used by North Korea , led the experts to conclude that a torpedo had exploded up to nine metres beneath the ship. That version has been disputed by both the North Koreans and their Chinese fan club, the latter suggesting it was caused by an American mine which came adrift. Those adhering to the more plausible unprovoked submarine attack idea suggest the explosion caused a bubble jet effect. This generated an enormous shock wave which broke the ship in two. The wording of the final report from the South Koreans, and a number of other countries, ourselves included, stated the Cheonan was sunk by a non-contact underwater explosion.'

A slight cough could be heard off camera. 'Perhaps you might explain the bubble jet idea to those who may have not heard of it before?'

Ash detected the modulated tones of the Information Officer from the radio broadcast. The Director gave a basilisk death stare to the speaker, before seeking the ceiling with his eyes. 'For those unable to search the internet,' he resumed, 'I shall explain, although time, my time I should say, is very limited.' He paused as he visibly gathered his thoughts.

'In an underwater explosion there has always been the assumption that the main cause of damage is caused by the shock waves. The direct impact from the explosion itself, if you will. However, there is a growing interest in how the bubble released in such an event also causes considerable damage to structures. This is because it expands and contracts multiple times, causing a whipping effect, that twists and bends around the structure. In addition, there are the billions, or trillions, of small bubbles that are attracted to any surface near the detonation, such as the hull of a ship. There they get up close and personal, forming a shape like a ring doughnut with water flowing at high speed through the centre. This creates significant local loads, and a sagging effect in the surfaces, creating notable damage. Considering the physics, as well as the catastrophic damage seen on the wreck of the Cheonan, it is a reasonable conclusion that the Queen Elizabeth suffered a deliberate attack through use of an underwater explosion.'

He paused and looked at whoever suggested the clarification, as if daring a question. None came.

'I shall now move onto how it was done. Or, how we think it was done. Because that is not only interesting in its own right, but it will lead to a conclusion of there being only one possible culprit.'

Ash sat up. This was going to super charge the spying game. The attack had already been characterised as 'state on state', and it sounded as if the intuitive guesswork, analysis and search for snippets of evidence in the waste bins of power brokers, in a world of unknown enemies and dodgy friends, was going to be re-set.

A known enemy, and a state at that. A new front. It would probably mean a gear change similar to the one which happened after Russia sent to attack opponents with a military grade nerve agent in the English city of Salisbury. This sounded like a whole new dimension. Ash shivered. Sitting in Thorswick, before a screen, with a hooting owl and moon spreading silvery light he knew the world would never be the same again.

'Everything we have tells us there was not a hostile anywhere near the multinational fleet that sailed into the South China sea. That, in its self, is odd. The Chinese, the most interested party to what we were all doing, were hanging back quite a long way. In fact, the nearest of their vessels, as far as we can make out at this early stage, was a destroyer some twenty-five miles ahead. All this, given their overt and threatening posture for previous such naval exercises in that region, makes this a notable response. If you like, this is a case where we have a dog that is not barking. And that makes us very suspicious indeed. This is also a case where something else went bump in the night.'

A sound came into the conference call. Three indistinct beats, which was played on a loop as if it were a message, its persistence and urgency growing with each repetition. It was allowed to sound for thirty seconds.

'We can thank the Japanese navy for this recording, which we believe is the start of the attack. If we have to look for positives in this ghastly mess then the fact it was an Akizuki class destroyer that was ahead of the main fleet, and the crew of the Sakaki were alert. These destroyers have some of the best sonar equipment around. Really world class. The Sakaki picked up this sound and sent it around. It has been identified by the Americans. This Ladies and Gentlemen is the sound of drone breaking surface before it flew. It was launched underwater through one of the tubes on a submarine that deploys decoys when it is attacked. It rises to the surface where it unfolds into an aircraft and takes flight. Once in the air it becomes the eyes and ears for an attack submarine. It will identify a target, from its profile, even the unique engine noise, send back the exact location, speed and bearing while also, in only a very few of the most advanced navies with deep pockets, being able to illuminate it to guide a torpedo. This "submarine launched unmanned aerial system", as it is known in the trade, can provide pinpoint accuracy against a specific target even if the potential victim is sailing in the middle of a fleet.'

'And what does this mean in the context of what we are looking at this evening?' The Director paused. 'The Sakaki very quickly launched its sonar arrays and went into hunting mode after picking up the drone as it transited out of the water. But there would have been time for a submarine to launch the damn thing and move forward under cover of thermals so it was not in the immediate search envelope. In addition, as the Sakaki was forward of the task force, its natural response was to look back for a threat to the other ships. Which it did with vigour. So, with every moment the distance between the Sakaki and the submarine grew.'

A display came up on the screen, which showed the position of all the warships in the task force when the Queen Elizabeth was hit and other points on the open sea. The marker for the Chinese destroyer standing off twenty-five miles ahead of the group started to flash. 'It is our guess that the submarine made for this destroyer. For all we know that ship could have taken over control of the drone while the sub dashed out of the search zone. Once close to the destroyer it could stayed submerged and then launch a sonar guided torpedo and explode it at a chosen depth.

The Director paused as if he suddenly remembered he was not addressing a naval academy. 'The best and richer navies have torpedoes that can travel up to thirty miles. The limiting factor in the past was trying to get a secure target solution over anything more than five miles. Having a drone feeding data and undertaking targeting takes all that away. The submarine, sheltering under the shadow of a surface ship showing no hostile intent, is able to launch an extremely effective attack from over the horizon. So, ladies and gentlemen. There is the smoking gun, and it was made in Beijing. They have this capability, and form when it comes to muscular assertion in the South China Sea.

'Thank you Director.'

'I haven't finished.' Again, the death stare. 'I would stress,' he continued without taking his eyes initially off the recipient, 'that this was a very sophisticated attack. Well planned. If the Japanese had not captured that bit of audio, we would not have a clue that a drone was involved. In addition, if we had cottoned on earlier to a submerged submarine we would not have been able to do anything about something moving away from the task force, nestling under a surface craft and which to all intents, benign. Setting the torpedo to go off metres below the hull of the Queen Elizabeth means we shall have to hunt hard for salvage evidence about the infernal machine on the floor of what happens to be a very deep trench. Without that any explosive residue found on the hull of the Queen Elizabeth will allow useful idiots to argue loud and long that a torpedo was not involved, and it was all due to something like a drifting mine.'

He looked suddenly weary, and this time he simply nodded to whoever was prodding him along. 'My conclusion is that the Chinese have slammed the door to the east in our faces. They picked out the UK's flagship and turned it into a colander. As a nation we have stated political ambitions to punch above our weight, and we cannot afford to suffer such a loss. This is a multi-billion pound boat facing a future as razor blades. They had the sense not to attack an American ship, but they have must have thought they were delivering a brutal reality check, while removing our ability to be visible in efforts to push back Chinese expansion.'

He walked away from the podium. Replacing him was the Information Officer, instantly recognisable from the clearly modulated tones. As he started speaking Ask also noticed that the lean, long faced man with a cleft in his jaw that looked as if it could harbour life forms, wore the party badge in the lapel of his blue suit. It suddenly occurred to him how rare it was seen to see any video, press conference or event from London that did not have the national flag in the background. The briefing from the Director had been free of this fixture, but the entwined red, white and blue with upward pointing arrow was something that seemed to be encroaching everywhere. Ash guessed that the Information Officer was a civil servant, but one that was proud to show his political affiliation. He wondered if this was a reason for the Director showing him such obvious disdain.

'I am sure that you would join me in thanking the Director for his frank, indeed, overly perhaps, frank appreciation. But, I would stress that the government, and I think I have some insights, are very cautious about ascribing blame at this stage. Particularly not to a country with which we have been successfully building so many economic ties.' There was more, but Ash guessed he would not alone in judging that whatever message of mitigation and deflection the Information Officer was trying to give would fall on deaf ears. As far as the present audience was concerned an insulted and assaulted military had given the orientation.

The video conference was ending with the Information Officer saying something about this being a good time for calm heads. Good luck with that, thought Ash as he took his mobile from the baked bean tin and switched it back on. As soon as it settled a call came in. It was Charlotte. Ash hesitated. As he did another call showed. Adrian Holesworthy. Ash took that one, cancelling out the other. His boss sounded tense. 'Your drone strike is on. Tonight.' A slight pause. 'You know, I always did think it was a good idea.'

Ash was surprised. 'I thought everyone would be concentrating on the Far East at the moment,' he said.

'Oh, not at all.' Adrian was sounding chummy, itself somewhat disconcerting. 'We can keep a broad view of our interests.'

'What about the Minister?'

A long, nasal intake came down the mobile. 'Vavasour Carrick- Rhodes is absolutely on board on the need for us to show resolution in all matters at this time.' Ash took on board the disparaging tone.

'All change then.'

'No, all the same. Just different. Well done for bringing this one home.'

The call terminated. He suddenly realised that the night atmosphere was fetid. Much hotter than it had been earlier. Going to the front of the cottage he opened a window to encourage air flow, before wetting a towel and heading for the bedroom. He took of his clothes and laid the towel on his chest. Next door the coolers hummed, keeping the computer equipment safe. Gazing up to the ceiling he ignored the illuminated mobile. If this temperature stayed he might be in the garden by midnight. But that was not the thought keeping him awake.

Soon missiles would be flying. Niggling away, in a place too far to be reached, was a sense that something was not quite right. At a time when all eyes were supposedly on the South China sea, there was a sudden rush for this harvesting in the Hindu Kush. One that would be brutal and well deserved, but the timing was off. And so he wondered.

Chapter 18

Balochistan

The deal to allow access for the mining of Lithium and rare earths in Afghanistan was always going to be agreed. None of those present, warlords or Chinese, were going to leave empty handed. It was only ever about payment.

All the same, protocols had to be observed. First there were the extended greetings between the main players as they and their retinues slowly accommodated themselves onto the floor cushions. Business was not discussed immediately. There were two rounds of sweet tea served in small glasses to be sipped first. The steaming liquid showing ruby red in the light from the tent flap. When the pleasantries slipped into talks the translators inched forward, listening attentively before murmuring into the ears of the negotiators. Jannat and Shameeza took no part. They sat near the entrance to the tent, both with their eyes lowered but missing nothing.

When there were words to be passed, the Chinese translator whispered to the woman. It was she who spoke to the man, who maintained an air of patrician detachment, in much the same way as Amanullah Tarzi and Mahmoud Ali. After listening with his head slightly inclined he would say something short and inaudible, often with a flick of his left hand which, in any language, could be 'just do it.'

The young woman, 'still mid-twenties?', guessed Shameeza, would lean back and think for a moment before gesturing to the translator to stretch nearer. She was, thought Shameeza, gorgeous. Slightly imperious perhaps, but she was used to that. It looked as if she had chosen the black jacket and long dress for modesty, and yet her movements suggested a lithe body. Perhaps even that of a one-time athlete.

When it came to the deal itself there was very little haggling. It came down to the amount for the facilitation fee, and the parameters had already been arranged. For face, there was a bit of toing and froing. Then nods and exchanges of looks of approval. More tea came while retinues worked their mobiles. Then the word was passed over the cushions. Money had dropped into accounts. More nods and then claps of hands. The meeting was over. It was time to celebrate.

Slowly, politely, the Chinese made for the entrance. Shameeza dodged out ahead to hold back the flap and escort them to their house. Looking back into the marque she saw the men craning over each other to read a screen. Jannat was making her way toward them, but turned and waved her away. She went, but registered the grim looks on their faces. Whatever they were reading was bad news. Or, at least, serious. And it looked as if both groups had received a similar message.

She could not wait to see more. The guests came first and were watching her with faces that managed to convey impatience without betraying a frown. The mud walled house picked for them was a hundred metres from the marque, standing in the midst of a mud walled compound and with nothing to distinguish it from other village homes. In fact it had been packed with new furnishings and rugs, the mud walls whitewashed and western style double beds imported. Each was made up with Egyptian cotton sheets. For the Minister the bed was a King. This had necessitated knocking two rooms into one, which left room also for a tiled ensuite shower room and toilet. Piped water was beyond the achievable, but there were buckets. Without a word Shameeza opened a cabinet downstairs to show bottles of 12 year old Scotch, French red wines and a VSOP brandy. A small fridge on top was marked United Nations Vaccination Programme. In it were bottles of white. Moving to a table she adjusted the bowl filled with Hamza apricots, apples and pomegranates. The team leader, looked at her as if for the first time, and said something. It might have been a 'thank you', but all the woman said was 'you can go now.'

She did, walking past and catching a zephyr of jasmine from her, and stale tobacco from the thin man. Outside she walked fast to the marque, but the entrance was barred by two men armed with assault rifles, and she knew better than to try and get past them. Instead she went to their accommodation and pulled up a chair to watch from the window. In the heat she dozed, but came to with a jolt to find Jannat staring at her from the doorway.

'What happened?' mumbled Shameeza.

'Quite a bit.' Slowly Jannat closed the door. 'They've been tipped off that a drone was stalking them here and was a gnat's away from blowing them up.'

'Shit.' Shameeza was awake now, her thoughts racing. 'But how did whoever it was know they were here?'

'They've been asking the same question for an hour. They think there's a spy.'

'Oh shit.'

Jannat looked at her evenly. 'Does the name Ibrahim Afridi mean anything?'

'No. Do they think he's the one?'

Jannat ignored the question. 'He's not someone in your wide spread family?'

'Not that I've heard of.' Shameeza was uneasy now. This was a version of Jannat she had seen before, but never encountered in the personal realm. 'Steely' was the word often used in the management magazine profiles of her. Right now it felt more than that. 'Who is he anyway?'

'Some sort of military type they killed,' said Jannat shortly. 'They think it's connected.'

'It means nothing to me.' Shameeza paused, looking for a change in the statue before her. None came. 'If what they say is true, they should get out as soon as possible. Apart from anything else we don't want the drone taking another shot when we have the Chinese around.'

Jannat nodded slowly. 'They don't think that will happen. In fact they seem to know it won't.' She paused. 'All related in a way.'

'And what's that?'

Jannat signed heavily. 'They have information that there is an insider working against them. When they went through all the possibilities your name was high on their list. They even considered the Chinese, thinking that assassination would a way to escape paying them off. But they have the money now, and the talks went well.'

She paused again.

'But it's not me.' Shameeza was searching her face. 'You know that. I set everything up.'

'And that makes you suspect number one as far as they are concerned.'

Shameeza was stunned. Wordlessly she read Jannat's coldness. The way she looked at her. Terror, so much worse that fear, was causing her heart to beat against her chest. She swallowed. 'But that is….' Shameeza faltered. That was unlike her. She wanted to say ridiculous. Looking at her boss and lover though, she had no idea what to say, or how not to make things worse.

'I have persuaded them that it cannot be you.'

Relief flooded through Shameeza. She half stood, wanting to embrace Jannat. To thank her. Tears were starting in her eyes. 'But that brings us to the second problem. Another one that makes them want to hang around.'

Shameeza subsided back in to the chair. 'I have managed,' said Jannat in a voice that sounded without any emotion, 'to show that you are trustworthy and loyal. An ideal companion and assistant. In fact someone who has admired them and all their works'

Shameeza searched her face. 'They are also persuaded by the elders that it would be an offence on all sorts of level if a wedding did not take place as promised.'

Jannat let the words sink in. She saw the look of relief on Shameeza's face change. First to puzzlement, and then consternation.

'It turns out Mahmoud Ali in particular has been following our careers with interest,' Jannat resumed. 'Having been assured that he does not need to shoot you and, having admired what he called your modest demeanour, he is prepared to marry you immediately so the correct customs and celebration can be observed.'

Now Shameeza stood, trembling, her mouth open. 'You cannot be serious. You of all people.'

'Understand Shameeza, as far as he's concerned you are either a spy or a wife. The choice is dead or alive. I have done my best.'

'No, I won't.' She blinked. Then. 'I can't.'

'It's the only way. You'll be married tonight. The Chinese will be guests. The whole village is ready, and this is a man who would react very badly to humiliation.'

Shameeza was in shock. Her worst nightmares, the ones about forced marriage, a life of seclusion, uncompromising days and nights of repugnance were tumbling across her mind. She was grasping now. 'But if that happens, it won't be for real will it? I mean, not you know, the night, and I'll still be leaving with you tomorrow won't I?'

There was a noise at the door. Slowly Jannat reached across and opened it. There were a number of women there, some of whom Shameeza recognised as the wives of the elders. Two of them held out a bright red coat shalwar kameez covered in mirrored sequins, the bodice and arms stiff with gold embroidery. A Balochistan bridal gown.

'They will prepare you,' said Jannat. She looked at her, and Shameeza quailed at the lack of emotion. 'Embrace your new life.'

Chapter 19

RAF Bincton, Lincolnshire, UK

A storm was building. Big clouds. Ballooning grey at locomotive speed from a charcoal centre. Monstrous and dangerous edifices. Rising to meet her. Back off, she thought. Go back. But there was no time. Cutting off retreat. Vapour trails. Engines of destruction. Jets or missiles. Aiming for her. Missiles! Get out! A scream in her head. Get out! Her hand went for the ejection handle. Get out before it's too late. Pull the bloody thing. Get out before the storm, get out where the sky is still kissed by the sun. Tumble out. Somewhere new.

No. Another hand. Stopping hers. Stay. It's going to be alright. The hand moved again and she stirred. It's firm. Knowing. You can do this. What's a storm when you feel good? Dodge the missiles. Nobody cares. Just enjoy. An alarm was sounding. Urgent and pulling her away from the cockpit. Making her stretch. Feel the regret. The loss of desired warmth. A soft voice coaxing. It was her mobile.

'Action stations.'

'Flight?'

'Back to the mission ma'am', said the Flight Sergeant. 'Immediately. I am required to give a timing on this one. Understand, it's the real thing. Time of this call is twenty two, twenty nine. You have ten. Ma'am.'

'Flight, that's the same if I were sleeping in the bloody war shack.'

'Sorry again, Ma'am. But times a wasting.'

Maggie flung back the quilt and made for the shower, which she pivoted in without giving it time to heat. Within thirty minutes she was flight suited and booted, at the controls of a drone speeding to the spreading sun of a South Asian dawn. Squadron Leader Pickett was prowling around the flight desks, his jacket off and distinct sweat marks darkening the blue of his uniform shirt. He had spoken as soon as Maggie, Jack Stevens and Mike Thompson came through the door.

'This is the only briefing you are going to get. The target is as before. London has picked up that the Taliban leaders are plotting again. Planning another attack. This time on Westminster, as well as a city in the US. So, we are going to take them before they disappear. We are the ones who know where they are, and you are the crew from the aborted mission.' Maggie looked at him keenly. He sounded as if it were their fault the original attack was called off. He did not meet her eye, so she was able to observe in more detail the red eyes and overall crumpled effect. Obviously the no alcohol rule when the base was active had not applied at all levels.

'And they must not get away. We will be given a precise target at some point. We must follow through this time whatever the consequences.' he concluded.

It was the last bit Maggie remembered as she flew. They were high, as high as the drone would go. Staying clear of Iranian population centres and crossing the border into Afghan air space below Herat. Once well inside, Maggie set a new course, and gradually dropped down to 15,000. At that height the upgraded camera would be able to pick out pimples, and it was still several thousand feet above the highest peaks of the Sulaiman mountain range.

'Has there been any ongoing surveillance since we left?' she asked into her microphone. There was a long pause.

'Not that we are aware,' Mike Thompson replied eventually. Which was strange, she thought, as how else would they be able to get an exact target. In fact, it was not believable. There were always satellites keeping a watching brief. Those silent watchers, flying even higher. Never sleeping. The idea their targets had been left in an unseen limbo beggared belief. And the thought added to her growing sense of strangeness about the mission. Ever since she heard the driven voice of Pickett, giving more of a tirade than a factual need to know, she felt an estrangement, as if she were walking into a party she did not want to be at. She shook herself on her chair. They were closing fast.

'So, we don't know if the bad guys are still there?', she asked without much hope of a reasonable answer. Just a way of clearing her mental tubes as much as anything.

'From what we have been told there is no reason to think they've left.'

They know, she thought. Of course they do. Features on the ground were slowly becoming visible now in the early glimmers of dawn. It showed lurid purple on the jagged peaks, which threw long shadows into green and beige valleys. In a few places trees struggled for life amongst the corrugated folds and whorls that seemed to flow in their direction of travel. Pointing to the target. They were there almost too soon for Maggie. 'There you are,' she breathed, and Pickett ceased his pacing to come over to the control desks.

They looked at the screens. The mountain road was quiet, and it looked like more tents had been put up. The pickups they had in the cross hairs less than a day before were parked and scattered among the mud walled courtyards that surrounded many of the houses. Around the centre were the local buses. Smoke came from a number of places and Maggie guessed that women would be preparing breakfast, perhaps with freshly baked bread. She shook herself again. Focus up she thought. Imagination in these circumstances was not healthy. Over the roof of one of the houses close to the central area and the wedding tent was a washing line with flapping black burghas.

A message came up on screen from someone somewhere. The targets are in the house with the washing line.

'That's it,' said Pickett. 'Hit them. You have the target.'

The cross hairs appeared on the screen, the centre squarely in the middle of the flat roof. Maggie wondered if the missile would cut the washing line in the flash before it smashed at huge velocity into the centre of the house. Jack Stevens was on the ball. 'It's acquired.'

Pickett took a breath. 'Fire!', he ordered

'Hold!' Maggie was looking intently at the screen. Had she turned she would have seen the Squadron Leader throwing her a look that flashed anger. 'What on earth?', he managed.

'I call the firing. And we haven't had time to look over the area to avoid other casualties.'

Slowly Richard Pickett walked to her station and leaned over her shoulder so they were both within the rounded curve of the console, shielded from the rest of the room by the banks of screens. His breath over the side of her face was whisky soured, his voice low. He muted the microphone. 'I can't leave that off for long,' he said. He was being Richard. 'Too many listeners.' She was shocked at his boldness, and felt herself shrink away within herself.

'You must understand Maggie,' his voice soft and reasonable. 'You have to behave. This is not the time for your scruples. This is the job.'

Maggie knew all about his attitude to her scruples. 'It's one thing, sir,' she said meaningfully, 'to know the target. It's another to know for sure there are no children or others inside.' She paused. 'As you well know. Sir.'

He breathed heavily, sluicing her again with fumes. He seemed to be debating the mute button. 'Don't blow this, Maggie,' Richard said. 'It's a nothing thing. Look around at the screens, where we are. They're killers, plotting in that far off place. Thinking they can't be touched.' His arm was on her chair, and she felt it move as if it wanted to pat her, like a dog she thought. 'We can stop it. Now.'

Thompson spoke up from somewhere outside their bubble. 'London is asking what is happening.'

'It's all good.' Pickett moved across her and flicked up the arming switch.

'No, it's not. We check out everything first and if we do it, it will be when I say.' Maggie was still on mute but her voice carried around the room. Pickett dropped his hand, and enveloped hers. The one gripping the control stick. Lightly at first, and then gently squeezing with an experience that could do such a thing without sending an aircraft into a spin, while making her expel a breath as his touch ignited a shock of outrage.

'You don't have to blame yourself', he said as, with a spasm like movement that turned into a grip of steel, he pressed hard. Her finger squeezed down onto the firing trigger. It was an attack of barely a second, but her body jerked convulsively. His hand was off the scene of the crime immediately, travelling up with a careless flick to unmute their systems. They were back on the airwaves.

'Missile away,' Richard Pickett announced.

'Abort,' Maggie hissed at Stevens. She was stunned, blinking as he released her. Looking up she saw that her co-pilot was starring fixedly at the screens ahead of him. Looking desperately at her console again, she saw that an override had been activated. She was not in control of the drone, or anything else for that matter. It was as if everyone was in some kind of play with her as the only one not knowing her part.

The missile was on the beam and heading straight for the house where a freshening wind caused the women's clothes to billow as if they were figures in an animated ghost story. 'There must be women in there,' Maggie pleaded. 'Look at the clothing for fuck sake.'

All eyes were on the screens, the play having become a tableau of still figures watching with an audience elsewhere taking in the enormity of their performance. The inevitable flash burned white, before the black image of a spreading flower grew across the screens, the petals spreading where the house had been. No doubt, thought Maggie dully, they would soon be able to see the shattered remains of the whatever around the epicentre that was once a home. She slumped back in the chair. Her body following the contours of the furniture, her whole sense violated. Again. She closed her eyes, the anger resurging to match her humiliation, spreading like the image. The room was coming back into her consciousness, chipping a way back into her thoughts. Over at the other console Pickett, she realised, was speaking, breaking a convention that everyone should just shut up until at least the dust had settled.

'Thanks very much one and all,' he said with the emphasis on the all. 'A good show. The right questions were asked, as they definitely should be', and here Pickett cast the briefest of looks into the airspace above Maggie's head. 'I will be heading off to London for a noon debrief, and I shall be saying how well this Squadron has performed. There is', he went on as he turned away from her, 'always likely to be, what shall we say? Yes, some creative tensions. Well, I for one welcome that kind of thing, just as long as we are all on board when the difficult decisions are made.'

He might have said more, but Maggie was on her feet. Standing initially at attention, she turned sharply and marched with quick regulation strides to where Pickett was addressing the room. His back was to her. If he noticed her movement, the style would have suggested a sharply given salute as a prelude to a formal exchange. He half turned, single eyebrow ready raised. It was an uncertainty competing with the jut of his jaw.

Out, wide and fast her hand came up. The slap catching him under the right cheek bone, the palm catching his nose and a nail cutting into an eyebrow. It was not the type of blow that might be given out of irritation, or as a quick fire response to an unwanted congress. It was a shaker, a potential jaw breaker, with the arm carrying the energy of a chest full of anger. Reeling back with a shout of pain, Pickett would have fallen but for Thompson managing to shoot out an arm.

There was an appalled silence. Maggie watched the man with folded arms as he slowly straightened, blood from his nose adding new dark patches to his shirt. Fumbling, he brought out a handkerchief and held it to his face where it filled. When he did finally look at her, she saw something approaching trepidation in his eyes. Given their background he should be worried.

'Flight Lieutenant Johnson,' he said through the linen. 'You're confined to your quarters.' He snorted slightly and looked as if he swallowed blood, an action that seemed to cut away at any reserve. 'Get out, he added venomously. 'Bitch.'

Maggie swung around in a way that would have pleased a drill instructor, and walked off. She knew better than to go to her console to pick up her things. The last thing she wanted was to accused of tampering with the thing. All the same, she could not help noticing the screen as she walked for the door. The drone was still flying over the site. Kept in position by satellite and auto pilot. The camera showed a huge black circle, with what looked like a rock sculpture garden of weird shapes around the perimeter. And amongst them were people. Some moving and others not.

Chapter 20

Balochistan

The detonation lifted the bed, and broke it. Shameeza was thrown to the floor amidst the blood stained bedding and tear soaked pillow. Winded, she lay for a moment, ears ringing, as all around came rose the sound of screams and crashing. At some point that night she had become dumb. Dulled and inert. Her pleading for time had come to nothing. A brief moment of fight was knocked out of her, while any resistance rendered impossible after being tied to the bed as he called her 'whore' and 'spy', amongst other things. The tears came while he was still with her, and strangely that seemed to disconcert Mahmoud Ali more than anything else. As she wept he knelt beside her and stroked her hair, before withdrawing in the darkest hours of the night.

The freeing of her hands allowed Shameeza to curl down to her ankles. The solid wooden bed legs had separated from the frame and hung on her legs like elongated shackles. The deep seated pain she was experiencing suggested injury. Something that may yet require a doctor. There was still some bleeding. Oblivious to everything she picked at the knots. The wailing and shouts were, for the moment, nothing other than a soft underscore to her own suffering and repugnance. Suddenly she retched, her eyes smarting and watering as a thick, foul smelling smoke penetrated the room. That, more than anything else, forced her to move. To do something to change from the foetal.

She drew herself painfully onto all fours, the movement causing her to take a series of sharp breaths as if, she thought vaguely, she were having contractions. The smoke was getting thicker all the time. Somewhere there must be flames because their light flickered through the shutters. Dimly she remembered it was to best to be under smoke. Feeling around amongst the soiled sheets she found the encompassing black bourka that Mahmoud Ali had brought to her room and said she was to wear whenever out, or when other men were around. Scrunching it up to her face, she sucked in air through the material and crawled slowly and toward the door.

It wasn't locked and opened into a courtyard. The cries and confusion beyond the perimeter wall were much clearer now, the sounds and sunlight blocking acrid smoke coming from the somewhere in the direction of the house prepared for the Chinese. Slowly, carefully Shameeza got herself up almost upright and steadied herself against the door frame, the folds of the hated garment still pressed to her face. There was no one around. Whatever had happened must be involving the whole village.

Just getting away from that room, and that bed, seemed to help clear the miasma in her brain. One thought was bubbling through with an increasing tempo. Escape. Getting away. It was not going to be easy. She had picked this location for its remoteness. It would be impossible to walk away. Even if she were fit and able. She would also be quickly recognised. How that man would react if she were caught did not bear thinking about.

Miserably she gave vent to a series of hacking coughs which tore at her insides, making her gasp between coughs. The Bourka. Shameeza pulled it away and held out the crumpled garment. Wearing it would turn her into nothing more than an ignorable wisp, able to move and barely seen. Slipping it over her head, she welcomed it's stuffy, humid embrace. Bunching the harsh material in a fist and bringing it up to her nose as reasonable considering the smoke. Taking a breath she opened the gate, opting for a quick slip through and closing it behind her.

Fifty metres ahead of her much of the facing wall of the compound of the Chinese had been blown flat giving a clear sight of a ring of rubble where the house had been. Men were working all over it, shouting and gesticulating. Some were also going down into what must have been a crater in the centre from where smoke was still coming. In the far corner of the compound a burned out vehicle stood steaming as a couple of youths threw buckets of water.

On the lip of the crater stood Jannat talking to Amanullah Tarzi and the rapist. Beside them were two shapes, which looked as if they were wrapped in blankets or carpets. From the arms and gestures, their conversation was animated. They stopped as heads appeared above the lip and a small group came up carrying between them the body of a man, a bloodied naked arm hanging limply. Even at that distance Shameeza could tell it was the Pakistani Minister.

A thought suddenly came to her. Jannat was the only person who could have done any arranging about what happened. She was the only other person with all the knowledge about the location, the meeting and who would be there. She had also put up Shameeza as a sacrificial, possible spy. Whatever was done here, and in whoever's name, it had to be down to her.

'Move old woman.' The instruction from the man coming toward her was followed by an expletive.

'Would you talk to your mother like that?' she mumbled. The way Shameeza was holding herself she realised was helping the disguise.

'Piss off I say, and make yourself useful over there.' He waved his rifle barrel behind her. 'There's wounded.'

He watched her limping and clutching her side head toward where there were people milling around. The smoke was beginning to dissipate, the devastation and damage to a number of buildings being thrown into ever sharper relief by the morning sun. As she got closer to the group she saw some were bleeding and dazed. Most were men, who she guessed were guards. There were a few women huddled in a dark corner a few metres from them. One of them hugging a child as the infant stared out with wide unblinking eyes.

The compound where she and Jannat stayed seemed to have escaped any damage, but going there to look for her mobiles, papers or anything else was impossible. There were armed men at the door shooing anyone away who came even remotely close. She looked back and saw the two warlords and Jannat walking slowly through a gap blown in the walls by the explosion. Shameeza swallowed. Her mouth was dry. Her body so parched it had given up sweating. There was nowhere to go. The bastard would discover her missing and start a search. And if found there was no hope. She would be lucky if he even offered her a life of misery and seclusion in Kandahar. She stood there, wished herself dead.

A coach started up. Wounded were now being half carried or stretchered toward it. An idea, half formed, started her feet toward it. Under the bourka it was stiflingly hot. She swayed. Her legs sending her weaving. A man tending the male wounded was looking at her. His mouth moved. Shouting. Pointing at her. Shameeza was slipping to the ground. Everything working in slow motion as she passed into blackness.

Chapter 21

RAF Bincton, Lincolnshire.

It was the Flight Sergeant who escorted Maggie back to her quarters. Alex Hayman was coming to the end of his service, having seen most things one way or another. During the short journey to her apartment he managed, without barely a word spoken, to convey a complete lack of judgement. As they got out of her car, he sniffed the unnaturally warm night air.

'The seaweed pullers,' he said, referring to the meteorologists, 'say one of those tropical storms is coming. Humid before the stair rods. If it isn't like a soggy blanket already.'

Alex "Handsome" Hayman was the sort of non-commissioned officer found as leaders in any age. Effortlessly, he seemed to be able to know what was happening, and who was doing what to whom. If there was dormitory where a new recruit was being picked on then woe betide the culprits. Those involved might be seen running around an airbase before first light having kicked off their session with a punitive kit inspection. If an officer was unwise enough to notice, a way would be found to mind his own business.

'Flight what are those men doing over there?"

'Birdwatching sir. They're also taking the opportunity to fill a few sandbags having noticed the base is a bit short. Very public spirited they are sir.'

He was also the one who handled other trouble. The soft word of mitigation, reassurance for unsure recruits and a sympathetic ear for the occasional mother at the camp gates. Backing all this up was an impressive record of service, some in places that could not be formally acknowledged, along with a rare ability for comic mimicry. He was much in demand for the latter at leaving parties and the station Christmas panto.

'You're off soon aren't you Flight? You told me you had a place lined up in Great Yarmouth.'

'That's right Ma'am, and kind of you to remember given your current cvircumstances. That little bit of dreamland fell through when they cut service pension payments and gratuity. Made it a little less practical, if you see what I mean.'

She remembered now. The statement about how the government was grateful for the work of those in the public service, and appreciated how they were willing to receive less in the face of the overwhelming hole in state finances. Her 'sorry', seemed inadequate given the circumstances.

'Nice of you Miss.' He hesitated. 'I don't know what happened in there. But if it was something to do with the attack, we just have to fire and forget. No use dwelling over milk that's already down the drain. It's what we do after all. If you think too hard about it then we would never go about it in the first place.'

She looked at him. This man of the service, who sounded regretful, and even a bit angry. 'What I am saying is, you can't blame yourself. But if what happened was about something else, then good on you. I saw his face. The man is a disgrace, if you pardon my opinion.' Hayman paused.

'Let yourself in Ma'am. I was only told to bring you here, not to stand over you. I'm off for a subsidised breakfast before they take that away as well.'

Getting into the flat, Maggie threw herself onto the bed. It was incredibly hot and airless. She was soon aware of the first light stretching across the airfield, and by then Maggie knew that she was a very different person from the one who first came to these quarters. Killing she could accept under the rules she signed up to. Fighting for ones' country, with all the tools available, was not a problem. It was different now though, and not just because of that house covered in washing lines.

Belatedly she pressed the remote for the fan on the dresser and enjoyed the movement of air cooling on her contours. Indefinably, without any formal alterations, there had been those institutional changes. Nods and winks. A different culture over the drinks. A harder edge to the expectations. It was so very difficult to work out when this started. It was a sea change without a storm.

A zephyr soothing into gusty. All slightly rolling before the third pandemic and the collapse of the economy. Before the current government. When the flag waving started. By that stage the waving looked more like a nation drowning, turning in a whirlpool of misplaced pride and self-regard. She got up and looked at the dawn.

The airfield was at peace. Orange lights headed off toward the fens marking the main runway. Way off on its inland cliff was the floodlit cathedral of Lincoln. Both, in their way, bastions of state. Maggie took a breath. She was not only finished but she would commit the crime of leaving. It was as if a lever had been clunked down and her train could not go back.

The telephone rang. Literally with a bell. The old fashioned thing, still using copper wires, a wall connection and a closed circuit within the confines of the base, was one of the few ways of communication that was considered relatively safe from Chinese ears. She guessed who it would be.

'Maggie.' It was him. 'You certainly got me one there! But I can get you out of this. I don't think London will get to know. The talk is all about the strike. And everyone in the cockpit knows the tensions we work under and, as married men, we get how some of our colleagues might at times have regular issues.'

He is unbelievable, she thought. Gently she placed her hand over the mouthpiece in case the arrogant shit read the wrong emotion from the quickening of her breath.

'I would have talked this over with you at breakfast, and introduced you to some of the lads from the fighter squadrons.' He paused meaningfully. There was the bribe. The reminder of a wish unfulfilled, and a career still to be had. 'Mind you, I would have had to explain the bruising.' A short laugh. Very forced, to her ears.

'Anyway, I will be driving down to London in an hour and I thought I would keep the team briefing until after then?' The slightest rise at the end invited the possibility of dissent, which she did not provide it. 'Good. Anyway. I thought it best if we all meet for a fuller briefing when I get back, so I give the full starting prices as it were, straight from the horse's mouth.'

My God, she thought.

'So, I'll look forward to it.'

She put the receiver back on the cradle and went to the wardrobe to pull out a bag, a plan forming. Leaving was not going to be easy. The base was on lockdown and heading out the door was desertion. It might even, given the circumstances, be seen by the military as desertion in the face of the enemy. That would be a something else that could be thrown at her. Right up there with slugging a superior officer in front of an enemy being blown to pieces several thousand miles away. Getting through the main gate would mean a lot of questions. Attempting to pass through any of the other entrances would mean a fast turnaround and a call to the service police.

Quickly Maggie changed and packed a bag with the things she valued most. For a moment she eyed her uniform, ready pressed and hanging. Lingering she took in the newly acquired extra ring on the shoulder and wings of a drone pilot. There was more than a little regret as she slowly closed the door and looked at herself in the mirror. She was dressed in civilian clothes, and on any other day, in any other context, she may have let herself think she was dressed to kill.

At the front door, holdall in hand, and computer bag over her shoulder, she looked back at the place she could have called home. Stepping out of it would be an irrevocable step. Her own Rubicon. Setting her jaw, she stepped out and into the gaze of Flight Sergeant Hayman.

They eye-balled each other for a moment.

'Flight Lieutenant,' he managed conversationally after the briefest of pauses.

'Flight,' Maggie said wearily. He was carrying a silver foil square she noticed, and the hallway smelled of bacon.

'Thought you might need some breakfast.'

'That is really lovely of you,' and she meant it.

He looked at the holdall, without meeting her eye. 'Of course, you might prefer to eat it inside. With a plate.'

'I am sorry Flight. I truly am. But I am not going back.'

Carefully Alex Hayman placed the silver package on the floor between them. And as he stood up he put both arms at his side. Not exactly to attention, but enough to be formal. 'Desertion Ma'am. Is a nasty word. And I don't think it is one that should be applied to you.'

'It's not….,' and Maggie hesitated. 'Flight something very bad happened in the cockpit today. Something I cannot accept. There should be an enquiry, and I don't think there will be if I stay here. It will be submerged. Drowned in a boy's club. Drinks in the mess and a favourable posting for me before I get really embarrassing. But I'm finished in every way. Except for wanting to make sure nothing like this happens again.'

'It won't be an enquiry. I would be a court martial.'

'And I will face that consequence, but I want something to come out from this.'

'And I imagine if there is a court martial some reputations other than yours will be on the line.'

'That may be true as well Flight.'

'I can understand why some seniors may not want that to happen. Especially those who were drunk.' Hayman contemplated the silver package between them for a moment, before picking it up and tearing the sandwich in half. 'Nothing like a bacon butty when the going gets tough,' he said as he handed a piece to her. 'What's the plan?' he asked through the first mouthful.

Maggie took a bite. It was delicious. She knew her exit idea was fragile and as she explained it, it sounded worse than ridiculous. It looked as Hayman agreed. Finishing the butty he took out a handkerchief and wiped his fingers fastidiously, before fixing her with an expression that did not need words.

'On that basis,' he said, 'the most likely scenario is that you are arrested and you'll be worse off. The best thing would be to go into that room behind you, think very hard and resign if you have to. Don't bother about thinking of trying to fight it. No one ever likes a whistle-blower, whatever they say. And the military dislikes them more than most.'

Regretfully Maggie shook her head.

Hayman sucked air up through his nose, in a gesture that pulled his mouth into a grim line. 'If you are not going back in there, then what you are going to do needs a bit more support.'

Maggie picked up her holdall, went forward and kissed his cheek. He blinked. Before continuing gruffly. 'Make sure you are at the gate in exactly thirty minutes. And don't give away too much. Just be entitled. Keep them talking until something happens. This weather will help as well.'

The promised rain had started. The first drops falling as heavily as dollops of cream. 'Don't do anything to risk your pension Flight. I won't have it.'

'Kind of you to worry about that pittance, and I won't. There are other things in life though. Some of us appreciate bravery. And you're not the only one who doesn't like a lot of the stuff going on.' He looked at her keenly. 'Get yourself a coffee. But remember. Thirty minutes on the dot.'

She made it as scheduled, approaching the gate in driving rain. Squads of armed soldiers stood around taking what shelter they could while staring across the barbed wire and road to the demonstrators collected on the far verge. It always seemed to Maggie that their numbers seemed to grow whenever there was a drone strike, and it was odd how they heard so quickly. Around them were civilian police, their glistening poncho style capes hiding the weapons they always carried for this duty, the deep hoods looking like cowls on monks.

Drawing up at the barrier, she waited. The rain bouncing off the bonnet and the windscreen wipers barely coping. Inside the main gatehouse she saw several people watching her, each with an expression suggesting they were loath to leave the dry. One even raised a hand as if to start the whole gate opening negotiation through sign language and lip reading. An arm reached out and a window opened. It was the sarcastic policeman from the other morning.

'Base is closed up Ma'am. No one in or out, or should I say, In, out, in out.' There was laughter behind him that just reached the car through the drumbeat of the rain. Someone in the gatehouse started to sing loudly, 'In, Out, Shake it all about.' The policeman turned to his audience with a grin that seemed to extend to the back of his head. When his face returned to the window, he added, 'No hokey pokey. Okay dokey?

There was more laughter, and Maggie felt the heat rise to her face. She deserved it. Her plan relied on them acting to habit. Seeing her dressed up and not daring to question when so often she was followed out of the gate by the Squadron Leader. She smiled at the gatehouse, and shook her head. Winding down the window a short way, she shouted. 'Corporal, I don't know why you think that is appropriate. But I have an appointment.'

The Corporal looked as if he was trying to think of something else funny to say, when someone handed him a telephone. He listened. Asked a question. Maggie busied herself, trying not to show too much interest. Her face had got wet when she opened the car window. Dabbing around her eye liner with a tissue, she surreptiously took a quick view in the rear mirror. Coming from the administration buildings was Pickett's staff car. It had just rounded a corner and but for a roundabout, it would soon be on the straight heading for the gate. He would be heading for London. The meeting at noon. In less than a minute she and the gate would be in clear view.

Sweat broke from her armpits, her breath was coming in shallow draughts. Hoisting a smile she looked at the gatehouse. The Corporal did a circular movement with his hand indicating they needed to speak. She brought down the window, this time all the way, bringing in more rain. 'What?'

'That lispy scouser in the Wing Commander's office says you have an appointment at the Hospital.'

'That's right.'

'Why didn't you say?'

'You didn't ask.'

He looked at her before turning back into the room. 'I don't like it,' she heard him say. Turning back to her, it was if he straightened. 'They said it was something urgent. But we've been told that the base is on lockdown. I think I'm going to need a pass.'

Maggie looked into the wing mirror. Her arm was now soaked. It looked as if the staff car had come off the roundabout at regulation speed, but was now accelerating.

'Here comes Squadron Leader Pickett now,' she said. 'This is your chance to question the Wing Commander's instructions.'

The Corporal swung round, and seem to blanch. 'Get out,' he hissed at her before slamming the window shut. Ahead of her the red and white barrier was rising, the half drum bafflers smoothly dropping. With a catch of breath she starting slipping forward, allowing her car to make the speed. Within seconds the staff car seemed to wake up. Its front flashing, even switching on the blues, the sound of its horn coming in morse like pulsating alarms. Maggie hit the pedal. Electric cars don't lurch, and its sensors would not allow collisions. The barrier was causing it to sound a panic collision and 'brake' flashed onto the dash. Just when the car would have done just that, the barrier slipped out of sensor range. A shout came from the gatehouse. The Corporal was running out of the door, his clothes becoming dashed in rain. Some of the soldiers half started forward, uncertain and confused. Someone yelled. But she was through, passing the demonstrators, some of whom pointed their mobiles to capture the moment. Behind her the staff car stopped, the barrier now having started its programmed journey down. In her mirror Maggie saw Pickett standing in the rain gesticulating at the corporal.

'Thank you, Flight Sergeant Alex 'Handsome' Hayman', she spoke aloud, as if making a prayer. Thanks for your gift that allowed him to pull off lisping Liverpudlian. A civilian cop seemed to give her a smile as she went past. It was, after all, nothing to do with him what happened in there. Maggie breathed and shook out her shoulders. Thorswick next stop. She knew she was storing up a lot of trouble. There was no way she would not be caught. Strangely though, as she settled into the driving seat, she felt free.

Chapter 22

Thorswick

A crack of thunder and rain splatters as hard as hail woke Ash. He enjoyed the feel of the rain dropping heavy on his skin for a moment, before going inside. The night had been oppressively humid. As drops became a deluge the temperature broke, and he felt the familiar relief that came with the monsoon.

Preparing a kick start coffee in the kitchen, he wandered around with his mobile having downloaded the video of the drone strike. He looked at it first after setting up the Italian machine, and again as the heated water squeezed through the grains. Sipping the Ethiopian blend he squinted at the images for a third time. Something was wrong, or at least, not quite right. Sighing, he went upstairs to his computer, shrugging into a T shirt and shorts on the way.

There was a lot to wade through. The report on the strike, written in language as dispassionate as the way he felt. An analysis on how the deaths of the two Taliban would disrupt their de-stabilisation efforts in the region and planned international terrorist attacks. A congratulatory message for his work. In the general messages was a compendium of media, national and international, on the inch by inch progress of the Queen Elizabeth. Some names of the fatalities had come out, and families were talking. So too, were those with people on board, complaining that they were getting no news. Amongst them, with a whole page to herself as she tearfully held a picture of her sister, was Charlotte Dayton. Ash read every one of the words, and looked again at the image. The mass of flowing blonde hair, the looks and figure made for that particular tabloid sympathy that comes with sexual seasoning.

'Now there's a well I won't be drinking at anymore', he thought. Quite apart from not answering her calls, again, she was on her way to becoming a media sensation. The trajectory was predictable. Charlotte would soon be a staple of the news talk shows, the TV sofa sessions, all with regular bouts of Downing Street tea and sympathy. They were already a step away from starting on the poor Charlotte line, the last thing he needed was to be identified as the person lending a shoulder to cry on. In any case, right now there was the problem with that video.

He put it on the big screen, and leaned back into the chair to watch it again.

'Got it.' The cross hairs were set on the only house with washing lines on the roof. 'What are the chances?' Ash breathed. Ever distrustful of coincidences, that must mean there was someone setting things up. Someone he did not know about, and who could communicate. Who was able to spotlight the target, and tell London where to hit.

Ash went back to the news pages. A statement about the drone strike was being given limited coverage. Hardly surprising, given the breathless, blow by blow reporting of the battle to save the Queen Elizabeth. Most news outlets simply repeated a statement that UK forces had acted against known Afghan warlords responsible for a number of atrocities in the past with 'Defence Ministry sources' saying the two men were believed to be planning terrorist attacks in western capitals.

Some of the quality outlets mentioned their names with links to the aid worker killings. An online analysis site in Asia said the two men 'thought to have been killed' had worked hard in the last few years to clear their reputations, and had emerged as power brokers anxious to bring new trade opportunities to the poverty stricken country. Ash smiled ruefully. The ambush on the road to Kandahar, and the assassination of his mother and father, gave the lie to that.

Downstairs he went to the kitchen and took out a jar full of rice grains, which he emptied into a pint beer mug. From it Ash recovered a round, grey capsule that would have been instantly recognisable to generations of photographers as the packaging for a roll of camera film manufactured by a company that failed to appreciate the threat of digital cameras. Flipping the lid with the thumb of his left hand he tipped out sovereigns.

Methodically he packed a small rucksack with a camouflaged poncho and an old running shoe. In a small, zipped pocket he placed the three gold coins, each wrapped in linen. In a long open side pocket he put a telescopic baton that could be opened with the flick of the wrist, and a knife with a spring loaded short, broad blade. Partially serrated. Finally, he switched off his mobile, removing the battery and the card. There would be no electronic trace of where he was going, and he would be silent.

Rain was still falling steadily. Ash, a son of the Himalayas and the northern plains, was used to being soaked and dried alternately. As he jogged he knew the rain would reduce chance encounters. The countryside seemed deserted. He saw not a sign of anyone as he went on a wide circle before getting to the crossroads. The tree stump he had identified as a possible site for a 'drop' on his morning runs was just beyond the drainage ditch by a holly bush. After another quick look around, Ash slipped off his rucksack and took out the trainer. He scuffed it up in the wet and mud before placing it by the stump. The drop was on.

Ash's hide was in the woods, where he was able to look down on the drop. He spread out the camouflaged poncho and got beneath it, lying flat on the ground and feeling the wet mud cool his body while the smell of the woodland floor filled his nostrils. A mosquito buzzed in his ear, but he stayed still letting the birdlife settle. The earthy hollow was a compromise. From here he could check the package, leave the sovereigns, slip back into the woods and get home without having to head back down the lane or across open fields. The disadvantage was not being able to see right down the lane and get an early view of who was coming.

It was still raining, water pooling on the poncho and dripping across his view. Above him a blackbird abruptly stopped it's singing.

A vehicle was coming up the lane. Ash tensed. It was a short Land Rover with a canvas top, a real museum piece, its old engine noisy and smelly. As it went past Ash saw the man driving. He was bearded and with a black and white dog in the front. It splashed its way through without stopping. An estate or farm worker, Ash speculated. Or someone wanting to look like one. Doing a good job too, if that were the case.

Slowly he twisted his wrist to look at his watch. Just after eight. The birds resettled. A woodpecker started knocking on wood, and a wren set off a noisy song. A small deer peeked from the hedgerow beyond and contemplated a route to the woods. The minutes ticked. The mosquitoes were biting now, itches erupted on his back, legs neck and face, the darkness under the poncho extending their night's feeding.

A sound coming up the lane set off some birds. Way off to the left. Cackling and calling crows started up from the trees. As far as he could tell it was at the cross roads. He could not hear anything like a car, but then the taxi was electric. He waited. It was a good ten minutes by his count. Could have been less. When Collier came into view he was walking very slowly, looking left and right, his sallow face a mass of lines and his clothes wet through. The black T shirt clung to his frame. In front of him he held a red show box bearing the logo of an expensive sporting brand.

At the stump he stopped and looked around. Rain plastered down his hair and a strand fell down over an eye. Taking a hand off the box with exaggerated care, he flicked it back.

There was something in the way he did that Ash did not like. He stared at the man, watching carefully as he took a last look round and turned to the stump. From up the road came the sound of a shotgun and from behind Collier a pheasant rose into the air with a loud, excited two tone cry. He spun around, both hands still on the box, a wild look on his face which only settled after another scoping of the area. Another couple of shots. The farmer or estate worker with the Land Rover, thought Ash. The repeated shots seemed to reassure the taxi man. There was country business going on. It was not about him. Squatting down he placed the box, stood up and stepped back just as it exploded in a deafening blast.

Chapter 23

Thorswick

A retinal imprint of Collier dissipating in a grey and red cloud stayed as Ash drove his face into the ground. Debris flew, hitting trees and ground in a malevolent pitter patter that drowned the rain. Something heavy fell on his poncho. He stayed down, breathing fast and shallow, hearing dulled, heart thumping. Only when the air was getting further into his lungs did his heart start to steady, and he risked a look to where the bomb had gone off. The smell and metallic taste of explosive lingering and familiar.

Tilting up, Ash took in the scene. Nearby trees were scorched and blackened, the branches flayed, with fresh wood exposed like wounds. The holly bush was lopsided. Beneath it were slashed and discoloured remains. Ash knew he had to get away, and fast. Somewhere from the lane came the sound of a car being driven off at speed. He was not alone.

Slowly and carefully Ash pulled himself back further into the wood before righting himself behind the trunk of an oak, stuffing his rucksack with the poncho. Using as much cover as possible, he headed back toward the road every sense alert and the knife in his hand. Staying well within the tree cover he got a view of where they had parked. There was nothing there. He moved forward slightly. No car anywhere.

Slowly and cautiously Ash trotted. Only when he was on a familiar route, and he was as sure as he could be that no one else was around, did he start into his familiar running pace. Further into the woods he went and pushed himself hard up the hill, extending the pain by taking a detour over the ridgeline. He ran with the hood of running top over his head, even when the rain had stopped and all the time checking, checking and checking. Holding occasionally behind trees. Taking the brief moment to let his thoughts flow as he scanned the paths and cover. With gathering strength a strange conclusion was forming.

He was not the target. Finding Collier would have been easy. Not hard either to put in the squeeze and get him to take the bomb to the drop. Because he knew what was in the box. The nervous, double handed carry was a giveaway. Also, Collier had been told to leave it by an old trainer. And what does the bomb turn up in? It was a shoe box for running shoes from a sports company. Whoever did this was having a very black joke, and expecting him to get it knowing he would be around afterwards. There was a possibility Ash realised that the bomb had gone off accidently. But no one would allow an amateur Like Collier to handle an unstable device anywhere near them, let alone travel in the same car with it. The more Ash thought, it was more likely Collier was given the package and from that moment on he was a dead man walking. The message to Ash was clear. It was useless to fight, and he should behave.

Passing Poacher's Cottage he turned into the village to see Robinson father and son outside the Post Office with Walter "Well" Able.

'Did you hear that bang?' It was Frankie, the post master who asked. Ash came to a halt. On the other side of the green were two lady dog walkers talking and looking at the surrounding hills, while their animals sniffed and looked bored.

'What bang? In the village?'

'No. Up there somewhere. About twenty minutes ago.'

'Lady with the collie said she saw smoke.' This from Able.

'I was on the other side,' said Ash. He took out some earphones from his pocket. 'you don't hear much with these things in.'

Able sniffed. 'Don't see the point of going out in the country if you are just going to have them in your ears.'

'Fair Point'. Ash was looking up at the hills. 'Perhaps it was someone shooting?', he suggested.

'You should have heard it,' said Freddie Robinson. 'I was inside the shop helping dad with the newspapers, and the windows shook. I thought they might actually break.'

'Anyone going to have a look?'

The three looked at Ash as if this was the first time they had thought about it. 'Well,' said Able, 'most of that up there is old Bert Halston's land, and he's never one to encourage sightseers'

'Typical farmer,' said Frankie.

'Tell you someone who might be already up there,' piped up Freddie, 'and that's Ben Whistledown. He's always up and around early. Says he goes tree bathing.'

The three longer term residents of Thorswick exchanged looks. 'What?' said Ash. There was something in the look between them that suggested something not being said. Freddie looked at his father as if to ask permission, but it was the older man who spoke.

'Ben likes to do that. Tree bathing he calls it. Says it's something he picked up from the Japanese or some such. Always wandering around in the woods. Says its calming and eases stress. Often suggests others join him.'

This time the other two smirked.

'Sounds like a nice thing to do.'

'Yes. Thing is he likes to get his kit off when he does it. He's often been seen. He doesn't do anything. You know, like flash his todger or anything. If people are bothered he just wanders off. There have been times though when he appears unexpected like, and then there can be a bit of a to do.' The postmaster nodded across the village green to the dog walkers. 'Those ladies for example. They say they've given up going up there first thing as they've seen him several times. He dropped round to the house of one of them to explain. Said there were real health benefits. She was politeness itself, and because she seemed interested, he asked her to join him while setting out the clothing rules. Well then the vicar got involved, she being in charge of the church flower arrangements and all.'

Ash kept his voice as flat as the catch in his throat allowed. 'You think he might be up there now?'

'More than likely.'

'Surprised he's not down here already,' added "Well" Able, 'given that bang. Stupid bugger likes to give out news, and this time it might be more interesting that the usual foreign stuff.'

The others nodded agreement, while Ash weighed the possible implications of a wandering nudist where a man had just been blown up. 'I'm often up there in the mornings,' he said, 'and I've never seen him.'

'He's seen you though. Said it a few times.' Able focused on Ash's rucksack. 'That's all a bit heavy for a morning run isn't it?'

Ash ignored him. If Whistledown saw him this morning, he would know which side of the hills he had been on. He may even have seen him running from where body parts lay scattered amongst singed trees. The last thing he needed was discussion about his morning running habits and why he seemed to carry a lot of kit while doing it. 'Terrible news about the Queen Elizabeth,' he offered by way of distraction. Once that discussion got going he left them to it. Everyone, it seemed, was now a navy expert.

Back home he put the card in the mobile and switched it on. It may, he thought as he did so, be time to give more thought and attention to Whistledown. The man seemed a bit of a joke. Always in the hope of an air ticket arriving for some far away disaster spot. There night be more to him. Acting as the local clown was not a bad cover.

The mobile was vibrating continuously. Not with calls but with downloaded messages. It was pinging and lighting like a pin ball machine on speed. Still with his mind on the lanky Whistledown, and without too much curiosity, Ash flicked the screen and reached to put some bread in the toaster. As an afterthought he turned the dial down to low. The last thing he wanted was the smell of anything burning.

His attention snapped to the messages. Amongst them was an increasing flood of news updates. With the sensation of growing dread he scanned the toplines and then opened a video from a chaotic open air news conference, and full in the frame were Amanullah Tarzi and Mahmoud Sher Ali. The strap line running under the pictures said 'Surviving Afghan leaders vow revenge'. Turning up the sound he heard them pinning blame on 'colonialist dogs of the United Kingdom' and their 'fellow carrion eaters'.

The coverage on the attack itself was graphic, stomach churning and vitriolic. Ash quickly came out of it, looked at more recent messages and read with disbelief. He kept pressing on more and more stories as he struggled to understand. The house destroyed, he read was hosting a visiting goodwill delegation from the Chinese government. Ash's eyes widened. The toast popped in the toaster. Beijing had just called for three days of national mourning. The man leading the goodwill mission to meet Afghan leaders in 'a neutral setting and in a spirit of mutual friendship' was Zhang Ke, the brother in law to the Premier and the man responsible for procurement across the whole of the country's armed forces. From the official picture being put out by the China News Agency, Ash immediately recognised the man who had travelled through Karachi airport on the false passport.

Ping. A profile from the Financial Times popped up. Zhang Ke, Ash read, was a noted 'China first' exponent at the heart of the Communist Party establishment who was considered to be a far seeing, major strategist. As such he was credited with maintaining the major shift of resources toward offensive capability in space, on the internet and China's ever expanding industrial espionage.

Ash sat down heavily on a kitchen stool. Someone like that would be a prime target for anyone wanting revenge for the Queen Elizabeth. But a hit on such a figure was on an entirely different level from knocking off two Afghan warlords. The fallout now was likely to be unpredictable. He remembered how he was rushed for details about who was in the Chinese delegation. How that pressure caused him to bypass usual safety protocols when speaking with his man in Pakistan immigration.

Ash absently bit into some dry toast. It was only after he sent the passport details that he was told the strike was back on.

143

He remembered the video image and the missile heading for a house with washing lines, and the speed with which the UK government got out a statement saying the strike was aimed at terrorist leaders. As he continued trawling through the news and social media sites he saw how some government friendly outlets were saying if a mistake had been made, then the Chinese leadership needed to be asked why senior figures were meeting such notorious killers.

There were a number of messages from an unknown phone. With a sinking heart he realised they were from his Immigration Officer asset in Karachi. They were not supposed to be contacting this way. He must be in trouble. The first texts confirmed it.

'Hi, I know we spoke about meeting to go on holiday. Have unexpected leave. You up for that?'

And then. 'Do need to get away for a long break. Call me.'

'My God,' thought Ash. He looked at the timings. An hour apart and sent at about the time he was sitting in the wood, mobile off and waiting for Collier. Time lost. He needed to get hold of Holesworthy and arrange an evacuation, even though every instinct told him it may already be too late. He was about to ring when his mobile lit up and, with a leap of hope, he answered.

'My Friend.' It sounded as if Hassan, the Immigration Officer was relieved. 'I am glad that we can have a last word.'

No, thought Ash desperately. This can't be happening. It was not just the choice of words. Hassan's tone was one of someone checking out but who is glad that a loved one had made it to the bedside.

'I sent you some messages earlier but it seems now that a holiday is out of the question.' It sounded as if Hassan was outside. On the flat roof of the yellow stone, colonial era apartment block in Karachi's Haqqani Chawk. It stood imperially proud, a proud face set against modernity. Ash could hear honking vehicles in the crowded streets and thoroughfares below.

'I now have some other friends at my door. What a pity, our families have always worked so well together.'

There was the noise of something breaking, and then, calmly, 'I don't think you could have helped me this time my friend. But I did want to speak with you one last time. I just wanted to know if you knew who was going to receive that gift when you called last night. Perhaps, if I had known, I might have, well, done a few things differently.'

Ash nearly choked. 'Really Hassan, I had no idea. It was just something routine they wanted urgently. If I had thought there was any chance of this....'

'Hush. Say no more. And yet they wanted something so urgently.' There was a long pause and Ash could imagine Hassan breathing in an air pungent with spices, fetid garbage, fried samosas and fumes from the bustling life below.

'Well, I suppose you cannot make an omelette without breaking some eggs. You are not to blame "Abu Bakir". In reality I probably never stood much of a chance in this world. The more I see of it the more I think I am more suited to a different age. As it is, I shall soon be dancing with daffodils.'

Ash caught a sob. Hassan Khan, a lion of a man. One of his best agents, while being fiercely loyal to what he wished his country could be, was repeating his desire to wander in the Lake District with his wife. For the last time he was quoting William Wordsworth. What was it? 'And then my heart with pleasure fills, and dances with the daffodils.' Ash knew Hassan was asking him to look after his wife, because all hope of anything else was gone.

'Now I need to destroy this thing before others get hold of it. Good bye my friend.' Ash knew then it would not just be the mobile and SIM card heading into oblivion amidst the mouldering rubbish below the old fashioned apartment block. And he wept.

Chapter 24

Thorswick

Minutes passed. Hassan, a man who loved the type of English where people were 'walloped', and a good thing was 'Top Banana'. Ash took a shuddering gulp. Two deaths in an hour. There was a very good chance now of Ash's entire network being rolled up as the Chinese and their allies went on the hunt. The very least he could do was save some. Upstairs he moved around the computer desk to the window. Leaning against the wall Ash slipped open the slats for the topmost shutter. Up on the hillside a tractor with flashing amber light was making its way down the lane.

Not without sympathy Ash reached for a pair of binoculars. The tractor stopped a few yards away. A man in blue overalls with a flat cap got out and eyed the flayed hedgerow and trees. Getting closer, he stopped again. He peered, his body becoming rigid. Nearer, his hand moving to a pocket again and pulling out some kind of rag, which he clamped over his mouth and nose as he pushed forward. Looking down he moved something with a booted foot. Swivelling away, the rag pulling from his face, he doubled up and retched.

Slowly Ash closed the slats. At the computer he filed a three line report on Hassan. It was all the obituary he was likely to get in service terms. He sent a note also to human resources. The wife in Cumbria, he knew, was Hassan's chosen beneficiary. Sighing, he pushed the button on the desk light. The call to Adrian Holesworthy could not be put off any longer. When they connected the other seemed as subdued as Ash felt.

'My contacts are under threat,' Ash began. 'There is no doubt I have lost one. There's a good chance of losing some others. We may have to get them out.'

A long pause. 'It's a very difficult context at the moment.'

'Not as difficult as it is for them.'

'Yes, of course. Just not sure if we have the capability at the moment.'

'Can we at least make the sure we contact our opposites and tell them to lay off? Give them an exchange or something....'

'I'll see what I can do. Send me something.'

From the tone of his voice Ash could tell Holesworthy was preoccupied, while making all the right noises at relevant points. Ash felt as if faces he knew were watching as he argued their case. People they had depended on for years to provide information, but who may soon be in cells with experienced torturers. Their families wailing. At the mercy of stone faced officials, handing out slaps as they tossed their homes. The regular silence from the other end did not offer hope.

'I'll get you something,' said Ash evenly. Then, 'what exactly happened with the drone strike last night?

Adrian drew breath. The drone had hit the intended target. It was understood that this is where the Taliban leaders were. Why the occupants were the visiting Chinese, rather than the intended recipients was something they were trying to work out. There would have to be some sort of inquiry. And here Adrian Holsworthy paused. Bureaucrats, thought Ash, do not like inquiries.

'Of course,' Holesworthy resumed. 'We said we attacked terrorists plotting attacks on the west. One would think that would provide enough embarrassment to prevent them from admitting they had such a high profile delegation in their company.'

'The drone went in,' said Ash, 'after I was asked for details about the Chinese delegation. That makes me wonder if the targeting was switched to revenge the Queen Elizabeth attack.'

It was as if he reached down the virtual wire and given Holesworthy a punch. 'No, absolutely not. You can't think such a thing. There are safeguards and controls. I mean, that would suggest a complete takeover of a very considered process, that has been honed over years. I cannot imagine why a professional would come to such a conclusion.'

Ash heard the underlying tone. The desperate desire to convince. The faux shock. So it was true then. Not for the first time Ash had to remember that Adrian Holesworthy was a master of vacillation and prevarication, skills that allowed him to hold several different positions at once. In the current febrile atmosphere no doubt his political masters thought he was on side, while the angry military considered him one of their own.

Ash continued to listen as a tissue of lies was woven into a blanket. Idly he turned off the table light, slipped the top panel and looked out at the hillside. A flashing blue light was showing through gaps in the hedgerow as it headed up the lane as if it were a firefly drawn to the amber luminescence of the tractor. The last of the rain clouds were going. Sun was playing across the sodden fields and woods. Ash suddenly realised it was very steamy. It was going to be a very long, humid day.

'And the very last thing we would be doing is tweaking the dragon's tail when the Queen Elizabeth is still at sea. So, I hope that's settled.' Holesworthy finally halted.

There was nothing to be gained from going further down that rabbit hole. Ash did have one other question, although he was conscious that the clock was ticking. Before the hour was out he should set out the case for saving the lives of all those who had worked so tirelessly for the British state. 'Was there someone else acting for us there?', he asked. 'Only it looked as if the house was marked by all that laundry.'

'Good God,' Holesworthy exploded. 'What on earth are you smoking down there? You're coming up with some pretty fanciful stories, is all I can say. Get a grip Ash, you're wasting my time.'

Ash expected that to be the end of the call, but Holesworthy stayed on.

'Something odd did happen last night around the strike,' he said. 'It seems the RAF pilot refused it. Said there was too much risk of civilian casualties. When ordered to get on with it there were some words, or some such, and she was confined to base. Anyway, she skipped. Took herself off and is now flying without instruments, as it were.'

For the life of him, Ash could not see why any of this would be his concern. 'The military police will no doubt get her,' he said helpfully.

'Quite. And a patrol car did spot her on the motorway but got called off to another incident just when they were about to pull her. In fact all the police are busy at the moment. The car number plate recognition system has crashed, along with systems controlling electronic motorway signs. In fact systems have gone off line all over the place.'

Holesworthy paused. 'Apparently, our domestic colleagues have some unique concerns about this woman in particular. And they want her found. Her picture was snapped by demonstrators as she left the base. It's since appeared on a number of sites with a heading "The Murdering Bitch".

Ash was still not getting it. 'OK, well that all sounds very domestic.'

'Agreed. And the whys are only being released on a need to know basis. Domestic are really hot on this for some reason. And it's being emphasised by the upper floors here.' Ash could tell Holesworthy knew more. 'All I am saying is that everyone is being asked to keep an eye out, but they don't want it talked about outside the family, as it were.'

'OK.' In his head, Ash was mentally compiling lists of people he wanted to get out of trouble, and thinking up the trade-offs that could be made.

'This errant drone jockey may have a connection with your neck of the woods. When I saw that, I thought you should know. I can't ask them directly, as I don't want to show any particular interest. After all, you're not really there, and we don't operate at home.'

Ash dragged his attention back. 'Do you want me to look for her?'

'Not at all. Far from it. Just be aware'.

'Ok,' thought Ash as the call ended, then why on earth then are you bothering me with it? Swiftly he started writing. He knew who in his network would be most at risk. The tricky bit was sorting out the pressure points that might be brought to bear. Highlighting the peccadillos of the ones with influence operating in London, their girlfriends and boyfriends, the politicians who stashed state cash in British banks, the British fellow travellers and useful idiots living within UK reach. It was not a long list. He omitted Safedeen Khan, and not out of old school loyalty. Rather it was the thought that adding Safedeen to the pickup list would lead to questions about his link to a fatal bomb explosion in a Cotswold wood.

The message took him longer to compose than anticipated. He was sending it through the coding system when his mobile lit up. It had detected movement outside. Quietly he went to the front of the house. At first he thought there was no one there. It was only when he checked the sides that he saw a figure peering through the letterbox of blue cottage. Quietly he went down the stairs, picking up the knife as he did so, and flung open the front door.

The figure next door shot upright. It was Ben Whistledown. Taking in Ash he languidly walked around to his gate. 'Thought I would just check if new neighbour was at home and not bothered by all this.' He waved an arm at the hill side, reeking of insincerity as he smiled at Ash. 'Quite a thing.'

The lane was now strung with flashing blue lights. 'It's like a fairy necklace,' said Ben. Ash kept watching the activity while taking in what he could of the speaker. Up to this morning, he had dismissed him as a dreamer and harmless eccentric, but the more he thought about his curious habits the less he liked.

'I wonder what could have happened,' Whistledown added.

'Who knows?'

Whistledown turned to him and smirked. 'I very much think you know something.' Before Ash could ask what he meant,

Maggie's car drove into the driveway next door and out she stepped.

Chapter 25

Thorswick

Maggie was hoping to get into Blue Cottage, close the door, and howl. Instead she was confronted by two men gawping at her, and dictates of common curtesy demanded she say something. Fortunately, there was an obvious distraction. 'What on earth is happening up there,' she asked, pointing up the hills. 'Police were steaming down the roads on the way here'.

Fleeing the airbase she assumed the police would be after her very quickly. The first flashing blue lights in her rear view mirror nearly caused her to be sick. But that turned out to be ambulance. Throughout the journey there were quite a few police cars speeding past her, with a number tearing up the other side of the motorway as well. Much more than usual.

Somewhere near Daventry, a patrol car did slot in behind her and a churning pit formed in her tummy as she prepared for the worst. She was so preoccupied she forgot to change lanes and tangled with the stream of traffic joining the motorway. That alone would have been cause to pull her in, instead it swooped off with the two men inside giving her a steady look of curiosity. After that she got off the motorway and took a cross country route. Driving into Thorswick she felt a sense of having landed after a difficult flight. It did not last long. Getting out at her cottage she saw the hillside.

In the fields there was a lot of activity. Handlers with dogs on long leads were sweeping around the hedged perimeter, while figures in blue overalls were wrestling upright a large, white tent.

'I've no idea,' said Ash. As he spoke he was aware how the other man cocked his head slightly without turning his face away from Maggie.

'There was a loud bang on the hill early this morning,' Whistledown said. 'I do hope no one was hurt.'

'How strange,' said Maggie. 'what was it"

They shrugged. Together. 'Did anyone see it?' Maggie was trying. Engaging her new neighbours in decent conversation about a curious incident, when all she really wanted do was to get inside, put a pillow over her head and have a very long, private, howl.

'No,' they said in unison, chiming thought Ash irritably, like a bloody clock.

In the way people do, Maggie registered the false note and, unbidden, her forehead puckered slightly. Obviously this was some local mystery she was not going to be told about. Sod it, she thought. As if she cared anyway. Soon enough these two curious blokes, and everyone else in this tiny world, would have her arrest and court martial to gossip about. Saying how lovely it was to see them again, she swung up her bag, shut the car door loudly, and went into blue cottage. In the dark hallway the first thing she saw was a distinctive envelope with the thick red edging of the Immunisation Service. It was correctly addressed to her at Blue Cottage, and usually would have to be signed for.

Everyone knew what such a letter meant. Usually it was about being behind on your vaccinations, and came with a requirement to take action immediately. Failure to do so risked large fines for each day of delay. In the meantime there were restrictions. The date of delivery, in red on the letter, was a week ago. So, should have got it when she was last there. Another puzzle was that Maggie was fully up to date on her jabs.

The envelope too was surprisingly heavy, as if contained more than the single sheet summoning her to fulfil her civic duty. Just at the moment the last thing she wanted to do was to go to a vaccination centre. Her name would ping up immediately on all sorts of systems, the Immunisation System having data sets that enabled them to track, isolate and, if need be, confine. She ripped open the envelope, and blinked. Because inside was another envelope. And it was of a type she immediately recognised.

It was as stiff and white as an undertaker's collar. The last time she had seen such a thing it was the letter from a London law firm telling her she had inherited the cottage, and directing her to a local solicitor for all future dealings. Out of curiosity she once called the city number at the top of the letterhead. Not that it did her much good. The person she spoke to said they could offer no more information.

'We are simply fulfilling the terms of a bequest,' said the man patiently. He repeated the phrase several times, before concluding in a kindly tone, 'I really don't see how I can be of any further use.'

Somehow a letter from that firm had found its way into an official 'red' envelope of the Immunisation Service. She checked it again. It was not a forgery. And it had been sealed. With a beating heart she realised a lot of trouble was being taken to disguise whatever was in the envelope.

Inside this time was a brief letter drawing her attention to the enclosures, which they had been instructed to get to her by secure means at a given time after the property transfer. The enclosure was five pages of firm, old fashioned handwriting, from someone who used a fountain pen without making a single crossing out or blob.

The first line had her catching her breath.

'I am your grandfather'.

She looked at the address. 'Blue Cottage.' And the date. Two years, and three months ago.

That first line stood alone. The writer obviously had a sense of drama. Someone who allowed time for the best words to be absorbed by his audience. Maggie remembered a few times in her life when an envelope in the same azure paper arrived at the council flat to create ripples around her grandmother, with tears often following. Not ones of sorrow, but more, she judged, of regret. How her drunken mother, when she was around at such moments, would spit words, cursing her lot, the way they lived and always with a preamble in a lost, little girl voice of 'Oh goody, is that from daddy?'

Maggie swallowed hard. 'I regret, profoundly,' she read next, 'the path I had to choose. It meant not sharing a life with the woman I loved and bringing up our child. I have to believe if I had been there, and able to provide the care and devotion they both deserved, things would have been different. You know better than me the heartbreak, desolation and awful personal consequence.'

That she did. Her grandmother had been strong. Keeping the family together. Picking up the pieces. Making sure Maggie was clean, tidy and fed for school despite her drug addict mother. What difference would a father figure have made? she wondered. It was a question that had always been there for Maggie, a prism for every emotional fissure.

'I worked for the secret service,' she read on. 'I was set to give that up for your grandmother. We had been together secretly for years. I was married, of course, which complicated matters. My employers were never sympathetic about unvetted liaisons. Life with your grandmother though would have happened, but for a mission that, in my mind, was going to be the last. I should not give you any details, but I will. You deserve at least that. Not only because the damage done to your family, but because you are in a very great danger and will have to be careful for the rest of your life.'

Maggie blinked and read the line again. Danger? Her head jerked back as if the writing was suddenly giving off a bad smell. She flipped over the pages. There were several to go.

'In fact, you and the family were always in danger because of what I did. While I was alive I kept an eye on you, along with help from others who knew the score. Now I am of an age, and with a terminal condition, I have made certain provision that goes beyond you getting Blue Cottage. What is impossible to arrange is total security.

'The reason for the threat is that the tail end of what I achieved is still whipping around.' Maggie noticed the wording and the sense of pride in what had been done, even if it came with unfathomable outcomes. 'On that mission, the one that should have seen my departure after a good, if routine career, enabled seeds to be sown for creating a nightmare of betrayal and suspicion amongst the Russian spy agency. To cut a very long story short, I met a man who was already 'tail up', as we liked to say. In other words, after a number of contacts, tentative as first, he was showing an increased willingness to flip and work for us. I was in contact with him when we were still at the 'eye catching across a crowded room' stage of the courtship. On that last, fateful, mission he leapt into bed. Our man was not a spy as such. He was a drone within the system. But an important one because he was easily camouflaged amongst hundreds of others changing over the systems and files. Taking reams of paper, making them digital, scanning and, for us, inserting nuggets of fool's gold.

'When he finally committed we already had a complex operation poised to go. Over years we had developed plausible scenarios, with the whole picture only being available if you drew a line between the points. These dots were to be seeded throughout their systems. In themselves they meant nothing. If joined together they would create a case suggesting considerable, and widespread, betrayal.

'It became evident on that mission however, although he was fully on board, our man wanted me to continue as the one doing the hand holding. Leaving the service, while such a prize was on offer was not possible. Years of work had got us to where we were, and I have to admit there was considerable vanity involved on my part. Your grandmother said she understood. She was also very wise. She accepted the decision, but seemed to sense that whatever I was doing might bring danger close to home. For that reason, she insisted that we have a total separation, that our daughter would never see me again, and any contact would be on her terms. Very occasionally she did reach out through a system of codes and contact systems, but we never actually met again. I was not in a position to refuse any of this. And she was completely right.'

The tea was acrid and nearly cold. She would have to get some milk she thought vaguely. Next door she could hear movement. Someone coming down the stairs, and the door opening. She went to the front of the cottage, the letter in her hand, the pause being welcomed as if her mind need time to absorb before tackling the final page. From her window she saw Ash heading down the path and taking a right toward the post office and the other road into the village. She remembered the shop, and wondered if it would take cash. It was unlikely, even out here. She might have to try though. But for the biscuits there was nothing to eat. The thought drove her back into the kitchen where she opened a few cupboards, knowing she would find them empty. She would have to think of something, otherwise she might as well make a call and hand herself in. Something she may well have to do but she would rather do it in her own time, when she was prepared and not because she needed food. She shook herself. She was distracting. Having been told her life was in danger, she was going about looking for crumbs because it was just something she could do. She needed to focus on the implications unfolding in the neatly written script.

'Maggie, our scheme succeeded better than we could have dreamed. All it required was for us to light the blue touch paper at different points for the Russians to join up details in their files. It led to the termination of many of their better operatives. And when I say 'termination', it really was a brutal cull. Unfortunately, it not only involved those we were glad to see out of the picture, but there were suicides amongst some of their families. At least a baker's dozen of the players and partners died by their own hands, unable to cope with the fall from grace, the loss of prestige apartments and all that went with their elite lifestyle. Children too suffered as they were expelled from schools or universities. It was an unintended consequence.'

She heard the disclaimer. The tone. The official word when unfortunate results are hitting the headlines. What is said to keep disciples when a bomb hits a hospital. Or for that matter, a missile takes out a wedding party. Images of broken families, suffering in their bewilderment came to mind. Hard faces perplexed at the ruination. Sitting in dark flats, the air as cold as the judgement. Recriminations and tears amongst people for whom it would be better not to think about. This was a very familiar world. One she already knew how to compartmentalise from her own work.

'We were not of course, operating in a vacuum. Such a success attracts jealousy. There were also spies amongst us who heard whispers. Some of these sleepers started to build their own picture. A pointer was drawn when I did a bit of backdoor support when your grandmother felt threatened by criminals on the estate where you grew up. It was as well your grandmother had insisted so long before that I should be out of your lives. Because there were soon people going around the area trying to find who might have a connection with someone in the secret service. They drew a blank, while we watched. But they were able to add a few extra dots to their own picture and my wife, unfortunately, found out that I had been less than faithful and might have had a child. This became common knowledge within the upper reaches of the service. We know it made its way into the identikit profile the opposition was building on me. We know there was also speculation that the 'other family' may have been of Caribbean origin, based purely on the majority residents of the estate at the time.

'To cut a long story short, a new head of the Russian Intelligence service steadied their ship, dug deep into the causes of their crisis, caught our contact and extracted a lot more about me before the inevitable execution. He also swore an oath, something that has been maintained by his successors. In effect it was 'hakmarrja'. An Albanian blood feud. The obligation to kill the offender, or their family, until honour is satisfied.

'The end of the operation meant I was finished, and given a new cover. I did extract a promise that protection would also extend to your family, but I sometimes wonder if that was wise given the leaks and the hunger of the Russians. With my death though, the only remaining target for their revenge is you. And I really need you to understand that you must never assume this threat has gone away. You will forever be a target. And I am truly sorry.

'It is time I finished. Do not trust too easily. Avoid those who ask questions. Run if you can at the slightest thing that doesn't seem right. If you need help, call the law firm. Ask for Peregrine Fawcett. They will know it is you. Maggie, I was there when you passed out at Cranwell and I could not have been more proud.

He was there? Maggie tried to think through the spectators, the ranks of parents and friends, all dressed as if for a wedding or a baptism. The day of polish, bands, dignitaries and bombast. The connections seeping through the martial ceremony. Was there a sole face paying attention to her? A stare that spoke? She could not recall any such thing.

'A final attempt to provide for your safety is in the loft. Behind the chimney stack. They are tools I hope you never have to use. You should run before you have to use them. Now, burn this letter. This <u>you must do</u>.'

Maggie remembered again. How the letters were read and set alight. The paper made into a wick and introduced to the gas flame in the kitchen. Her grandmother, poker faced, performing as if it were a silent, religious rite. Her mother, no longer requesting a sight. Satisfying herself instead with curses, and a final 'yeah, Daddy. Burn. Burn in hell for all I care.'

She sat for a long while, she simply did not know what to do next. At first thought it was all too fantastic, but there was enough said that fitted into the mysteries that had pockmarked her life. It explained a lot about her grandmother. Why she was like a scenting dog, sniffing the air when out and about. She was looking for danger. At the thought of her grandmother, a small smile came to Maggie's face. Taking the letter to the stove she lit the gas and held the end into the flame. Holding it as the fire spread and she remembered, even more fondly now, Evelyn Mary Johnson. Feeling a new and stronger connection to her granny as the flames consumed the letter and started toward her fingers. Getting an insight into the life she chose. The fear she must have felt every day. Her suspicion of strangers now understood.

This fear, she realised as she crumbled the ashes, was her inheritance. What she had imagined was a daily, routine caution felt by many around her because they were black and living on a bad estate was nothing compared to the menace outlined in the letter. The new constant which would now be directing the rest of her life. A very directed and personal threat Evelyn well understood, but which her mother, tried to block with chemical oblivion.

'Fear,' she murmured. 'I greet you.'

Upstairs she got a chair and stood on it to push open the loft hatch. The light on her mobile showed a dusty space that extended over the other cottages. It was an area that was obviously seldom used. She heaved herself up and made her way over the joist to the chimney breast. Amongst the cobwebs was a wooden box with faded gilt letters announcing a company that provided the King with 'fine garden games'. Croquet in particular. Maggie opened the lid, and gasped. Not daring to touch. The thought occurred to her that the contents would be enough to give the police a lot more to talk to her about, and ensure twenty years in jail.

Chapter 26

Thorswick

'I'm So Happy!' The quote was everywhere. Along with pictures of a smiling Charlotte in the UK next to one of sister Abby giving a thumbs up from a hospital bed. The story was everywhere. How Abby had been got onto the last helicopter to take injured from the Queen Elizabeth. The Thai medic on board the aircraft got a message out to the fleet and a doctor on the Turkish warship put up his hand to do the surgery having performed similar operations. He was brought over to the American carrier and Abby was now sitting up, and according to the Navy press release, asking about her shipmates and wanting 'revenge on the attackers'.

Quite a few of the pictures had Charlotte arm in arm with a 'special friend'. Brian, she said, has been incredible, and 'it is at times like this when you really find out who you can rely on.'

Ash sighed. At least she is still thinking of me, he thought sourly. A rabid pro government news site proclaimed 'Victory' and in much smaller letters 'for brave Abby.' Readers here would have been forgiven if they missed out how many other nations were involved in the effort. The text made it sound as if Abby was saved through British pluck and highlighted her desire to take on whoever had crippled the Queen Elizabeth.

What images there were of the British ship came from news agencies of other countries. To Ash it looked as if it was far lower in the water. Another site noted that the female commander of a Japanese destroyer died from a broken neck after being thrown down stairs when the ship was struck by the wave caused by the explosion.

He turned to the messages. A formal picture of Maggie in uniform filled the screen. The accompanying text giving an outline description. "Aged 27. 6 Ft. tall. Slim build. No known domestic address." Also a justification. "There is concern that she might be in danger. Due to the nature of her role the security services have become involved in the search for her. All officers to note and contact headquarters as soon as seen."

Ash put his head in his hands, his eyes closed. It was a train smash. If he called it in, Pandora's box would spring open. Home intelligence would get interested about what he was doing there. They would then start drawing the links. It would be very unlikely they would ignore him being within a quarter of a mile of a bomb that killed. And any answer would suggest he was working on home turf without their say so. At which point he would be skewered, and whoever was occupying the senior desk in the lingerie section would throw him to the wolves.

Another message flashed onto the computer. It was an IFAT, or notice of Immediate Foreign Agent Threat and came with a very different picture of Maggie. It was of her at the wheel of a car. A snatched image like those taken by photographers when a celebrity has been trashed in court and is being whisked away. Mouth grimly shut, eyes wide over whitened knuckles on the steering wheel, the windscreen reflecting pearls of rainwater. Not glamourous, but recognisable.

To justify the IFAT more detail needed to be given. Ft. Lt. Johnson, it was conceded, was the last known relative of an agent. Because of the work related actions of this individual, an established threat exists. However, it's not believed that Johnson herself is aware of this. Anyone approaching her must be circumspect in what they say, but stay with her until armed assistance arrives. Headquarters to be alerted immediately on identification.

It was Russians, Ash thought. It could not be anyone else. The age of the former occupant of Blue Cottage meant he would have been battling a resurgent Russia. And Russian spy agencies had a long habit of including family members in their vicious vendettas, while getting themselves embedded in Britain.

His duty was clear. He should call it in, go around to next door and make light conversation until the cavalry turned up. Because Ash was under no illusions. The alerts would have put blood in the water. For all he knew the sharks were already circulating. Any watcher would have asked why a search for that individual was not being left to the heavy boots of the military police. Someone doing searches on leaky systems would provide more information to the dumb computer banks trawling for the last living relative of a hated enemy. Artificial Intelligence would super charge the search, come up with too many associations with the missing Maggie Johnson and establish correlations about what was known about her mysterious grandfather. If she ended up as another notch on the Russian revenge list, a yellow spittled, poisoned corpse within a few yards of his home, he would be torn apart. At least assassins might be stalled by not knowing about Thorswick and Blue Cottage.

He stood up and grabbed his mobile. They should have given me a gun, he thought bleakly as he prepared to send the message to headquarters. A bleep announced another urgent from headquarters. Maggie, coloured in red with added devil ears, was being auctioned by something or somebody called 'The Laughing Gnome' who would give her precise location to the highest bidder. The sale was closing within an hour of the first posting, or in forty minutes. Ash went to the page on the dark web. The price in a crypto currency he had never heard of, was running as a ticker on the page. It was rising, fast. There seemed to be a lot of interest.

Whistledown. Ash had watched the speed with which he had left Maggie's cottage after she arrived about an hour ago. That left twenty minutes to set out his stall on the dark web. He checked out 'The Laughing Gnome' on search engines and simply got the song by David Bowie. The lyrics seemed to mock. Quickly he searched Ben Whistledown. Nothing known on his systems or the benign web, other than he seemed to have been around a lot of trouble spots without being associated with any government or agency.

He was prevaricating. There were enough police on the hill to flood the village within minutes, get hold of Maggie and take Whistledown away to be shaken by professionals to see what fell out. At the very least, she would be safe, the flower arrangers of the church might sleep easier, but he would be road kill.

He put the computer into sleep. It would, after all, he thought, only take minutes to do a final check. It was time to see Ben Whistledown.

@@@@@@@@@@@@@@@@@@@@@@

It was the women who saved Shameeza. On the coach carrying the wounded to hospital in Quetta the only person with any medical skill was a man, so it was left to the women to see to their own and the children. It quickly became obvious that Shameeza was not injured in the same way as everyone else. Not that she knew much about the journey. Drifting in and out of consciousness, she was unaware of the discussion that took place around her, and the call made to a trusted relative instructing him to meet the coach. While the others were taken into the hospital in Quetta, she was helped into a car. As if it were happening to someone else she saw a gold bracelet being handed over, and her face being held in both hands as she tried to speak. The gesture being oddly reassuring.

The driver said nothing to her on the drive to Islamabad, and now she was waking up properly because someone was demanding it.

'I need you to speak to me.'

Slowly she was re-entering. Reluctantly. Coming around to the noise of someone talking against a background of corridor noise and beeping. The first thing she saw was a ceiling. On her finger was something, and rising above her a bottle with some liquid in it. Slowly Shameeza turned her face to see what could have been a doctor by his white coat and neat, black hair streaked with grey. She was obviously in some kind of bed, and in a room. Looking around she saw they were alone.

'You're in a private room,' said the man. 'At a hospital in Islamabad,' he added in case she had not realised. 'You have had surgery. Do you understand?'

Shameeza nodded. Beside her was a monitor. Doing the bleeping.

'I am here to make you an offer.'

She was getting more alert now.

'You are not safe. The Americans have been tipped off that you are here and, as far as they're concerned, you are the wife of Mahmoud Sher Ali.'

'I'm …' Shameeza started. And then stopped because the man was raising his hand.

'I know,' he said. 'But they will take you. On the other hand there are others who want to hear much more about what happened and the deal you helped set up. They can offer you safety and a new life.'

'I don't want a new life. I want my old one.' Her throat was dry.

'That's not possible, 'I'm afraid,' he said as if this was really a personal regret. 'You are faced with little choice, he went on, and Shameeza noted that he also had a stethoscope.

'If your 'husband', discovers that you ran from him you're dead. And being the wife of a terrorist in an American secret detention centre, I imagine, would be appalling. On the other hand I work for people who have a better understanding and interest in all that you have done, and will look after you. If you agree we can get you away immediately on a medivac flight.'

'You're not a doctor are you?'

'No, but on this you can trust me.' He smiled briefly.

'Why?' After all she had been through it seemed a fair question. A memory of Jannat's face as she was consigned to a life of marriage rose through her struggling mind.

'Fair point. Let's just say that my principals feel that throughout their recent dealings there has been manipulation, and they were not entirely in control. So whoever was pulling strings is someone setting themselves up against national states. Some kind of supra-national able to take power. That is something that is particularly odious to the people employing me.'

He stopped there and there was a very long pause, the silence being filled by the monitor. Eventually Shameeza nodded, and it was understood by them both. The man stood up and patted the hand that did not have a canular. 'I shall make the arrangements. It's a good decision. I believe someone with your business connections will flourish in Shanghai.'

Chapter 27

Thorswick

Going to Poacher's Cottage broke every commandment. Ash could hear the sandpaper tones of his father as he headed for Ben Whistledown's home. "I don't want you even getting out of bed in the morning without a plan.' Advice repeated nearly as much as 'you must analyse the threat, know the risk. Have five ways to counter.'

Even before he turned the corner Ash could smell the pungent, sweetly sour smell of rotting apples from the orchard. He stopped at the rickety wooden gate, contemplating the weed strewn path. 'There is no greater sin than ignorance. Remember this.' His father, training his son and quoting Kipling's Kim.

He took a swift look back at the village. It was quiet. People were probably staying inside to avoid the fetid heat as temperatures, once again, started to climb. Above the elms and oaks slate dark clouds were creating bulbous mountains, dimming the hot, autumnal sun. Over at the Manor lights were on in some upstairs rooms. His nose prickled and he sniffed deeply. Taking in the air smoothly, pushing the sensation around his brain, pulling back his cheeks like a wary animal. Letting it alert his senses.

He got apples, and the pungent fermentation going on below the trees in the garden. The sweetness of the rotting fruit and acidity caused his saliva glands to react. But here was something else underlying that acidity. Fish. Rotting fish. He honed in and savoured the smell. Loving it.

He knew it. A smell as old as Asia's trade. He could have stayed there, welcoming the siren's song while a part of his brain pushed away the tentacles wrapping him in a dangerous embrace. Suddenly from inside came music, as if someone had turned up the volume. It was that song, rising like a challenge through the walls.

'Ha ha ha, hee hee hee'. There was no uncertainty now. The Laughing Gnome. There may have been other ways into the cottage, an open back door or French windows onto the orchard. But the sound was the kick Ash needed. He shoulder barged the door, once, twice. Each sending a cleansing shock through his body. The shoulder protesting, and the sharpness of the pain down his back welcomed. The frame burst on the third, the elderly wood splintering and sending him spilling onto the floor of the cottage, landing on all fours in a hallway now lit by sunlight falling around him.

He was up in an instant, tense and crouched ready for an attack, his eyes darting around. The smell of rotting fish was strong. Blackened foil strips lay on the scored wooden floor boards. The music and smell was coming from a darkened room to his left. Slowly he straightened, and Ash again felt the familiarity wash dangerously into his being like an engulfing tide.

'Christ,' said a drowsy voice from the room, 'you could have knocked.'

Slowly Ash went to the doorway. A few shards of sunlight escaped the closed drapes sending triangles of light into the room. He stood in the doorway knowing that beyond lay a danger that was nothing to do with whatever the man inside might attempt. Dust swirled in the searching sunlight and it was as if the air was solid with menace. In the corner of a couch was Ben Whistledown, his eyes bloodshot and rimmed, an open laptop bleeping at his side, and a half empty cola bottle on the floor. As Ash took in the room, the computer played that annoying snatch of song.

'Another bid,' said Ben. 'Ching, ching.'

'The Laughing Gnome,' said Ash as a statement.

'Ha ha, ha, hee, hee, hee', sang the computer. 'I'm going to be so rich,' slurred Whistledown. 'There's people really wanting that babe.'

Ash felt as if the self-protection part of his brain was telling his feet not to move. Taking the first step over the threshold into that drug soaked room felt like a move threatening his own destruction. Crossing the few steps he kept his eyes on the computer. Whistledown made no protest. He seem merely amused as Ash swept up the machine and started to hit keys. 'You're too late,' was all he said.

Four minutes to go.

Ash kept on with the keyboard. The screen showed a running total against a clock counting down. A couple of clicks proved to Ash he could not get into the site and shut it down, his every action seemingly mocked by a hooked nosed goblin like figure jumping with each new bid. Whistledown was right. Already the bidding would buy a house in London's Mayfair.

He was getting nowhere. There was an option being offered to a remote registry. Inevitably a password was demanded. Ash dropped the computer into Whistledown's lap and smacked him hard around the face at about the moment it landed. 'Stop this thing,' now he ordered. For good measure he grabbed a handful of hair to get his attention.

'I couldn't even if I wanted to,' said Whistledown, his voice slurring and struggling, 'and it wouldn't make a difference.'

'Explain.' Another twist of the hair.

'It's all out there. Set up to succeed. I don't have to do anything. In fact I can't do anything now.'

Ash gave the hair another twist.

'I mean it's all remote. Operated so the biggest bid will get the details as soon as the crypto dosh is registered. On platforms like this one signs up to certain conditions, if you see what I mean.'

"No I don't. Just imagine I don't get any of this.' But he knew. The criminal sites in the deepest parts of the dark web facilitated blackmail, extortion and kidnapping. They took a cut of everything that passed through them and were not run by the people who appreciated cancellation. Once committed it was all or nothing. Within the service there were specialists able to break in to such systems, but even they would need time.

'I think you know,' Whistledown was saying. 'These things are set up so it all goes on even if the police get involved,

169

or people want to back out of a deal. So even I can't stop it. And that entire programme will erase itself anyway.'

Without letting go of his head, Ash picked up the can of Cola and shook it. 'And what if I pour this into your computer and let it eat the hard drive?' He was scrabbling now, out of his depth as the timer counted down and the cartoon gnome continued its demonic capering. Two and a half minutes.

'It wouldn't mean anything to me,' said Whistledown. 'My crypto account is secured elsewhere. Mind you, the people who may want to dig around in the computer later to find out just how bad a boy I've been might wish you hadn't destroyed their play pen.'

He seemed so sure of himself. Stoned and secure. Apparently not worried about what might happen to him in the future. It was, thought Ash, as if he were protected.

'Right now, I guess you might be thinking of working me over. Pouring water over my face, stretching back my knees so the ligaments scream', Whistledown was rambling now. 'But you don't have the time, do you?' He surveyed his hands, stretching them out before him as if they were something new, or an offering. 'Perhaps you could snap my fingers to get me to do something, anything to stop this thing? That might be quicker.' He raised his voice into a whine. 'Please sir, I did what I could to make him talk, I snapped each one his fingers. It just didn't work. I think it must have been the drugs sir. He just didn't seem to care.'

'I was thinking more of something more permanent. To make sure you will never enjoy anything from this.' Ash was back on the computer, the machine nestling in the crook of his arm, tapping keys one handed.

'You mean kill me?' The red eyed face peering up from the sofa seemed amused by the idea. 'That would mean another body happening rather to close to you wouldn't it, and I can't believe whoever you work for would be too pleased about that.'

Without thinking about it, Ash subsided onto the coffee table so he could address the keyboard with both hands. The screen told him he had one chance left after two failed attempts. 'I don't think anyone will be linking that amateur bomb on the hill to me.' He muttered. A bit of him wanted Whistledown to keep talking. His brain logging new information while he tried to find a way into the computer.

'Amateur?' Whistledown seemed insulted by the word. 'Why amateur?'

'Trust me, I wouldn't use something that goes off so early that the courier gets it.'

Ben snorted. 'We wouldn't either. The bomb was detonated remotely. We wanted you to see it.'

Ash was nodding. Whistledown was giving a lot away. There was confirmation that it was not a booby strap for him, just a brutal message. And then there was 'we', and the pride coming through Whistledown's drug soaked speech. It might explain why he was so confident. 'I'm in,' he said.

Not 'in' completely, but at least Ash scored a hit with Whistledown, who stared back. For his last attempt Ash dug deep, reckoning on all he knew of the man opposite. He was a functioning drug addict. One who had travelled and liked to remind people of that by wearing an Afghan hat around the village. Then there was the skulking around, a secret life as a naturist but one that he wanted others to join. From what he had revealed he was a bit part player with people who did not like to be considered as incompetent when it came to bomb making. The 'we' had to be Safedeen Khan and a link to Pakistan, a country heavily involved in heroin trafficking. It also made a connection with Norman Ellroy.

All in all Ash assessed the man now giving him his full attention was one of life's outsiders, a voyeur who wanted to be on the inside instead of always watching. He remembered the false note struck over the name of Ellroy's racehorse. The ultimate insider sports accessory. Buzkashi. He typed it in. Capital B. It worked.

The screen changed. It was asking for a biometric confirmation. Whistledown's thumb perhaps. Or forefinger.

'Looks like I will need that finger of yours after all,' he muttered. One minute to go.

Incapable as he was, Whistledown was shrinking away and looked as if he heading behind the sofa. All he actually managed was to slump sideways and his wrist was an easy grab. 'Which one?' demanded Ash as he pulled the man onto his knees and, wrenched the thumb onto the pad. The screen stayed unchanged. Thirty seconds. Whistledown attempted to hit with the other hand, twisting as he did and Ash felt the finger he was now gripping against the screen dislocate with a pop. Whistledown screamed, and Ash registered the fact his pain was not entirely cushioned and he was therefore not as high as he thought. Pulling him close he gave him a subduing slap. It was also not that finger.

Ash twisted the hand ready to use the second digit. The goblin gnome was cantering again, its frolics now more manic as the counter hit the last quarter minute and a triumphal trumpet started. The sinister grin of the goblin was growing now to fill the screen. And then it stopped. Died along with the voluntary at fifteen seconds. Or rather the screen went blank except for a message. Connection lost.

It was as if oxygen was suddenly sucked from the room. Whistledown stopped whimpering as his hand was released. 'What have you done?' he managed.

He was looking like a wounded animal with a damaged paw. The thing was, Ash knew he had not 'done' anything. Certainly not enough to shut down the programme. He had barely started. The computer showed no internet. Digging out his mobile he saw there was no network either. Swivelling the computer round he showed it to Whisteldown, who deflated back into the sofa, holding his injured hand in the other. 'You bastard,' he moaned. 'that was my chance.'

'A chance to do what?' Ash had taken the computer back and was clicking keys. The machine was sound, but anything needing connection was inert.

'To escape. Be useful. Anything really.'

'Useful to who? And for that matter, escape from what?'
He was responding from habit. Ash was still wondering at the
computer.

'You know.' Whistledown reached behind a cushion and
fetched out a tobacco tin. 'Join me?, he asked. 'And don't pretend
you never have. It takes one to know one.'

He had Ash's attention now. More so as the tin was
popped and he saw the full plastic bag with powder nestling
amongst creased foil rectangles.

'From what I heard you were quite the junky.'
Whistledown was using one of the foils to add powder to a stained
spoon he had recovered from under the table.

'And who could have told you that.' A bit of him was
wondering if the internet would come back, and if it did, whether
the clock would start again with the Laughing Gnome doing a last
caper. But his focus was on the preparation as adrenalin forced his
heart beat.

'I think you know who I heard that from.' A cheap, orange
lighter was being flicked, its sparks flashing.

'Tell me.' It was as if the snake was now in front of him,
its hood moving slowly from side to side.

'I can't tell anything. That's why I needed the money to
get some wriggle room in case I need to get out of Dodge. They're
doing heavy stuff.'

'Keep talking.' The powder was being heated and turned
into a brown, viscous liquid that looked like a particularly nasty
cough mixture. And the smell in the thick smoke. Fish rotting in
the sun. Ash needed to go, or stop that smoke before it was too
late. 'Put that away,' he said, his voice too thick for his own good.
Stretching out he knocked aside the spoon and seized the tin.

'Fuck you man. You're nothing, and if he gets his way,
you're dead meat.'

Ash stood. 'You make it sound as though there's a debate.'
Whistledown must have realised he had said too much and given
away something that Ash needed to know. He looked up with

desperate eyes and then at the tin, which Ash started tapping lightly. 'So tell me what you know, and I might give this back.'

'No way. I can't.'

'You say that now, but I'll just wait around to see how long you last.' Ash needed air, he was already feeling heavy and far too interested in the effects of the smoke. He walked across to the French windows.

'I can do without that stuff.'

'Sure you can,' Ash said smoothly, because they both knew the score. 'I reckon from the bag that this represents a few days for you. So if I were to tip it down the toilet it might mean you eating turkey. But it's here when you change your mind.'

'You bastard.' It was loud, and sounded as if it were made up from all of Whistledown's remaining resistance.

Ash smiled ruefully pulled back the curtains and tried the double doors. They felt as if being opened happened only once in a blue moon. Whistledown would not being going anywhere. He was tied body and soul by the promise in the tin. And Ash really needed to clean his lungs. Giving the aged handle a yank he felt it give and pushed open the doors with such force that two quarter light panes cracked loudly.

'Hello'. The voice came from amongst the apple trees. A figure was detaching itself from amongst the apple trees. It was Maggie, and she was looking at him curiously. How long had she been there, he wondered. Long enough to hear the scream? 'I was picking up a apples,' she said. 'I need to ask Ben if that's alright.'

'I am sure it is,' said Ash.

'Still better ask.' She took a few steps toward him, coming into the light with a cotton bag hanging off her shoulder, and stopping a few yards in front of him. She knew. Something. Ash stayed put.

'He never bothers. All sorts of people pick up here. They'd go to waste otherwise.'

'All the same.' She cocked an eye at the door behind him, her gaze slowly slipping down to the laptop he still held.

Ash hesitated for a moment. He need to get Maggie to trust him. She was not going to go away, and all she would see if she went inside was a pig sty with a drug addict. He was sure Ben Whistledown would have enough wits about him to play along and pretend nothing was wrong after what he had tried to do. He came to a decision and stepped away, with a brief wave of his hand. 'He's inside, but please understand, I'm a friend and he has a problems. He may not like to be seen like this. We often have to protect him from himself.'

She looked at him curiously and seemed relieved he had stepped a good way from the doors to let her in. There was the briefest of pauses before he heard her cry out, followed by the sound of apples falling and rolling. Ash smashed through the door, laptop in his right hand ready to swing as a weapon as he charged. His one thought was that Ben Whistledown must have attacked her, but as he came in Maggie shrank away. She was standing alone in the centre of the room, starring at the sofa. Ben Whistledown sat where he had been left. His eyes wide open with a small round hole trickling blood coming from the centre of his forehead. He had been shot.

Chapter 28

Maggie bolted. She crashed through drapes and French doors, smashing more panes as she headed for the far side of the orchard, her mind racing through options. Wood absorbed bullets. The back of the property gave that cover, if not escape. She needed to put distance between herself and Ash.

Long grass slowed her legs. Branches whipped at her, and she fell near the last of the apples trees, her arms barely getting time to break the worst as she pitched onto the ground. She lay there winded, her breath refusing the come as ordered. Panic rose as her system resorted to getting air through short, fast sobs. She knew she had to get up. To evade. Willing her breath to steady, she sensed through her body to feel out any damage. Her arms hurt. But nothing serious. Her legs too were fine. She had slipped. Not been shot. Skidded on rotten windfalls. She was getting a ground level view of them now. Dozens of them in various shades of red or fungi brown amidst the long grass. Large wasps chomping holes in them as the smell made her think of cider and hay barns.

She had to move. She was a witness to murder. What was the guy's name? Ben. Wilder something. It must have just happened. She may never forget the face with a bloody trickle moving down to drop off the nose. Fresh. A witness and alone. Although that, she realised suddenly, had changed.

'Stay down. Don't give him a shot.'

Somehow, he was ahead of her. As far as she could tell he was by the fence, some distance away. Had she been knocked out? She could not see how he had got there. And now he was trying to make it appear that there was someone else around who might try to shoot them. At least he was not standing over her head and about to blow her brains out. He was also speaking quietly, making it sound as if the order was kindly meant advice. For the moment she did as he said, lying prone and listening to the buzzing of the wasps while her breathing settled and she gathered her wits. He had the drop on her, that was certain. But with each passing moment she wondered why she was not yet dead. Eventually she risked a look up.

'Don't do anything sudden.'

He was sitting back on his haunches, positioned so he could see her and the cottage, his arms out in front of him resting on his knees. A very foreign look. He was a few yards away. His hands, she noted, were empty. Hanging loosely from his wrists as his eyes stayed fixed on the cottage. He did not appear to have gun, and so she moved to start sitting up. His eyes briefly washed over her. 'Quietly,' Ash said, 'the wasps don't like sudden movement. Be careful you don't put a hand on one as you get up. They sting like buggery. And stay low.'

He was not sounding like a killer. Or at least, not one that had her in the cross hairs. She got herself upright, uncomfortably aware that something ripe and rotten was seeping through the seat of her jeans. Both of them were head level with the tops of the grass. 'Let me go,' she said.

It seemed, at first, he hadn't heard her. Ash's attention was still at the end of the orchard. Behind the mask of his watching face though, he heard her tone, and her fear. How she was afraid of him. He suddenly realised that her dash from the house was not because there was a hidden, homicidal gunman around, but because she thought he was the killer. Seeing it from her side, he supposed that was obvious. After all, she had seen him walk out onto the patio from the room. Barely thirty seconds later she had gone into the same place to be confronted by Ben Whistledown with a hole nature had not designed.

Getting her on side in this mess had just got a whole lot harder. If it were possible to sigh inside about the unkindness of fate, Ash did it. Casting a quick look in her direction he saw that Maggie was now also looking at the cottage, taking in the little chocolate box of horrors. 'Maggie,' he said eventually. 'I can't let you go. It's too dangerous.'

He could have chosen better words. He was thinking how to tell her she was a target because of what her grandfather did.

About how her picture was lodged in the brain of every jihadist and fellow traveller as the death dealing bride of the devil, and why the only logical answer for the professional wet job on Whistledown was the assassin was still in there. Before he had a chance to start though, Maggie turned to him and fixed her eyes on him. 'Whatever happened here,' she said, 'whatever the reason for what you did, you don't need to do me as well.' She took a deep breath. 'I have good reasons why I won't go to the police. We can both walk away. You can go as far away as you like, and I can say I wasn't here. When they come looking, that is. I certainly won't be ringing them.'

Even to herself it sounded particularly lame. As far as this man was concerned, she was an officer in the Royal Air Force. As such, he would expect her to be straight onto the police to report a crime, and be a willing witness. This odd man, sitting back in long grass untroubled by the heat, could not know that running to the authorities was a long way down her to do list. The bottom line was that she was a witness, and even as she tried to layer conviction into the plea, Maggie knew she was going to have to fight for her life. Shifting slightly her fingers found a stone. Her hand flexed around it while she eyed the best target area with a trained dispassion. A crunch into Ash's face might be enough. Smashing the rock into his head would be certain. It was a deed that would have to be done with the swiftness of a snake strike. At the thought, her leg muscles tightened under the stretched denim.

'Don't.' It was all he said. But it was as if her muscles, once ordered, were unable to stop. Her pounce was like a cat's, followed by a swinging arm, the rock scything the air. It was all it found. Ash was rolling back and away, coming upright on all fours. Maggie sprawled, the energy of her swing not having been staunched by ending in his head. He could have thrown himself on top of her, but he let it play. She came up fast. Ready for another go. Her eyes locked on his. She would have done it too, but for a searing, burning pain in her shoulder. She yelped and dropped the stone. Her other hand going to the shoulder as she fell on her knees, her mind crashing to a stark conclusion. Her back was to the cottage. He had warned her. This is what it felt like to be shot.

'Told you,' said Ash. 'Those wasps hurt.'

She stared at him angrily. Her shoulder felt as if a branding iron was being pressed into it. If there were to be a fight now she would be even more at a disadvantage. Even as she paused, taut and ready to spring again, numbness was spreading up to her neck and down her arm.

'You don't have to be afraid of me.'

'There's a dead man in there saying otherwise.'

'And he was trying to sell you to the highest bidder. Your face leaving the base after the drone strike is all over the dark web. People were paying good money to find you. Very good in fact.'

The sting felt as if it was entering her nervous system. It was her face now falling under its effects. Her right eye started to droop. He was looking at her even more closely.

'Are you allergic?'

'I didn't think I was.' She was trying to concentrate on what he had said. Whether it could be true, and how it all worked with the warning from her grandfather. With a dizzy sense of embarrassment she found herself shaking her head. Meanwhile, Ash was picking leaves from the base of an apple tree and chewing them.

'That stuff about selling me. It's a bit much to expect that such a thing would be happening here.' She was trying to find the horizon now. To get on an even keel, and make sense of what was happening. 'I don't understand why you would even know this stuff.'

He hesitated. 'Because I work for the services. You know, the secret ones. And so did the previous owner of blue cottage.' He let those words tell as he took out the wad of chewed plant and rolled into a ball. Being so blunt was a gamble. She could still see him as a killer. Even if the revelation went some way to earning trust.

Maggie's eyes were puffy and half closed from the sting, but he caught a flash of something more appraising than aggressive. 'I'm going to put something on your shoulder that will help.'

Half crouching he went behind her. 'I would prefer it if you didn't try that again with the rock.' Just to be sure he stayed on his toes, ready for a leap back while keeping his tone light.

'T shirt on or off?' Without a reply he pulled the material up from the waist as far as it would go, moving his hand up before placing the saliva soaked wad against on the round, red mark and continued to hold it there.

'It isn't just terrorists and their mates who may be after you thanks to that picture,' he went on. 'Because of the activities of the man who, I think, was your grandfather, we know the Russians will want to get you. Right now, there are a lot of people looking for Maggie Johnson. A lot of data crunching around you as well.'

Maggie let him speak. What she was hearing chimed with the letter, unless this strange man had composed the thing and slipped it into the gardening brochure and vaccination envelope. Ever so slightly she shook her head again. No, that would not explain the covering letter from the legal firm. Or the stuff about her family background. None of that had ever gone onto the internet as far as she knew. As the balm worked on the sting, she realised the desire to reject what Ash was saying had a lot to do with a sense of being robbed of exclusive and precious knowledge. Private stuff, she wanted to process in her own way before the inevitable knock on the door.

All that did not change him being the most likely person to have killed Whistledown, and her position as the only witness putting him on the scene while blood was still oozing. As things stood he also still had a hand on her left shoulder, a hand under her T shirt with the palm against her bra strap. It would be an easy to break her neck.

'Better?'

'It is. What did you use?' Keep him talking.

'Plantain. It's good for stings anyway, and seems to work particularly well when these new form wasps have a go.'

'You've been there.'

'It's not just people who throw rocks around they don't like. Runners too. In fact most of the village at one time or another has been stung.'

'I still can't believe a place like this has spies or dark web terrorists. Or the likes of you. As she spoke, Maggie stifled the irreverent thought that he was not the first distrusted man to get a hand on her bra. 'As I say,' she added pointedly, 'It's better now. And thanks.'

Ash slipped his hand out and stepped away, leaving Maggie to pull down the T shirt. He settled himself opposite her, back on his haunches, feeling her disbelief. 'The first rule of the spying game is that you can't believe anything. It is truly a hall of mirrors where even friendships can be a deception, and where wrong things are done to do to achieve the goal. Right now you have to choose. It's hard I know. You have been here for five minutes and someone is dead. And a man you barely know is telling you that you are now going to have to rely on him to save your life.'

Ash paused to cast a look at the cottage. It was as still and silent as when they had run.

'You need to understand that I am going to stick to you, and am duty bound to protect you until people come to take you in. You can try to run. You can fight. You can decide that I am a murderer, and that you are afraid. You may not trust me, and think what I am saying is rubbish. None of that is going to change what we now have to do. If you still have difficulty, remember that I know who you really are. And who gave you the house. That should give me some credibility about who I say I am.' A thought seemed to occur to him. 'Also I haven't killed you. Can I borrow your mobile?'

'No. And it's not working anyway.'

Ash looked at her thoughtfully. 'Run out of battery? It was a question.

She fished it out. 'No signal. There was one, but it went about half an hour ago.'

'In that case, we need to go and speak with the police on the hill. They probably won't believe me either. Presenting them with another dead body should get their attention though. At least we will be able to speak to my people and get you somewhere safe.' He stood up, being careful, she noticed, to place himself well under the apple tree. He was still worried about a shooter in the cottage.

'They've gone.'

From her position Maggie had a view of the hill where the bomb had gone off. Ash swung around. The hillside was quiet, restored to bucolic tranquillity with the only movement coming from the sheep as they recovered their grazing. Even the white tents had been packed and taken. From this distance it looked perfect, the shattered trees already absorbed into the background. Ash took it in, fear sucking at his reducing reserves of confidence. The mobiles going down at the same time as the internet was unheard of. A bomb that claimed a man's life would not, in any normal world, be packed away as if it were a pub fight.

'What do we do now?' At least, he thought, she said 'we'. Maybe she was on side after all.

'Or put it another way, what would you do if I were not here?'

He turned to meet her raised eyebrow. How typically officer class, he thought, with a flash of anger. 'We,' he emphasised, 'should go to my place and hunker down until the mobiles come back. Your place isn't an option.'

Maggie's eyes narrowed. 'Your place?' She made it sound as if it were the type of invitation she was used to, and not welcome. 'But, what would you usually do when faced with this? She waved her arm back toward the cottage.

'If you didn't do it, and if you are what you say you are, I think you would be down there trying to find out what happened. After all, if there was someone else, and they wanted us dead, they would have come after us by now. Or,' she added reflectively, 'killed us while we were gawping at the corpse.'

Not necessarily, he thought, but she had a point. She was also standing.

'So let's go,' Maggie said.

Chapter 29

Maggie led the way. Walking with deliberate strides, her heart a steady beat, mind dulled. When she was on a mission there was focus and, in a strike, a controlled, disciplined rush to be channelled. What she felt now was something very different. Her feet were moving forward, heading toward possible danger, but with a robotic like compulsion. There may a killer, but walking through the sapping humidity and trees she felt resigned. It was as if after all the turmoil and confusion she wanted resolution. Even if that meant finality.

'You should stay back.'

Ash was walking behind, taking a cautious approach, but one that would make it harder for a gunman to get them both. Or, possibly, it was his way of adding theatre to his story that someone else shot Ben Whistledown. At the same time another train was running. She was marrying up what he had said about her father with the information in the letter, and how so much of it matched. Even so, there was also the dire warning about not trusting anyone.

'Not much point in busting in,' he said. 'I think we telegraphed ahead.'

Telegraph, she thought. What age was that from? She was still mulling that one as he went through the French doors.

The room felt particularly dark after the sunlight, and quiet. Undisturbed. That, to Ash, was the worst thing. Hair prickled to attention on his scalp and arms as his eyes took in the open eyed corpse, the tin of drugs on the window sill and the laptop. There was a complete lack of anything to say someone else had been there. It was all exactly as when he left. Surfaces caught in the shards of sunlight showed settled dust. He took a deep, slow intake through his nose. There was not a whiff of any new odour. Looking across the room the door from the hallway was as he had left it. Ajar. The laptop too was where he had put it. Surely the killer would have taken that.

'Quiet,' said Maggie grimly. 'Isn't it?' Ben Whistledown's face showed bemusement, an expression matching Ash's own.

'I'll check around,' he said. The kitchen was a health hazard of encrusted dishes and pans piled high in the stone sink. Flies buzzed lazily in a shaft of sunlight while others crawled over the hardened food spills. The unbroken spider webs around the window were decked with cocooned fly bodies. Ash moved carefully across the sticky lino and tried the back door. An old fashioned key refused to budge in the rusted lock. No escape there, and no one had been through it, he reckoned for months, possibly years.

Back in the hallway he stepped over the splinters of his entry. As far as he could tell, nothing had been disturbed. No crushed pieces of wood to mark someone else's passage, or the debris having being replaced by a master ambusher used to camouflaging. There was only one place left to check. Reflectively, he eyed the stairs, but if that was the hiding place before and after the murder, then someone would need the gift of levitation. Because there was no way to get from the stairs to the sitting room without treading through the debris. Even so, he would need to check. Grabbing an old golf club from a hollowed out elephant's foot by the door, he started up.

The bar boards creaked. Each one, all the way up. Try as he might, it was noisy. Anyone upstairs would be laughing, except Ash was sure upstairs would be empty of threat. He would have heard if someone came down while he was with Whistledown, let alone if someone was rushing back. Ash was still careful though. On the landing he listened before using the club to push open the first of the two bedroom doors.

It was small. The opening door nearly scraping the far wall. It was also empty. Again, Ash stayed for a moment to listen, but the only sounds came from downstairs. It sounded as Maggie was shifting furniture. Ash took a step down the landing, trying to be as light as possible but the floorboards creaked betrayal with every step.

The door to the second bedroom was half open, so he pushed it wider and stepped back. In this one the wooden floor boards were covered with rugs and kilims, and fleetingly Ash noted the poor quality. Staying on the landing he looked through into the room. It was empty except for a rumpled double bed by the window, with a stool beside it supporting a clock, lamp and an old style transistor radio.

Ash was more than a little curious. He had not seen a radio like that in years. It used to be a feature of homes and tea houses where he grew up. They were around for quite a time after other places had succumbed to the convenience of listening on a mobile or computer. This one was wrapped in a floral cotton dust cover of the kind that spoke of south Asian markets and ubiquitous sewing machines. Ash picked it up, feeling the familiar.

'I've got something.'

With a last look around Ash went downstairs. Maggie was pointing to something behind the armchair facing Whistledown. He went over and saw what looked like a broken toy. It was black, and split in a way that reminded him of a dissected frog from school biology.

'It's a drone.' Maggie did not wait to be asked. 'And cutting edge at that.' She sighed deeply. 'The things I fly are Jurassic these days. A flying totem for states. This on the other hand is something else entirely. I'm not an expert on these tiny jobs, but it is more like something from your world. An assassination tool. From the bits and pieces it looks like it can listen and shoot a single bullet. From what I've heard they can be targeted on an individual, through voice or visual recognition. Even smell, and DNA. I would say it was already in the room listening to the two of you, and then someone decided to press the trigger.'

Ash looked down again. Now he knew he could see the mangled rotor blades, melted and loosely twisted around the hard barrel of the body. At least, he thought, the discovery put him in the clear as far as Maggie was concerned. It sounded as she was accepting he might really be from a world where covert killing was part of business as usual. 'How long could it have been here, do you reckon?'

'Hard to tell. If it was on the ground behind that chair doing nothing except listening, the battery could last for days. As it is, at the end, it just needed to rise up, zero in and fire.' Maggie looked thoughtfully at Whistledown. 'It was his expression that led me to it,' she went on. 'He looked puzzled. Perhaps even amused as if he saw something unusual. Or funny. So I started hunting around.'

'You think it was placed here rather than flew in?'

'Either, in all honesty. They're not noisy. When you were on the patio, did you hear anything?' Ash shook his head. Only the wasps.

'If what you say about this man is true, then he seems the type someone might want to watch.' They were silent for a moment, the thought occurring to them both there might be other drones close by and listening. 'What's that you've got?' They looked at each other, their eyes communicating the threat, and the need to talk about something else.

Ash held out the radio as he took a step to get closer to her. 'A tranny,' he said. 'Old fashioned, fail safe technology.' He switched it on. It was fantasy to imagine the sound would prevent any bug from filtering out their conversation, but it might make life more difficult if they whispered. Twiddling the volume, he turned it high as a carefully measured voice made metallic by the cheap speakers filled the room.

'As already announced by the government, the police and armed forces will take extreme measures under the Emergency Powers Act if faced with looters who do not immediately disburse.'

They looked at each other, shock registering in the long pause left by the announcer.

'Due to the shutdown of a number of vital systems, including traffic control, power, as well some isolated cases of disorder, people are being urged to stay in their homes and off the streets. In the face of this extraordinary situation the Minister for Security Mr Carrick Rhodes has ordered all U.K. national internet service providers to turn off the Domain Name System and the Border Gateway Protocol of their services. In a statement he said this temporary order will isolate the country from the world wide web, or internet, and will be restored as soon as possible when the security situation allows. Please stay tuned to the radio and television for further updates.'

The announcer was replaced by classic music. It was something familiar to anyone who travelled in a lift. Music to be ignored, and not in the least bit stirring. Ash twiddled the plastic dial on the side to switch to other stations. They were all playing the same piece.

'Vivaldi,' she said. 'On them all.' Ash went across the room and flicked the light switch. No light. Fishing out his mobile he saw no internet or phone connection. That's why the announcer had spoken about old fashioned steam radio and television. 'It's an attack,' he said. 'Cyber. Has to be.'

Maggie nodded. 'War by other means. It would explain why the cops have gone'.

'Sounds like they're busy'. He paused. Too busy to look after a bombing and murder. Ash sucked in his breath.

Carefully Ash replaced the broken machine. Even with a cyberattack the top level security communications back at the cottage should be working. It was built on a separate network at great expense, with secure components from vetted suppliers. Raising the alarm would mean a rinsing of historic proportions. Handing over Maggie alive was probably the one thing that might go in his favour. 'We need to go,' he said picking up Whistledown's computer.

'You know there may be more of those things watching us.' Maggie did not bother to say the rest about how they could be picked off with ease. She shivered slightly and looked out at the garden through the French windows. After all, where there was one killer drone there was likely to be more. Everything she had read about these bugs is that they were best used in swarms, attacking as needed with others poised to strike.

For the briefest of moments Ash touched her shoulder before opening the French doors and stepping into the garden. Yes, he knew.

They didn't need witnesses to their retreat from the murder scene, so Ash took them the long way round. Silently they went up the lane, each of them wondering if their lives were about to be ended by a machine not much bigger than a finger. At the long hedge they turned and used it as cover to get to the back of Ash's cottage. Getting into the kitchen they immediately felt the type of relief that happens when you step into air conditioning on a summer's day.

Thanks to the thick walls the place was naturally cool. It might have been a moment for some of the stress to fall away, but Ash had barely taken two steps into his home when he knew something was terribly wrong. Dread flowed through his system as Maggie halted at the unmistakable sound of a pistol being fed a bullet. Her head swivelled as Ash stepped forward ready to take the shot. Perhaps it would give her time.

'One move,' said a voice. 'And I shoot.'

Chapter 30

'Keep calm. "Ash"'. The emphasis on the name. How it was a joke.

For Ash the words and tone sparked equal measures of fear and relief. Everything might soon the over, but whatever happened he was dealing with a known commodity. Not a stranger in the dark, a drone rising up in front of him, just a six year old morphed into a professional assassin.

'Safedeen.'

'The same.' A Glock automatic freed itself from the depths of the hallway and Safedeen Khan steadied himself against the door frame. The gun was pointed, Ash noted, straight at his heart. Behind him, Maggie stood frozen.

'Good of you to drop in.'

Khan said nothing. Barely moved. Only his eyes moved over them both, his pupils like black pearls. Good technique, thought Ash grudgingly. Not rising to the invitation to respond. Safedeen was a man going about his business to the very best of his considerable ability.

'Turnaround.' A pause as the gun moved slowly in a circle like a hypnotising cobra to illustrate the order. 'Both of you.'

So this was it, thought Ash. It was going to end in a badly lit, narrow hallway in a cottage far from where he loved. The choice was a bullet in the front if he made a fight of it, or the back of the head if he played along. He looked straight into the eyes. 'Leave her,' he said. 'She's valuable. To some.'

A gambit. Make the person think you have valuable information. Buy time. A flicker of expression passed Khan's face. It was sardonic. Amusement forced a zephyr through his nose. 'Value,' he said, as if the thought was new. 'Oh, you're right Ash. She might be. Perhaps to the kin of my relatives killed in her missile strike, for example. I am sure they would love to meet her.'

He paused, and then motioned the pistol again to indicate that the turnaround order still applied. 'And on your knees, with hands on the back of your head,' he added.

As Ash got down he felt the press of the gun on his neck as Whistledown's computer was taken from under his arm and the mobile removed from his pocket. At the same time he noticed woodworm holes in the side of the stairs, and caught himself thinking how this would be the last thing he saw. The tell-tale burrows of destruction.

'In fact, you should have died in that ambush I set for you in Afghanistan,' said Safedeen as if it were something of mild academic interest. 'You might as well know,' he added, with a twist of the muzzle.

Ash had sometimes wondered, especially when he heard that Khan had been in the area. 'Me? Why? Us being old cricket team buddies and everything.'

'Hardly buddies, I think.' Ash was surprised by the almost friendly tone. 'But, it's true, there was some regrets along the way, after all when someone we have known a long time passes then we do lose a piece of ourselves.'

He paused. 'Please do excuse this bit of old time religion Flight Lieutenant. And talking of that I would hate anyone to think that any of this has something to do with religion, or some kind of deep layered colonial hangover, although this man's family has been something of a multi headed demon in the land of my birth. No, I am afraid "Ash" you were a highly effective craftsman, and our world just got too small for us both. Everywhere I went to work I felt your breath, or I trod on your toes. Altogether it was becoming too much like a badly conducted tango. Something had to change.'

Safedeen was running his hands over him, flighting over his torso, a searching hand to the groin and then down his legs while the muzzle of the Glock continued its grind into the base of his skull. Nobody bothered to search someone you were about to kill, Ash thought with relief. It was easier to search the dead. Beside them Maggie tensed, in a way that signalled a move to the

191

two professionals. It was immediately rewarded by a sideways slap to the head. The gun staying very still on Ash.

'Don't,' Khan told her, 'even think about it. And as for you, Ash, your system is down, wrecked actually. Also that taxi man left a note at his squalid little bedsit describing you in really quite precise detail. More than enough to have you implicated in that ghastly bombing, if we need to.'

"We" thought Ash. Interesting. Safedeen finished the search. He did not bother to frisk Maggie. Quietly, beside them, she was seething. The blow stung, but she knew better than to try any heroics. Best to sit quiet and soak it all up. Quite apart from anything else there were people talking about murders and a stitch-up in front of her as if she was invisible, or worse.

'Stand up both,' Safedeen ordered. 'Norman Ellroy wants to speak to you. And that involves a trip to the pub.'

At the front door Safedeen holstered his gun. 'I think you both now know,' he advised. 'We can kill you at any time, so please just do as you are told.' With a nod of his head he indicated the front door, which Maggie opened.

Outside there were people dressed in black shirts and trousers playing on the cricket pitch. Most were men, and one was wielding a cricket bat as if he were playing baseball. A group were taking it turns to lob balls at him. A successful strike brought exaggerated cries in false English upper class tones. 'By Jove sir! And even an "Egad.' They were from the Hall.

'So much for the curfew,' Ash muttered, while Safedeen glowered as the players packed up bat and ball and preceded them to the Nag's Head. The road outside the pub was like a car show for millionaires. It seemed every make of super car was represented, and in colours that made it look as if someone was playing automobile snooker, with a new Indian electric marque providing the vivid pink. Ash clocked off a blue Bugatti, two Ferraris in red and sunflower yellow, a low lying red Lamborghini that looked as if it were snarling into the nose of the latest attempt to revive the Jaguar marque. It's classic Green bonnet end to end with a white McLaren. Closest to the pub was the car slated as the

192

most expensive and luxurious in the world. A black four wheel drive Rolls Royce from China.

After the evening sun, the inside of the Nag's seemed particularly dark. The place was lit by faux lamps, which, given the circumstances may have been intended to rekindle a fondness for an age when lungs breathed paraffin fumes and were coated with soot and tobacco. Norman Ellroy rose from the gloom of a snug his face lifting a smile when he saw the computer in Safedeen's hands. With his shiny face reflective in the flickering lights he was for all the world, thought Ash, like an aged chucky doll.

'What can I get you?' he said in a way that suggested lines learnt from a book on pub etiquette. And then, without any apparent irony. 'My shout.'

Chapter 31

It was Safedeen who went to the bar for her tonic water and his pint of lime and soda. 'Nothing stronger? Well I can understand that. Although I hope we can all relax'.

With a sweep of his arm Ellroy left the seating choice to them. Ash placed himself so he could see into the room. It was fuller than usual. Close to the dark oak panels of the snug were three couples, each in their way of the same build and professional watchfulness. Goons, thought Ash. Mercenaries. And as such, good up to a point. Each must have been allowed a car to drive.

Despite the curfew strictures, there were also villagers corralled further away on the other side of the pub, talking in subdued voices. In fact, the whole place was quiet. Having the likes of Norman Ellroy dropping in with heavies was bound to be a downer. Ash looked across at Maggie. It was the first time he was able to look at her properly since they were jumped.

She too was subtly taking in the sorroundings having chosen a seat with sight of the entrance, while also being able to observe Ellroy. Her face was a mask, just the barest flicker of an eyebrow at Ash showed she was alert. Not that Ellroy was taking much notice of her.

'Call me Norman,' he said to Ash. 'If our talks go well then we shall revert to Mr. Ellroy.' The billionaire smiled benignly. Except with his eyes. 'I do so hate waste,' he said softly. 'That is why I am particularly annoyed about the car you wrote off. It was so,' he paused, 'It really was so,' he searched for the word, 'unnecessary.'

This was a man, Ash recalled, who made his first fortune with a shopping app developed at university. This enabled the harvesting of personal data for marketing, political targeting during elections and for security agencies. Even before the wars in Europe and the Middle East he developed military applications to link data with small killing machines. As a result his cheap, smart drones could be found in the tool box of every government, rebel and insurgent across the globe.

'The cost is immaterial, it is more about the indulgent destruction of something I thought was beautiful. Those aged vehicles are, to me, more desirable than a Matisse or Van Gogh.'

Ash was aware that Norman Ellroy defied black and white assumptions about sides, loyalty or nationality. Being such an enigma gave him access to a vast array of leaders. An individual to be always wooed. 'To be honest, your response to my hand of friendship was a surprise. It did though suggest a certain spirit which was, shall we say, interesting?'

Ellroy paused. It seemed as good a time as any for Ash to add his own items to the agenda. 'Before we start,' he said, 'did you press the button to kill Whistledown, or did your man to do it?' They both knew who he meant.

'Usually,' Ellroy said thoughtfully, 'When faced with such a question, which might be considered accusatory, I might choose to take offence, and not say another word. But as you are currently, shall we say, bug free and I also own the pub, which was swept before I arrived, we can have candour. I think we can be even more secure as the mobile system and internet are down, which means most means of eavesdropping are inoperable. In a way, it's quite refreshing.'

He stopped for a moment while he took in Maggie thoughtfully, as if reminding himself there was a third person with them who he didn't own. 'In my position,' he began, 'problems are sometimes posed by former associates going freelance with the skills and insights they have gained. I cannot say how extremely vexing that is. For the individual you have alluded to, one might have hoped that a period of convalescence in the quiet of the countryside, along with the odd game of cricket, would have been helpful. When such an opportunity is rejected it may leave very few options for those concerned with a bigger picture. Do you follow me?'

Ash did. Whistledown was once of use. When such people went off the rails for some reason it usually ended badly. 'It's still murder,' he said.

'Not necessarily.' Ellroy seemed pleased about something. 'Is it murder when you, Ms Johnson, send a missile into a house? States are regularly conducting killings through their forces in third countries. Yet, the action, and those who do it, are given legal protection. One of my companies is speaking to a number of governments about providing an immediate termination for those in their own states committing criminal acts. In fact, Ben Whistledown's death may yet prove to be his most useful contribution yet. It provides a wonderful example of how to stop a bad man and prevent a terrible tragedy.'

He had their undivided attention. 'Think about it,' Ellroy continued. 'An individual or group are in the act of something that is criminal and harming others. The police are stretched and a very expensive resource. Behind them are overrun courts and packed prisons. A whole system bursting at the seams, costing tax payers a fortune and giving very poor returns. And you can see the crime happening. If there was a process, perhaps with a judge viewing the real time evidence before allowing a termination, then we have a nasty situation resolved, less cost and perhaps even lives saved. Prevention by drone to me is a very obvious extension of having so many security cameras around, and indeed having drones flown by the police. It provides an option for immediate intervention.'

'Someone agreed to this?' It was Ash who spoke, but from her expression, it could easily have been Maggie.

'Agreed? With what happened to my former employee? Well they didn't disagree. Nor did we tell them where this was happening. There was considerable interest in securing your safety Ms. Johnson, and I am confident there'll be no recriminations. After all, even if that unfortunate man was tracked and prevented from enjoying the fruits of his macabre auction, the Russians would probably have exacted their revenge by then. Believe me, a lot of people are very happy with the solution we were able to provide.'

'And if they're not?'

'Ash, if a story does come out here in Thorswick about a local villager being murdered, then there is more than enough forensic evidence linking you to the scene. In that case you will no doubt be serving the interests of your adopted country behind bars as a convicted killer. Your bosses and their political masters would much prefer that version to the truth. And there was also the slight matter of the poor chap who died in a bombing.'

He paused and then sighed as if he could tell he had not yet convinced his audience. 'Have you heard what is happening here on the streets? The police can't cope. Imagine though if they could immediately identify and neutralise the ring leaders. That would certainly get people staying at home like good citizens. And, even if such approaches are not adopted in countries that purport to support out dated judicial systems, there are countries with vast territories where the state is weak. Think of jungle clearings where drug lords and illegal gold prospectors are decimating the rain forest. The rain forest we so obviously all need. A drone operated by a small teams could deliver justice to known law breakers without having to send hundreds of troops, while encouraging the righteous to stay out of the way of machines that will know if they are ever tempted to go off the reservation.'

Norman Ellroy looked over to the bar where Khan was beginning to muster the drinks. He dropped his voice slightly and turned directly to Ash. 'Before Safedeen returns, he said, 'I need to share with you my dilemma. You see Ash, he really wants you dead. But I have an interesting idea that could work for us both.'

Chapter 32

Nag's Head, Thorswick

Without apparently moving Norman Ellroy managed to give the impression of squirming in a self-satisfied way. His head lifted up with the pleasure of the thought he was about to deliver.

'I've had quite a job reigning him in,' he offered in a way that suggested a huge favour. 'As I say, I really don't like unnecessary waste. While I do like to give those working for me some freedom to have their moments, I know you have networks built over generations. In many ways you would be the balance for similar assets Safedeen brings to the portfolio. The two of you create quite formidable value. It might easily transpire however that changes in South Asia mean I don't need you both.'

There it was thought Ash, the challenge. It was him or me. To the side he saw Maggie lifting here eyebrows as she got the implication. Something was about to be offered from which there could be only one winner.

'Khan has seen the light, and some time ago threw in his lot with me while maintaining a position within his home intelligence service. But he knew that tying oneself, in this day and age, to the disparate and chaotic interests of a failing nation is nonsense. There are more powerful influences at work. Around the globe there are a handful of people who bestride our collective fallibilities. When they call, world leaders stop to listen. They, or I suppose I should say "we", reinforce our data power with networks to harvest value. The data is neutral, but people,' and here Ellroy paused and looked across at the village side of the pub with something like distaste. 'well there's another thing.'

'People in my position,' he resumed, 'are the inheritors of what they wanted. A shift away from national power structures started when the first container ship arrived in a port and unloaded goods for customers hungry for fridges, televisions and whatever else lit their rockets. They never worried about where they were made, just as long as it fitted their budget. Gone were the days when people looked to the local factory for a job, gone too were days when national borders were sacrosanct. Poorer people followed the goods, seeking a good life as their lands became inhospitable sometimes by war or by becoming dust bowls. From the moment they touched a keyboard, I and few others owned them in a way states never did.'

'And the consequence?' Ellroy obviously did not expect an answer. He took a sip of beer. 'With globalisation multinational companies took economic agency from people. With social media even fewer individuals received the minds and souls of anyone posting. A child with a mobile is ours for life. We will know more about his mind that any parent. Mass data and artificial intelligence gives us everything, and is the gift that keeps on giving. The few who are masters in that universe are not buffeted by petty politics, nor concerned with the interests of outmoded national states. We are unaffected when regions are flooded, crops fail or people cross borders to spend the rest of their lives in miserable tents.'

Norman Ellroy fixed his eyes on Ash. 'With me, you can have the freedom to be your own man and make a fortune beyond what you could otherwise imagine. You and yours would be shielded. Safedeen, and anyone like him would be unlikely to come after you. Because if they did it would piss me off. And what I can muster, and where I can reach, really makes your current employers look very puny in comparison.'

It was feudalism, though Ash. A global version pure and simple. In an insecure world he was being offered his own castle. Just as long as he paid due homage and fealty to his lord, Norman Ellroy.

'Look at the mess this country is in now. Under attack and unable to defend itself. The Queen Elizabeth has sunk by the way, in case you haven't heard,' Ellroy looked distastefully around the pub.

'Currently China is handing out a lesson to your country. In retaliation for the strike on the Queen Elizabeth, your military overrode the wishes of the politicians and cherrypicked an opportunity that fell into their laps. Thanks to you. The result was that the Brother in Law of the Great leader is dead, and China feels the need to flex its muscles. In fact the great leader did not happen to like his sister's husband. He was getting far too powerful and rather to free with young women on his staff. However, needs must and they could not let the slight pass. While China is too invested in western economies to want to do anything too drastic. But it has been wanting to demonstrate its ability to hand out a spanking to moralising western countries for some time.'

'Only a mild punishment. That's reassuring.'

'It should be, because, those around me will profit. The UK will want to rebuild systems, and I can provide them. China will still want the deal they were trying to make in Afghanistan to go through. To do that I shall need your help, and those of Safedeen. One thing I will want is for two lynchpins in that process to be safe, however distasteful they are.'

Ash stared at Norman Ellroy, the other returning his look with unblinking earnestness.

'But I do have to accommodate Safedeen's concern to deal with you personally. It's all part of the tacit contract we have with each other. When we saw the data sent from your escapade with the Ferrari, he suggested he could beat you in a car race, and out it came. How you two were such rivals at school and, even for a time, afterwards. And it gave me an idea. One that will help me considerably. So tonight, on my track, you two are to have a race, each in a car of your choosing. If you come out first, then he has to accept your involvement. You coming second would suggest you are not expressing the commitment I need, and the offer is withdrawn. Khan, as winner, can then do as he wishes.'

Ash was incredulous. 'And if he decides to take the opportunity to crash me off the track?' Safedeen he saw was finishing his conversation with a purple haired bar maid who was having difficulty with the till now there was no electricity or internet for card payments.

'Then he will have got everything he wanted. Which, in its own way, is also admirable.'

He stopped as Khan loomed over the table with a tray. Ash looked up at him and smiled as he took his lime and soda. 'Thanks,' he said. Under the circumstances he really wanted to rub it in that it was Khan holding the tray, for all the world like a chai whallah. Safedeen got the reference and served him back a cobra eyed look of hate.

'By taking part in the challenge I shall assume that you have accepted the offer of working with me.' An emphasis on the "with".

'As an added incentive,' continued Ellroy. 'you will decide what happens about our renegade officer here.' He looked across at Maggie with no particular interest. 'I have not told anyone that I actually have her. For the moment she is under my care. If you accept the offer to race I will assure you, hand on the heart, I believe I still have....'

Ellroy paused here to see if anyone smiled at his joke. No one did. 'I assure you,' he went on, 'that she will be returned unharmed to the government whether you win or lose. If you win, then she's yours. If you wish to curry favour and stay with those who currently employ you, then I would expect you to provide me with whatever I need. Or, you may wish to use her to your horizons by moving her onto whoever wants her the most, or, if that is your taste, keep her. She would be safe from the Russians. I shall see to that.'

'How very sporting.'

'Thank you and yes, perhaps even like a medieval joust. Two knights charging on their steeds and battling for the favours of a lady.'

Another image from a bygone age thought Ash. It was an effort not to look across at Maggie. If he had he may have registered the briefest shock in a face that trying to remain as flat and expressionless as possible. Maggie's training, if kidnapped or held against her will, was to become an invisible person. The forgettable one in a group. Keeping that up in these circumstances was difficult. This person, this odious, creepy man, was speaking as if she were a commodity to be bought and owned. She stumbled over the thought. Nothing better than a slave in a market, and deep within a shiver went through her.

She contemplated the lamp on the table and snatched at the idea of smashing it over Ellroy's head, wishing it could be like those old paraffin ones and have blue flames enveloping him. He was within easy reach, but so too was one of the security men. He was a good looking thick set type of medium height sitting a little way off. Catching her eye he smiled and pulled back his jacket slightly to reveal the butt of a gun. He was daring her. Bitterly, she reeled herself in. They were still speaking about her.

'Oh, yes, Norman Ellroy was saying. 'I know all about the Russians and why they want her. Forgive the cliché but it's a wounded bear lashing out whenever it can safely get away with it. By the way, the people at what I think is described as the Lingerie Department have ordered your arrest. They seem to think you had something to do with the bombing on the hillside. They've told the police to leave it alone and they will handle it.'

'Presumably they were acting on the information received,' said Ash bitterly.

'That is exactly the kind of analytical skills I want to harness. Come in with me and the demise of Robert Collier, taxi man, will be something else you won't have to worry about.'

'Looks like I have no choice. I'll race.'

'Good,' said Ellroy. 'I may also add a few more cars programmed with your driving style from the data we took from your drive in my Ferrari. This kind of race attracts a lot of my friends and network and I am always interested in expanding potential markets and using such opportunities.' He rose, his bitter barely touched, and indicated Maggie with a flick of his wrist. Safedeen's hand on her elbow brought her unresisting to her feet.

'Don't worry about me Lofty,' she said looking at Ash. Then over her shoulder as she was guided toward the door. 'I'll be alright.'

Her eyes pierced and Ash knew he must try one last thing 'They will want her back. They'll be a big reward for that too.'

Ellroy stopped and barely turned. 'What they want and what they get, as far as I am concerned, are too different things. On this occasion, it could be decided by you. Accept my offer, win the race and you can be this young lady's white knight, or hand her over to whoever you choose.'

He turned and gave Ash the full benefit of his eyes. Blue, rheumy and wide. 'Refuse me and I shall decide where she can be placed in my best interests. I do tend, in that regard, to go with the strength. Not that her fate will be a concern for you, because ..., well, it won't be a concern shall we say. We shall start in an hour.'

He and entourage swept out and into the cars. The engines came to life and, as if for a funeral, followed the sedate progress of the black Rolls as it carried Ellroy and Maggie to the Hall.

Chapter 33

They had made a mistake. Norman Ellroy's security team moved with him. It was not their job to stick around watching a victim after their boss had done his thing. That was probably a daily occurrence. For all that, amidst the flurry of Ellroy's exit, someone should have stayed watching Ash.

The cavalcade was on its way to the Hall this must have occurred to Safedeen. A Lamborghini coloured and shaped like a cheese slice came to a halt. Safedeen levered himself out and walked back to the brilliant white McLaren. As he approached it he indicated with a circular motion and the wing door of the vehicle opened upwards as if it were going to swallow him. More gestures. Ash watched as the he driver got out, looked back toward the pub and dug out a pistol from his belt and handed it to Safedeen. He was the bat wielder from the impromptu game on the green, and who had dared Maggie in the pub to have a go.

Standing by the side of the road he gave mock salutes to the parade of cars as they passed the McLaren, and while he did that, Ash was off. Going out the back door, the one thought was Maggie's high, raised eyebrows and calling him 'Lofty.' It had to mean something. Reinforcing his thinking was that her grandfather was hardly a retired vicar with nothing more upstairs than old sermons. He ran from the yard of the pub and, once again, headed to the hedge line at the back of their cottages.

First stop was his own place. He needed to check to make sure communications really were down and create some delays. Cautiously he pulled open the back door and listened before stepping into the kitchen. No one inside. Another mistake.

Reaching for a coffee jar he smashed it on the floor. In the middle of the explosion of granules was a small greaseproof paper packet. Ash tore it open and dropped one of the gold sovereign and moved it with his foot so that it was barely visible under the cooker. Bending low he blew coffee around it. Standing up he surveyed the floor. He wanted it to make it look as if he had hurriedly grabbed something and some hidden treasure rolled away. He hoped a flash of gold would do what it has always done, which was to distract and beguile. Hopefully the mercenary would see it and spend time digging around looking for more. To sweeten the search he shoved another under the microwave. Try doing that with crypto.

Satisfied he went up the stairs two at a time. The computer system was completely wrecked. Wires were bunched like tumbleweed and screens smashed. Peering out of the window he saw McLaren man was at the back of the pub scanning the countryside. A lot would depend on what he did next. He could easily shrug, decide Ash was on the run and head back to the Hall.

Ash watched the debate unfold through the man's body language. His look around the countryside was intense. His body taut. This man was a hunter, and unwilling to give up. Turning he looked up at the windows of the Nag's Head, and thoughtfully at the line of cottages. Now there was indecision. Ash read his reluctance. Giving bad news to the likes of Safedeen Khan and Norman Ellroy was not to be relished. It might even be the end of a cushy number. Perhaps worse. It would also be best if he checked out all possible options before facing fury at the Hall. From behind the half closed shutters Ash saw the man turn in his direction and give the place a long hard look. As he did so his right hand twitched at his empty holster. It was a tell. The kind of unconscious shrug or tic from bowlers on the cricket field as they betrayed their intention to deliver a bouncer or full toss. The man wanted his nine millimetre, and that meant he was coming to the cottage.

Ash only had moments. A maximum of minutes. The man was on his way, walking steadily, eyes alert. Ash went to the landing with a chair, opened the hatch to the loft and took the chair back to the bedroom. The hatch was inches above his fingertips at full stretch. He crouched and leapt, grabbing the sill, and then dropped stifling a howl as the muscles in his back felt they were being ripped. He sunk onto his knees, head bowed and breathing deep. Looking up he prepared himself and slowly stood. This time he would have to leap better and ignore the pain. He counted down, took a deep lungful and jumped, his fingers closing. This time he breathed out with the pain, holding the woodwork, settling for a second before pulling himself up and into the loft.

Closing the hatch behind him he straightened and made his way across the joists. The cottages had been built according to their times. Daylight came from the eaves and the partition wall between his home and blue cottage was single brick, and stopped a good few feet off the slates . He had put stuff in the loft when he first moved in and had noticed how the mortar was powdery and crumbling. Bricks came off in his hands, which was just as well as McLaren man must be close and the sound of a wall crashing down would certainly bring him running.

Ash quickly made a hole big enough to step through, and saw immediately the prize. Opening the long garden games box he could have whooped. There was a carbine with, he quickly checked, a full magazine. Four smooth, round American made grenades and a presentation box the size and colour of a serious bible. Nestling in its carved space was a brand new Glock 20, the hand gun marketed as perfect for the beginner. The gun came with two magazines, which had been ready loaded with 10mm bullets. Whoever put this together had someone in mind who might not have time to mess around with padlocks and fiddle with bullets.

The last thing in the games box was a small, black rucksack. Perfect for a quick pack and run. Stopping only to load the Glock, Ash put the handgun into his belt and packed the grenades into the rucksack. Regretfully he decided the carbine was going to have to stay put. The firepower was sparking possibilities, and a plan. Mind whirling he went to the loft hatch for Maggie's cottage and dropped, knees soft. Downstairs he put his ear to the wall. From his kitchen came the sounds of smashing crockery and drawers being thrown onto the floor.

Opening the front door he slipped out and headed off at a jog trot to the church, using the trees as best he could to circle round to the road and the McLaren. Using the super car to shield him from the row of cottages he approached at a crouch. Reaching it he opened the passenger side wing door, holding it so it didn't flap up like a seagull's wing. Ash quickly scanned the interior. As he expected the driver's seat was set forward, the security man being below average height. He felt quickly under the driver's seat. There was barely room for anything. He tried to stuff the ruck sack into the space, but it snagged and stuck. Sweating, he took out the pistol and forced it home.

There was nowhere else to put the pistol but in the space under the armrest. He would just have to hope it wasn't found. There was one more thing to do. His time was nearly up. Even the dumbest Ellroy minion would know he must report Ash's flight, and the sooner that was done the better. Ash could guess at what the man would concoct to explain why it hadn't be done immediately. "I looked everywhere. Searched his house. He may have gone there first. Must have just missed him. Took a quick look in hers. No sign. Wish I was kept on him from the beginning." All that, with no mention of gold sovereigns.

Crouching along the ditch Ash got to the back of the pavilion and kicked in the door to the kitchenette. He had never been in before, and at first glance he doubted if it would have passed many health checks. It was from here that Maureen delivered a profusion of chips, with toppings of melted cheese and chilli con carne. Nothing else. The chip fryer was a venerable beast, the oil inside dark. On the shelving above he put a pack of plastic water bottles, pierced one with the knife so it dripped onto the stove and turned on the gas. Going into the bar he reached under the counter and sorted through the stock of bottles. An opened bottle of 12 year old single malt was right at the back, and he pulled it out.

Raising it to his lips he murmured 'Here's to you Hassan,' and took a reverential, substantial, swallow. A toast to his late asset in Karachi. Another swig followed before Ash splashed some over himself and poured half onto the floor. Taking a deep breath, he stepped onto the wooden veranda and straight into the starting eyeballs of his hunter. He was fifteen metres away, about to get into the supercar.

'Have you been following me?,' Ash demanded truculently. He stood for a moment starring out the man, before easing himself down to sit on the wooden steps, with the air of a world weary drunk.

'What have you been doing?' There was worry in the voice.

Not an obvious accent thought Ash, but almost certainly east European. A conclusion reached primarily through, what Hassan might describe as, 'the cut of his jib'. With some exaggeration, Ash looked at the bottle in his hand before answering. 'Nothing much.'

The man looked quickly around and back at the pub. Getting his bearings and working out how Ash might have got to the pavilion without being seen. 'Thought he had done a runner,' he managed eventually.

'Thought about it,' said Ash pausing briefly to take a pull from the bottle. 'Got to the church and then thought as I had been left alone there was probably a drone waiting to knock me off if I excused myself from the party. So I came here for a stiffner. Want some?' He waved the nearly empty bottle.

'No thanks.' The man was tracking the route. Noting how someone could use it and be unseen. 'Anyway you're wanted.'

Slowly Ash stood up and indicated the bottle again. 'No? Suit yourself.' With a last regretful look he threw it at the door of the pavilion where it smashed leaving a very small brown stain.

'Give me a lift?'

'No you stink. Walk in front of the car.'

Sensible of you, thought Ash. No point in chancing a chop to the throat from the passenger seat and Ash being gifted a very fast getaway car. Shrugging, he walked heavy footed for the Hall, the McLaren growling behind. Ash was sure the driver's eyes were never leaving his swaying back. Which was just fine and dandy as far as Ash was concerned considering what was behind the driver's seat.

Chapter 34

Thorswick Hall

Catching her first sight of Thorswick Hall Maggie felt like she was entering a film set for a cliché. It looked the perfect location for a drama on the doings of picadillo encumbered masters and their tightly buttoned servants. The honey coloured walls rose straight up from manicured, well-watered lawns, while the leaded, mullioned windows were like a hundred angry eyes as they reflected the red of the setting sun.

'Go straight round the back.' The words to the black suited driver were the first Norman Ellroy had spoken since sinking into the cream leather and walnut opulence of the limo. He seemed completely oblivious to her, a state that increased her sense of being a commodity. It was not, as far as she could judge, a case of him being lost in his own thoughts. It was more a neutral disinterest. Instinctively she felt he was not driven sexually, either gay or other, and, as such, she was a weapon down. She was resolved to be that quiet mouse as much as possible but gave a start of surprise, despite herself, when they passed potted trees shaped like spear points and rounded the corner.

'Impressive isn't it?' Ellroy said smugly. And Maggie said, yes it was, and was rewarded by an approving nod. The car came to a halt, and now it was Norman Ellroy who got out first and went around to open the door for her. 'Have a closer look', he said, his damp hand helped her down.

It was an astonishing sight. The whole back of the Hall was made up of glass sheets the size of a terraced house, each embedded in a framework of grey painted girders. It was as if the building had been cleaved and two violently opposed styles had been welded together without compromise. In their extremes each side demonstrated the extraordinary wealth garnered in their own times through exploitation.

'It's a garage for my babies,' said Ellroy. 'Watch.'

A central section of glass was moving, out and up, exposing a dark cavern through which a midnight blue, low slung car emerged. She could not be sure at first because of the tinted windscreen, but as it growled in low gear down a long ramp she saw there was no one in the driving seat. It moved at steady speed on the incline, taking the long sweep onto a semicircle of tarmac where it stopped, the engine dying. 'It's multi-story in there. The car lift alone in an engineering masterpiece.'

'And you were allowed to do this?,' Maggie paused briefly, she knew how that sounded, and this was not the time to be critical. Adding, 'I mean, it being an old building and everything.' This last bit in a tone designed to suggest that she for one would have no sympathy with those standing in the way of such progress.

'My dear, I can do what the bloody hell I like.' He paused. 'Here, and anywhere else for that matter.'

Like sausages, cars were disgorging smoothly at regular intervals. A spectrum of modern and classic forming a fan shaped spectrum on the tarmac with a few starting up, turning the hot evening air pungent with exhaust. It was an array, thought Maggie, conveying the same sense of menace and pent up power as jet fighters being readied for the off. Someone, somewhere, threw a switch. On came floodlights. Some from the steel girded building above them, warming the colours of the cars. Others around the park, through the trees, and glowing from behind a hill. A track. No, that's wrong thought Maggie. A circuit.

Ellroy caught her eye. 'Still work in progress, of course, but sufficient I think for tonight's occasion. Anyway, as a technician of sorts I am sure you will be interested in the master control room. Shall we go to the orangery?'

They walked past the cars. Some now had bonnets up, with men fiddling and engines gunning. The burnt fuel reinforcing Maggie's sense of being on an airfield prepped for action. Their steps took them to the other side of the Hall toward a hexagonal, flat roofed stone building covered in wisteria. It looked like a Victorian attempt at a summer house, but one handled by a clumsy architect. As she got closer she saw how the chapel like windows were blacked out. On the roof two white cabinets gave a clue to the current use.

The steel faced double door opened with a sigh after Ellroy had put his eye to a reader and they went into a sealed area. When the first door closed Ellroy opened the second, and Maggie involuntarily shivered in the cold of the air conditioning. It was dark inside, with lights blinking on electronic columns stacked behind dark glass doors around the walls. A large screen was split into boxes showing a map of the Hall along with live images from the park and racing circuit. There were also pictures from other cameras showing the main gate, the lanes around the Hall and the entrance to the summer house.

In the gloom Maggie saw two others seated in front of consoles on either side of a giant screen. Curiously she felt almost at home. Or rather, at work. One of the console jockeys, in a black T shirt, was taking the security cameras for a canter. Different views flashed up just long enough for an eyeball scan before being replaced. Lifeless, museum like rooms inside the Hall, and a wide hallway with a suit of armour. How very kitsch, thought Maggie. A panning movement from another camera showed what could be a car showroom, only this floor also had cars stacked into a space saving system like an airport long stay.

Ellroy went off to speak to the thin young man in a loose fitting purple T shirt at the other console. The images from security cameras now switched to show sections of the track. A drone must also be flying. It soared and dipped, speeding around the circuit, roaring over the tarmac. Testing out the racing surface was a Mercedes saloon, it's lights flashing over hoardings advertising motor oils and tyres. Each a testament to a bye-gone age.

'I expect you may be wondering,' Ellroy suggested as he came back to her side, 'why you are not constrained in some way.'

It had occurred to her. 'The reason,' he continued without waiting for a response, 'is prediction.' He emphasised the word.

'You will have realised that I am your best hope of being safe, and me keeping the promises made if the man known as Ash wins the race.'

He stopped while he put on a headset and adjusted a small microphone. 'As soon as I heard who he was from my colleague Safedeen I set up this little event as a demonstration of how data sets can predict outcomes. Everything known about him, his history, blood group, family background, where he has been, what he watches, everything. Including his cricket activities. The sensors in the Ferrari he trashed gave us more information about him than he could ever know. The conclusion was that he would face this challenge and what the result will be.'

'So you knew he would agree to this race even before you spoke to us today?'

'I did, and how useful it could be. One can speak about prediction capability to potential customers but there is nothing like a bit of red blooded sport to attract the eyeballs.'

'So I was always incidental to the plan.'

'On the contrary. You may have come late to the mix, but you have reinforced it. As you came into play we fed your likely influence on his decision making into the mix, and it turns out that this servant of the Crown has some curious characteristics. We know from his reactions tracked when he had a woman in the Ferrari, that he showed, strangely for someone in his profession, considerable empathy. I was curious to see if he would help her when she asked for help, which we know she did. Repeatedly. He didn't, but the data suggested strongly that this denial, if you like, would make it more likely to help the next to cross his path in distress. He was also ordered to look out for you, and protect you if necessary. That matters too. However, he was not brought back with us, so confident am I that he will take part and we don't need to use any other means of compulsion. This is an experiment, and it is right that we walk around it and kick the tyres a bit, so others can see that your knight had a choice, but our predictions proved correct.'

'And what are the predictions for the race?'

Ellroy gave her enigmatic smile. 'If I told you that might take away all the fun and thrill. In any case, Eric over there,' and he indicated the man in the purple T shirt, will be inputting and monitoring data right up to the last minute and that will affect our prediction of the outcome. Now, if you will excuse me, I have an audience to speak to.'

He paused as if he were expecting another question, and then he gave the answer anyway. 'I have my own satellite and fully isolated communications,' he said. 'As we have seen, you really can't depend on the internet these days.'

Maggie watched as he straightened up and beamed at a camera somewhere in the room. She hoped against hope that Ash had done a runner. Even if that meant uncertainty for her. It sounded all so set, so predetermined and somehow evil.

The screen came live to the room, and a super-sized image of Norman Ellroy filled the space before dissolving into a number of boxes each with faces starring back.

'How nice to see you all,' boomed Ellroy. 'And thank you for taking time, which I can assure you will be worth your while. Before we get to the main event I want to show you another business development that I have no doubt will be of interest to your governments. This is breaking news if you like and concerns an individual who was attempting to conduct activities against the interests of the state.'

Norman Ellroy waved a hand and the image changed. It was a static shot of a man sitting in an armchair starring at a laptop. It was Ben Whistledown.

'You already have police drones. But our troubled times call for their capability to be taken to another level entirely.' He paused and gulped some water.

'In real time this individual was tracked, but he was far from any law enforcement and what he was doing on line had to be stopped in minutes. National interests were involved. How many times has this happened in your country? Or even on your street corners? Surveillance cameras may pick up a drugs deal, a person about to kill another, or a robbery in progress. But how to interrupt it and deliver appropriate justice? I want to show you in this instance how something very unpleasant,' and here Ellroy turned to give the slightest smirk toward Maggie, 'was forestalled, and all in keeping with accepted norms of civilised justice.'

On the video Maggie saw how Ben Whistledown was looking up in the direction of the French windows of his cottage. He seemed interested, and mildly amused. Well he would be, she thought. That was probably the moment she and Ash met on the patio.

'A government Minister, having taken legal advice, authorised the use of lethal force just as police marksman would be allowed if there was a terrorist in the cross hairs of his telescopic sight.'

Maggie saw Ben's eyes move as he followed something up from the ground and his amused look became like a child seeing a toy. He then jolted, a red dot appearing in the middle of his forehead as he slumped back into the chair.

'So there we have it. In this case the individual was already under surveillance by an armed drone. But Ellroy Industries is talking to governments about having lethal and non-lethal loitering drone capacity as a swift enforcer in a civilian context. Believe me, with such assistance to police at your disposal your streets will be safe and crime free within days.'

On screen there were many smiles, some inaudible clapping and several Smiley emojis. 'Thank you. I thought you would be interested. It is entirely possible to programme drones to take action in wider fields of law enforcement. Take for example a situation where armed terrorists attack an airport, and civilians are hostages. In the future with Ellroy technology, you could withdraw your police, programme the drones to kill anyone armed. That way there is no need for police to conduct an armed intervention, no risk to the hostages and the bad guys don't trouble the courts. Perhaps you know in another scenario that all your targets are men. In Nigeria for example where militants raid girl schools and take them away. Drones could be set loose with instructions only to shoot men. Solid food for thought I think! If you have an individual's DNA the drones will hunt out just that person. There will be no hiding place. Similarly if there is an ethnic minority causing problems just the threat of drones being programmed against them will be more than enough, surely, to prevent them daring to challenge. If one were to link the drones to the type of listening devices people have in their homes to order a pizza then the drones could react to key words and take pre-emptive action. Really, the limit to all this is only our imagination.'

Ellroy paused again, to let the enormity of his vision sink in. 'So if there are no questions......, I will be back with you shortly when we move on to demonstrate our prediction capability.'

The screen reverted to the circuit. 'I think that went well,' and Maggie thought he would have said it whether he had an audience or not.

'Can I ask a question?'

Ellroy looked at her, and Maggie thought, briefly, it was the first time he had shown any real interest. 'Was a decision really taken by someone to kill that man, or did the drone decide for itself?'

At the console she saw Eric stiffen, while Ellroy gave her a joyless smile. 'Really, no that would be a dangerous step would it not? It went as I said. Otherwise one would have to set in coordinates that effectively predicted and prejudged someone with the ultimate sanction approved. And whoever controlled that would be God indeed.' He nodded at her in a way that managed to be both patronising and menacing, while out of the corner of her eye she saw Eric giving her a very long stare.

'Here we go.' Ellroy, now the ebullient host. 'As predicted.' The screen was showing the driveway and, with a pang of regret Maggie, saw Ash walking toward the array of cars, a white one following close behind. As he got close he deviated to stand in front of a figure clearly recognisable as Safedeen Khan. Only at that moment did she think his walk seemed unnaturally deliberate.

'Marvellous,' breathed Ellroy as he unconsciously flicked his fingers. 'This is going to be so exciting.'

Chapter 35

Maggie saw Khan muttering into his sleeve, his voice crackling onto the speakers. 'He's been drinking.'

The camera zoomed on the group. Maggie took in the downward cast of Ash's shoulders. Something in her stirred. If they were to have any hope of getting away they both need to be on their game, but Ash looked beaten already. He also looked unarmed. Perhaps he had not picked up her "Lofty" reference. But then he had been watched. Mentally she shook herself. She must not give up, or rely on anyone else. Walking toward Ash and Khan were men she recognised from the tables around them at the pub. A couple of them now carried carbines. The driver of the white McLaren was getting out and talking to Khan. She recognised him alright.

'Our man says he went to the pavilion and got into a bottle.'

In the control room, Eric looked up briefly. 'Given some suggestions in past history, drug usage and alcohol abuse were already factored into the prediction.'

Ellroy rocked on the balls of his feet for a moment. Maggie thought he looked annoyed. Even disappointed. He walked over to the control desk, while never taking his eyes off the screen. It was filled with Safedeen and Ash talking, with the latter's gestures looking particularly exaggerated. 'What are they saying?, demanded Ellroy.

No one answered. 'Why can't we hear them?', he seemed agitated somehow.

'The area is not rigged for sound. Or at least directionally.' Eric was typing, and did not seem in the least bit concerned about Ellroy's agitation. Maggie watched the reflection in the darkened glass doors that protected the system as his hands flew over the keys.

'But that's just stupid.' Angry now, the billionaire waved a hand around his mike, indicated it should be switched on. His breathing came onto the speakers. 'Choose a car, gentlemen. Let's get this show on the road.'

Both Safedeen and Ash looked heaven wards at the sound as an example from a new stable of super cars, a black Tampla Dragon was coming down the ramp. 'I'll take that one,' said Khan.

Not a bad option, thought Ash, but under the circumstances he felt at the very least he should be given first choice. He looked at array of cars. So far so good. McLaren man had answered truthfully when asked where Ash had got a drink, but not added anything else about him being out of sight for some time while he hunted through coffee granules. Right now the man was standing nervously watching, committed by his omissions.

Ash decided to up the stakes a bit. His voice slurred and petulant, he pointed at Safedeen's choice muttered about how that was not fair.

Safedeen almost grinned 'Fair?', he said, 'whatever else you hear, this was not ever going to be fair as far as you're concerned.'

The Tampla Dragon was a new kid on the block, built by a company with a headquarters in China which had recruited established designers and engineers from far and wide to surpass every known marque. They had produced a swooping, dashing vehicle with the low slung driver's compartment bookmarked by massive air intakes.

Ash waved his arm in an all embracing way. 'Is it as good as they say?' And then, without waiting for a reply because he already knew the answer, 'some of these cars are controlled from elsewhere aren't they. What's to stop Ellroy doing something to slow them or switch them off halfway through the race as if he's playing some kind of mad video game with all sorts of crazy car capers with us?'

Safedeen turned his head away from cameras before speaking. 'He won't,' he said with a certain grimness. 'He is using this to showcase the prediction capability of his quantum data systems. Therefore he really can't interfere in whatever happens.

Everything known about you and me has been crunched and when the race starts the viewers will be told the predicted outcome, and what are the likely key moments. That won't stop them betting on it. There are always those who will want to take odds against the favourite. Your Minister Carrick- Rhodes will be amongst them, using money from Ellroy to bet on a race between me as a known foreign agent and you as one of his spies. Think about it "Ash", your boss and security minister is taking time off from a national emergency and the downing of the internet to watch you die.'

'Sounds like he's prepared to see a lot of cars getting damaged. I thought he worshipped these things.'

'He does, but these are only the replaceable ones. He's see's this race as a dramatic way of making his point.'

'Get on with it!' The voice from up above, and around them. Caesar speaking.

'Sounds like this is our last chance to work out another way.' Ash did not think for a minute Khan would turn, he just thought he should try. He was very aware how a cloud of the 12 year old spirit was filling the space between them. 'We don't have to go along with this,' he added lamely.

'We do, actually.' For a brief moment it looked to Ash as if Safedeen would have liked to have said more. Their eyes met and then Khan looked away, touching his earpiece. 'It sounds as if we are now live. So go and pick a car.'

In the control room the faces were back on the screen along with a drone shot following Ash as he walked unsteadily down the lines of cars. Occasionally he peered through a windscreen or bounced a wing as if testing suspension. Ellroy watched, his eyes flicking around the assembled faces, his fingers clicking with impatience as Ash went down the whole line. His walk passed marques from what was now being seen as the 'Golden Age' of the supercar. Among them were an yellow, black streaked Lamborghini, a red Ferrari along with classic models such as an Aston Martin and the rally honed Nissan R32-GTR Godzilla.

Running along the bottom of the screen was a flashing yellow headline. "Early Prediction. Marginal call. Safedeen Khan to win. Mitigation against Ash 15% due to alcohol usage." This was being replaced regularly by "Final prediction dependent on car choice".

Having reached the end of the line, Ash very obviously shook his head. On the periphery the men with guns each touched their ears in in the time honoured way of security types listening to their communications. The one nearest then approached Ash.

'Problem?', he asked. He was an athletic man, probably the same age as Ash, with close cropped black hair untouched with grey, who slung his carbine behind his back leaving his arms free to cross as he stood several feet away.

'Yes, the car I want is not here.'

'Which is?'

'A Bugatti Veyron.'

A Veyron. The car with a cult status from before the first epidemic, which needed a special key for a mode that even professionals would fine hard to handle. Any serious collector with deep pockets would have one. Ash had never driven a Veyron and knew it would be a mistake to opt for such a beast. On the other hand he was interested in causing as much trouble and delay as possible.

The man went to his ear. 'He wants the Veyron,' he reported. He listened, arms behind and when they came back it was with the gun. 'Mr. Ellroy says you are to get on with what's here.' The gun ticked up. 'Now.'

Ash smiled, time to play to his global audience. Slowly he extended a middle finger, and leered in an "all men together" way. 'Guess he may have lost the insertion device, if you know what I mean. After all you know what they say about old men and sports cars.' With that curled his finger into a droop.

The other man's eyes widened, his face betraying an urgent desire not to be part of the conversation. He swung his rifle to smash the butt into Ash's face, which would have connected if it were still there. Instead Ash leaned away from the swinging weapon with an ease suggesting lubrication. 'Wow, easy tiger,' he said convivially. 'The man wants a race remember.'

'Pick a damn car,' the man spat. In the control room Maggie noticed that the Prediction on screen had changed. Mitigation had dropped to 3%.

'Why the change?, Ellroy's face was flushed. He had seen some laughter around the world.

'Nothing to do with me,' said Eric at the console driver. 'Data picked up that your man is not as drunk as he seemed. His reactions were fast enough when he thought he was going to be hit by that goon.' Across the darkened room, the security man shot him a look.

'Put me on the net.' Norman Ellroy hoisted a beam at the camera, 'You see from this little demonstration of humour by our contestant here how quickly the data reflects the monitoring and adjusts the prediction. In real time on a battlefield, on your streets or in a crisis such speed can bring you the result you want even faster.'

There were approving nods. Meanwhile Ash was back at the start and he pointed to the white McLaren. Turning around to catch any cameras, he gave a thumbs up. Opening up the wing door he got inside and lowered himself into the wrap around carbon fibre seat. And waited. The car was familiar. He had raced similar models in Dubai and at that weird track in Rajasthan.

'Are we going to let him use that one?' It was Norman Ellroy asking the question.

'Well we thought he would take one of the others,' said Eric. 'But that was lazy inputting as we just put in the variables for the choices from cars brought out this evening. But we can fix that. He tapped some keys. 'It's done.'

'I mean is there something wrong with him making that choice.'

Eric looked up. 'Well we have already refused him the Vayron, and the optics around refusing him his second choice might not work for your audience.'

Somehow, Maggie realised, the power in the room had shifted. Eric was not simply obeying Norman Ellroy's orders. He was acting like the project designer.

'OK.' Ellroy still sounded uncertain. 'Let's get this started. Switch on that McLaren. And put up the prediction.'

Maggie saw Ash's car start to move, being waved toward the starting grid by a man in an orange vest. A sleek black car was already there. Black and white, she thought. Quite a chess game. On the screen the faces of the world wide audience were intent, and then up came a flashing script. Final Prediction!

Safedeen in Dragon to win on a margin of 20%. High probability of incident/accident (10th lap).

Norman Ellroy turned to her. 'Nothing is certain, of course', he said smoothly and if his smile was intended to be reassuring, it was anything but.

'It's a big margin.'

'We know Ash has driven a similar McLaren before, and quite successfully,' said Ellroy. 'The Dragon is newer. While there have been a few teething problems, we have worked with the Chinese to make it a formidable performer. The choice of the McLaren suggests your white knight has gone for familiarity and agility. But this is a race that will almost certainly favour strength and robustness, rather than the more aged option.'

'Because it is a demolition derby?'

Eric snorted, sounding amused, while the billionaire looked ever so slightly offended. 'I was also referring to the characteristics of the man,' he said shortly.

On the run to the grid the engine sounded sweet, deep and throaty. Pressing buttons he adjusted the seat, letting his fingers trail briefly behind the driver's seat. They touched something. Leaning forward he turned the dial controlling the mode, and put the car into sport. He was as ready as he was ever going to be. As far as he could tell from the engine noise, the car was at perfect pitch.

As he slid down the final part of the ramp a figure emerged from the darkness and into floodlights. It was McLaren man, who smiled and brought both hands together pointing a finger as if it were a gun before exploding the hold like a magician showing there was nothing there. He winked. The message was clear. Fearfully, Ash waited until he was well past before he fumbling with the cover of the armrest, fighting the webbing of the seat belt to get his hand inside. There was nothing there. He flapped his hand all the way round, only pulling it out as he drew up beside the Dragon, and brought the car to a halt on the starting line and looked dumbly at the gantry lights.

McLaren man must have searched the car. He would have realised the smuggled weapon meant his lie about keeping tabs on Ash the whole time was compromised, but quietly removed the weapon. In the control room a new message was flashing, "Bets now closed." And then, another; "Likelihood of both drivers finishing low (7.79%) ".

Eric gave a low whistle. 'Sensors in the steering wheel of one of the cars has picked up a sudden spike of an additional stress factor, which is being read as a doomsday. Or in another words, one of the drivers believes he is not going to make it.'

'Which one?' demanded Ellroy, but Eric didn't need to answer. On screen the prediction changed again. Final. Incident lap 10. Dragon to win- 99%. And Maggie's heart sank.

Chapter 36

Ash looked ahead, barely thinking. The lights on the overhead gantry were flashing 30. The number of laps. There was no way his racer would last that distance, given the speeds he would need and the pummelling punishment along the way. He looked at the Dragon, and the Easter egg like composite that hid the driver. The McLaren had been his Trojan horse. Chosen because of the weapons hidden inside. In this race it did not stand a chance and nor, for that matter now, did he.

The lights ahead changed from five green to four. Two seconds later, three. The countdown was on. Ash shook himself. He was going to have to get himself into what was going to happen within the next few seconds.

The green lights had been replaced by five red. As in a professional race. The five held. They would be there for at least thirty seconds. He revved the engine, lifting it to a pitch that put the counter well into the red, the car throbbing around him.

Four. Now there were four red lights, and they would now drop every two seconds and when the last went, they were off.

Three.

It would be best to let Khan have the lead. Keep in his slipstream to save fuel. So what if the paintwork got pebble dashed. Have him in front. Far safer.

Two. One. Nothing.

The McLaren leapt for the track, took the Dragon's lane and sent sparks down its wing as metal seared and a light exploded. Playing the paddle gears Ash flexed for the first curve, his mirror telling him the attempt to crush the wheel arch of the Dragon had failed. Safedeen guessed the move, and how Ash was likely to use the only weapon available. The car. In the gallery Norman Ellroy was barely able to contain his fury. 'The bastard,' he screamed.

'Well that wiped the smile off the face of the Dragon,' said Eric, but the move had set the McLaren on an impossible line for the first bend. It was swinging, the back wheels slurring into the start of a spin. Catching up was the Dragon, charging past the trees where it seemed the McLaren would inevitably broadside to a violent halt. Beside Maggie, Ellroy sucked in his breath, and spat out an 'idiot!' as the car was enveloped in a puff ball of dust and gravel.

The wheel was following the skid, Ash allowing the steering to have its head. Only when a crash seemed inevitable did he apply power, pulling the swivelling vehicle back and ending with it facing the wrong way. Yanking the wheel and pushing the accelerator violently, Ash sent the McLaren in pursuit. Cold sweat fell from his armpits while the tyres screamed at the violence of the acceleration. 'Careless', he thought. 'Actually. Bloody stupid'.

In the control room Ellroy was clicking his fingers, now in apparent appreciation. 'He did well there,' he said grudgingly. 'At least now there might be some drama.'

Maggie saw the way he glanced across to Eric, how they exchanged looks before the operator's head went down over the keyboard. There was something about it she did not like. It was the type of understood communication when something did not need to be said. She had seen it countless times before. Usually when something messy was being planned, and nobody wanted to commit to saying it out loud, or leave a paper trail. As such it was all too familiar.

She was working hard at not being noticed. The race made this easier. The security man, she noticed, did keep an eye, but even his attention dropped as the laps mounted up and Norman Ellroy started to express his pleasure in a chummy way that seemed to rule her out.

'Fuck me, not literally of course! Ha!,' he said at least twice. After a few laps he looked again across at Eric. 'Time, I think, to send out some of the others,' he said languidly. He dictated the cars to go, sometimes by marque and also, Maggie noticed, by colour.

'Now perhaps, the Lambo.' And across the control room Eric hit the keyboard, 'and the Ferrari at the end. One should always add a dash of red!' Only when the fourth and last was travelling to join the track did a new camera angle show an empty driver's seat, and Maggie realised there were drones.

Ash meanwhile was calculating. The head up display of the McLaren showed speeds up to 180. But whatever he did, the Dragon stayed just far enough ahead to keep up a spray of dust and gravel. The sleek car was like a will of the wisp, occasionally enveloped, sometimes out of view on corners, the black paintwork mixing with shadows where floodlights were sparsely spaced. But as he flexed and parried, chose his line and gunned the engine Ash knew Khan was driving at nowhere near the capability of himself or the capacity of the car. He wanted Ash close.

The Hall was coming into view, the place lit up like a theatre. Eight laps down. The McLaren was still at the extremity of the Dragon's tail as they swept past the array of cars. Fewer of them outside for some reason. Nemesis corner fast approaching. He eased the car round having braked hard in the run up while the tyres were aligned and then toeing and heeling on the accelerator. Coming out he saw he had gained on Khan.

His shoulders and back were aching, so too were his thighs, as he tensed, braced and released many thousands of times. The aged McLaren at least managed the eccentricities of amateur handling, and a far from professional race track. The sport suspension was hard without making the frequent road crunches lumbar shattering. Even so most of his body felt as if were being tenderised by a meat mallet, while his neck and shoulders were so painful and tight they could have been corded cables. If it went on like this he thought grimly, death would be a relief.

On lap nine Ash saw the smoke. Carried from the village, he soon smelled it. The acrid tang coming through the vents as thick plumes started to fill the hollows of the circuit. The cooking oil in the pavilion kitchen had taken longer than expected to catch. When it caught the water suspended above it there would have been a dramatic combustion. It was something done at the last minute, without any clear idea about how it would help. But, when the odds are against you, do what you can to mess up the opposition's playing field.

In the control room at the Hall a mobile went off. Without removing his eyes from the race on the big screen, the security man fished out his device, and listened briefly. Ending the call, he put it on the desk and started to tap on his own keyboard. 'The cricket pavilion,' he said. 'It's on fire.' Then added unecessairily, 'the mobile systems are back.'

Ellroy at first did not react. Then, 'so?'. His eyes stayed on the race.

'A big fire apparently.'

"How?'

The security man looked over at Ellroy briefly before getting back to his screen. Maggie noticed how he also was holding up his mobile so he could see both screens at the same time. 'That's just it. Might be an accident. Just don't like the timing. We have all this going on, and it's going to get the villagers out.'

His voice was staccato. And accented, without inflection. For the first time since the race began, the security man became of interest to Ellroy. 'And what does that mean, get the villagers out?'

'I mean they will ask for help.' The man looked at his mobile. 'Looks like calls are already going to police and fire.' He paused. 'It's a distraction. If it was started deliberately it means there might mean your man is not the only opposition here.'

'Could he have done it?'

'No. My friend had eyes on him after he left the pub. He just sat there and drank. Then threw the bottle at the place.'

Maggie kept her eyes on him and noticed how he was not looking at her. The accent bothered her. The man's use of English too suggested he was translating in his head, keeping the structure simple.

A mobile was sounding again, this time from somewhere on Ellroy. On screen, a video call ID was showing. Ellroy seemed to come to a sighing, reluctant decision and answered. The face that came up was of an elderly man in a flat tweed cap with rheumy red eyes. The associated name was "Well" Able. Maggie remembered how the face looked at her grumpily when she turned up at the pavilion having had her car windscreen smashed.

'Mr. Ellroy!' The voice sounded as if the speaker had caught a lot of smoke and just finished choking. The soot stained image of "Well" Able filled the screen for a moment before the mobile tilted round to get a view of blazing building. The whole centre was being hollowed up, flames chasing over the reed roof. 'The cricket pavilion is on fire and we need help here.'

'Walter, what can I possibly do? Would you like me to call the Fire Brigade?'

'Done that, but they say they're too busy. Police won't come. Say they've got too much else on. We need some men, We've got out the hose but don't you have some kind of fire truck thing for that race track of yours?'

'Unfortunately, I have an event on, and safety first and all that.' Ellroy pushed a mute button that showed on the screen. 'What are we up to on the betting for this one?'

Eric did a couple of strokes. 'Twenty three million, three hundred and forty three thousand.'

The mute button came off. 'Yes, I am sorry Mr. Able, no can do.'

'But it will be destroyed.' There were sobs now.

Yes, it probably will.' A drone was now above the cricket green giving them a view of the burning buildings and a growing semi-circle of people. Black smoke was billowing from the centre of the thatch, pushing filthy grey pillows up to the drone as it side slipped to escape the embrace. A small group of men were directing an impossibly thin stream of water at the middle of the pavilion. Others were running backwards and forwards with buckets of water, the futility of which should have been obvious. As they watched a new flower of flame erupted in the centre sending sparks and burning wood flying. The nearest people scattered, the hose dropped to writhe like a spitting snake while a shudder seemed to go through those furthest away. Over the mobile came the sound of a boom.

'Explosions,' said the security man. 'Maybe gas.' He thought for a moment. 'Draught beer', he added.

Ellroy was contemplating. "Well" Able's expression was one of abject misery. 'Don't worry, I'll fund a new one,' the billionaire said eventually. 'Bigger, better. We can incorporate a few new design ideas. Bring it all into the modern age.'

'But that's not the bloody point is it?' 'Well' Able was broken, the tears flowing and his voice coming out as a wail. 'We don't want something new. We want what we have. What we know. There's some things that can't be replaced.'

Impatiently Ellroy cut the call and the caller ID left the screen. 'Let's get back to the race.'

Except on the high drone shot of the track, while cars of colours moved below, there was no sign of the McLaren and Dragon. Over the entire area a blizzard of black flakes was falling.

Chapter 37

The wiper blades were not coping with the smuts from the burning thatch. Thick oily residue smeared over the glass, and Ash strained forward against the criss-crossed safety belting. Visibility dropped by the second, forcing him to reduce speed. It would be the same for Safedeen, he knew, but conditions were becoming even more dangerous. A tight corner, bracketed by a copse, loomed through the full beam of the headlights, but the McLaren was a good metre off the perfect racing line. Cursing he swerved as a bullet exploded the side window by his head.

The McLaren spun. Ash thumped the seat belt release on his chest and struggled with the webbing before pressing himself down and across the seats. Even amongst protests from engine and tyres he heard holes being punched into the metal body. As everything twisted and juddered as the car crashed with force into the trees, Ash gripped the seat anchors. There also were the padded shoulder straps of a rucksack.

Ash slithered out, hugging the bag to his chest and then rolling to put as much space between him and the smoking wreckage as possible. Each time he went over he felt hard objects pressing into his bruises. Stopping to take another breath he heard a muted cough from his right.

'You really want to do this?,' he called and was rewarded by another bullet ricocheting off something by the car. Ash set off rolling again, but was sick and dizzy from spinning and smoke. There was also the smell of petrol. The crash, or the bullets must have ruptured the tank. He had lost any sense of direction. Dimly he saw something white. The smoke was beginning to clear and he made out words. 'The High Performer.' An advertisement. He made for it and launched a bunny leap to get over it, just as another shot smacked into the image of an oil can.

He lay panting, lungs choked from the noxious smoke, fighting the nausea. His body superheated and sweat soaked. Oily soot stung the cuts on his face and arms. His muscles ached from the driving. Peering between a wooden post and the edge of the hoarding he saw a figure slowly getting to his feet from a ditch ahead of the McLaren. The air really was clearing now. It was Khan. His gun hung lazily from his arm as he looked across at the hoarding. He was a hunter who knew exactly where his quarry had gone to ground.

Slowly he started his walk and Ash reached into the rucksack. Safedeen Khan would stand no chance of escaping serious injury at best. With his cricketing skills Ash was capable at hitting a wicket with a cricket ball at this distance, and the American grenades were exactly the same size and as familiar. It was almost unfair, and that thought was quickly suppressed. Khan could have walked. Or continued the race. He had opted for an ambush and was the one with the gun. Inside the rucksack Ash's hand closed, and his heart lurched. It was a familiar shape alright. Leather with raised stitching. A cricket ball. He dropped it and sought another. The same. He tipped the bag. Four polished red balls dropped to the ground.

@@@@@@@@@@@@@@@@@@@@@@@

'They stopped, ' said Eric as he tapped the keyboard. 'on the bend. Where the worst of the smoke is blowing,' he added completely unnecessarily. 'The McLaren is out. It seems to have lost fuel suddenly.' All this from the on board monitoring.

'What's the lap? Ten. Perfect.' Ellroy was delighted. 'As predicted. An event. In Lap ten. Proves the prediction capability amidst a wealth of possibilities. Presumably our two gladiators are at each other's throats, so again it will be right when only one finishes. Eric, set the cars others going. The punters still expect a race after all.'

On screen the super cars leapt forward. 'We can pick up what those two are doing to each other when that smoke clears. Put a drone over there so we don't miss any of the fun.' Ellroy was clicking his fingers again. 'I shall want to say something about all that. Give me a minute to think about how best to set it up.'

Maggie could see he was excited. The way Ellroy was working his lips, he may even be salivating. Perhaps, she thought, he got pleasure from pain, or seeing it inflicted on others. But there was also something else happening. Over at his bank of screens the security man seemed to be concerned with his mobile. While taking in the race he was tip tapping away, or looking down as anxiously as a lover waiting for a message.

Slowly Maggie took a step backward, and then another. Enough to take her more into the darkness at the edge of the room. No one noticed. Another step. Darker still. Sideways now. Stop. Ellroy was thinking up his next oration. Eric's keyboard was being vigorously worked over. The big screen was full of the four super cars fast approaching the smoke bank where Ash and Safedeen had disappeared. Another sliding step to the side and her hand closed over a fire extinguisher. It was the size of a wine bottle. One of several around to handle lithium battery or electrical fires. Gently she pulled it from the plastic bracket. It popped out. Maggie stifled a gulp. There was no going back.

Ping. The security man had received a message. Perhaps the one he was waiting for, because he was giving it a lot of attention. Two more side steps, an arm now flexed with the extinguisher. Whatever was in the message the man's body language told her it must be private. Because he was turning in on himself to take it in, head down and shoulders hunched.

'Smoke's clearing. A bit'

The security man's head came up. Maggie shrank back

'Get the drone in there.'

'Wow. McLaren's had it.' The security man eased back, looking up, his mobile temporarily neglected as he held it upright in his fist.

'Safedeen has a gun!'

'Of course he does,' Ellroy said to Eric as if he were a child. 'And Ash doesn't. Where is he?'

233

'He'll find him.' As the security man spoke Maggie saw the message page morph into a screen saver. It was a flag. Caught full frame in the wind. Red White and Blue horizontal stripes with something gold in the middle. Russian. He was stiffening, suddenly aware something was wrong. A person missing. His head turned to where Maggie should have been. Swivelling now, his body rising. Some sense warning him of danger. Perhaps catching movement in cabinet glass. His arm came up, breaking the full impact of the falling extinguisher. His cry was loud as he fell back onto the console with the force of Maggie's charge.

In a flash the other hand was up and at her throat, while the arm that had taken the blow thumping at her side. Each of these delivered with him grunting and grimacing. He might be injured but she was in trouble. The man was strong and trained. His fingers were like iron, and the eyes that held hers were not troubled by emotion. Just a cold intent as his good hand squeezed. She had seconds, if that. She was blacking out.

'They want her alive!' Not a flicker in the man's eyes, boring into her. If anything the fingers tightened at Ellroy's panicky call.

The extinguisher fell from her grip, the valve striking the floor. It went off, enveloping the two in a silvery cloud and directing a jet of freezing, burning gas at the man's ankles. He yelped, his grasp suddenly looser. It was enough. Maggie snapped her head forward into the bridge of his nose with as much force as she could. The man went backwards as Maggie pulled back, and kicked, landing the full force just below the man's right knee cap.

He yelled again and rolled off the console landing on all fours. Facing away from, readying to spring up. This time she kicked between his legs. Kicked in a way that would have lifted her foot up to her jawline. He screamed, dropping as he doubled up, hand going down. One arm reaching around. There was a gun, tucked into his belt. Under the T shirt.

The extinguisher was spinning on the ground, nearly exhausted. Scooping it up Maggie leapt onto the man and rammed the nozzle into his ear. This time he shrieked. Expanding gas colder than an Arctic storm was directed straight into his ear canal. As he passed out, and collapsed beneath her, she dropped the extinguisher and grabbed his Glock.

Which was just as well as Ellroy was lumbering at her with an office chair clasped in both hands as if he was going to clout her sideways with it. Maggie slipped off the safety, raised it two handed and fired.

The bullet hit the chair, the force knocking Ellroy to the ground. She had fired because she was not sure if she could even speak, and was not bothered where the bullet went. Only with him down could Maggie put a hand to her throat and feel the bruising and take large, painful gulps of air. Behind her the security man was fitting in jerky moves. A final spasm was so extreme it could easily have broken his back. 'Tie him to that,' she rasped, indicating the chair. 'Use his belt and yours.'

She was in shock. Both at the narrowness of her escape and how the violence had come so naturally.

'Why are you doing this? It really is unnecessary.' Ellroy stood slowly and undid his belt as a wet patch spread further down.

'When you said, "they want her alive", who are they?' Her voice was a hoarse, whisper. The action of speaking painful.

Ellroy was standing over the security man and hoisted a plaintive look. 'Why, the British government of course. Your people. No one else. I told you.'

She did not believe him for a minute, and her legs were wobbling.

'I think he's dead by the way.'

Right now Maggie needed the chair. Leaning on it she pushed it over to Eric who was transfixed at his console. Maggie sat down heavily and put the gun in his side. 'Show me what's happening,' she ordered.

He did. The drone showed Safedeen Khan in the middle of a spill over area by the white McLaren, looking toward an advertising hoarding.

'Shift it over left,' said Maggie. She watched the key strokes as he did it. There was Ash lying prone starring at some objects.

'Does this drone kill?' Maggie whispered. She dug the pistol into Eric again. 'Don't lie to me now.'

'No.' A pause. 'Honestly.'

Maggie looked up at the big display. The high rolling punters were looking puzzled, some obviously in conversation and gesturing toward their screens. The four data controlled super cars were storming around the track having lapped their stationary human opponents and were about a quarter of a mile away from doing it all over again.

'Right,' said Maggie. 'Here's what we are going to do.'

Chapter 38

Ash looked at the balls. He was finished. He would die knowing that the guy sent to watch him had pulled a funny having found everything. Well, Ash thought bitterly, I hope he chokes on whatever he buys with the sovereigns.

'Stand up Ash.' The call now from around the McLaren. Slowly he did, still holding one of the balls.

'What's that?'

Ash tossed it in the air and caught it. 'Never without one. And I thought it might remind you of the days when you weren't such a bastard.' He lightly threw the ball again, caught it and stood very still. 'Seriously, Safedeen. You don't have to do this. Norman Ellroy is playing us. Stay with me. We can get Maggie and the UK government will be very grateful. Think about it.'

'In case you haven't noticed, my family were never big on the Raj.'

'It's not about that anymore. Look around. It's about faceless goons like Ellroy. Running the world. And our people, our families, friends, compatriots, whoever they are. Just data fodder. Dictatorship by code. A new colonialism. We can do something here. Right now'.

"Ash". You and me? Against him? We would not stand a chance. If you had any sense, you would have gone with the strength when it was offered. As it is we have had to go through this charade with the cars, while you dream of saving that woman. Such things are from the past, Ash. You are showing what an anachronism you truly are.'

'God, Safedeen, listen to yourself.'

'Don't be so sanctimonious Ash. It's not as if either us have live lives on the moral high ground.'

Safedeen was shifting, He was steadying himself, crouching two handed for a shot it would be difficult to miss. Ash thought about throwing the ball. A desperate thing that would only work in movies. The last thing Ash would see was the look of contempt on Safedeen's face.

'Safedeen!' it was not a plea. It was a warning. Shouted as the background roar of the super cars changed and became a sound that was all wrong. Wrong speed too. Both men spun to the track. The yellow Lamborghini was peeling off the curve and heading into the spill over area, closely followed by the Ferrari. The other two cars were behind, having cut their speed as if they were attack dogs waiting their turn at the kill.

Only one of the men seemed to be the target. As if he realised that, Safedeen shot again at where Ash had been while leaping from the path of the onrushing Lamborghini. He was not fast enough. He was caught in a flesh flaying spray of gravel and dirt as the Lambo spun after him, the Ferrari tail side swiping Khan and pitching him high into the air before coming to rest beside the wrecked McLaren. The other cars were stopped on the bend. Their lights illuminating the devastation and where Safedeen lay on the ground, stunned but with a hand jerkily reaching down to his leg.

Slowly Ash walked toward him, his shoulder throbbing and a thin trickle of blood making it to the hand as he bent painfully down to pick up the gun. With every step the smell of petrol grew stronger. Safedeen's face, twisted in agony was covered in multiple cuts.

'He must have wanted you to win.' He groaned, and sounded puzzled. 'Those things went for me. Not you.' He gave a shuddering breath. 'How very strange. And you tried. To warn me, I mean.'

Ash shrugged, not wanting to get near. Even down Safedeen was a very dangerous man, quite capable of slipping a knife between ribs. Khan seemed to understand. 'Don't worry Ash. I won't be getting up quickly from this one.' He paused briefly. 'And I don't want to die by fire.'

From the wrecked cars they could hear the flickering noise of sparking electrics. 'So here's the deal. Look after me and I shall tell you what he has planned for your Miss Maggie.'

Ash did not reply immediately. A flame was starting somewhere, betrayed by a flickering light. Before the cars became a furnace he needed to resolve a nagging thought about the rucksack. In the light he had seen that the one carrying the balls was not the one he had put into the McLaren. Quickly he strode to the wreck and pulled the driver's door. It would not budge at first. The heat was rising. Pulling it with all his might he felt it give. With a leg up against the side he heaved again, falling back as it gave. Flames were now coming from the engine. Reaching inside he felt under the seats. There was something else there. It was jammed. Jerking it furiously, he managed to get it out. It was the one with the grenades. The other bag must have been from the impromptu cricket game outside the Nag's Head when he and Maggie were taken there at gunpoint.

'So what is he going to do?'

Khan had curled like a child asleep. 'He will give her to the Russians.' Safedeen's speech was now breathy. 'For two reasons. Ellroy always gives governments something, and right now that woman is giving the Russians a massive hard on. For another, many of the security guys men around here are Russians. They will do whatever Moscow ordered and Ellroy might find it easier to go with the flow. If I were you, I'd forget the girl and get home. He'll know where to find you. No doubt he will call in the favour for saving you. If you want a long life,' and suddenly the incongruity of what he was saying gave him another painful grimace. 'Well anyway, he's undefeatable.'

Slowly and painfully, Safedeen Khan rolled onto his back and straightened himself as best he could, placing his folded hands on his chest. The air was thick with smoke. 'Now do your part of the deal.'

He did, and ran. The flames around all four cars were growing, stronger and hotter. The pile of wreckage went up with a whump noise, and a shock wave that knocked him flat in front of a bronze Bugatti. It, and a green Arrinera, were idling throatily but backed off as he stood, swung around and roared off back down the track, their cockpits eerily empty.

I suppose the show must go on, thought Ash as we watched them. He felt beat. The race had taken a toll on his muscles and he ached all over. The shoulder that had taken a nick from the bullet was throbbing and still bleeding. He wracked off another series of coughs from the smoke, doubling up with hands on his knees, eyes streaming. When he looked up he took in the floodlight track, the front of the Hall, looking like a well-lit doll's house, and over the trees an orange glow from the burning pavilion. Somewhere, in this destruction, there must be communications. There was also Maggie Johnson. Safedeen's words stayed with him. The Russians wanted her and, whatever Ellroy promised, she was theirs for the asking. Slowly he straightened up, his eyes on the mansion. Grimly he set off across the track.

Chapter 39

The explosion from the ruptured fuel tanks momentarily parted the smoke, giving the watchers in the control room their first view of the devastation. It was Eric he broke the shocked silence when he squeezed out an awed 'wow'. He had objected when Maggie told him what she wanted, while being acutely aware of the muzzle rammed into his side.

'We can't just override their programming,' he'd argued. 'They're not able to crash. That's the whole point.'

'But they're learning from what the drivers actually do.' Maggie countered as she pressed the gun into his temple. 'So set them to remove any threat to the one they've learned from the most.' It was a gamble but the only thing she could think of to save Ash. She just hoped that his driving and ability to get results from a much more basic car would make him the more valuable data provider for relentlessly learning systems.

Eric had almost smiled. As his fingers flew over the keyboard Maggie realised he was like so many techies. He seemed interested only in how things work, and the possibilities the systems offered, while being oblivious to consequences.

Their few tantalising glimpses on screen were quickly closed down by smoke and smuts. Cameras on the following Bugatti and Polish Arrinera caught how the yellow Lambo did not crash, but set itself in a slide. They also showed an indistinct figure staggering away as an explosion as flames engulfed the scene. It was impossible to see who it was through the smuts and smears.

Ellroy was the first to speak. He was sitting now at the other console, the inert body at his feet. For a man who had recently lost bladder control, he did a very good job of sounding authoritative. 'So young lady, you've had your fun. I will stand by my promise to you but I suggest you get back to your cottage while I clear up this mess. First of all I need to speak to my punters and backers.'

Eric froze over the keyboard, unsure what to do, but with the nod from Maggie he reverted the screen to the faces and opened Ellroy's mike.

'Once again, what may have been unexpected to you, has proven how the predictions were right. An event in the tenth, as expected, with one man standing. We shall see which one would have won based on the data of the two men being utilised by the two cars still on the track. And so the race continues and all bets will be honoured accordingly.'

On screen various people raised their hands, or fists, but they dissolved as Ellroy snatched away his mike and the screen reverted to the track. He took a deep breath. 'As I say, best if you leave us now. And by the way', and he indicated vaguely, the prone figure on the floor. 'Even this I can make go away.'

His voice trailed away. Maggie waved the gun and nodded at Eric to move aside, which he did, shrinking up against one of the system stacks. 'Turn around,' she said, which he did.

Seated at the console Maggie did a few key strokes of her own before getting up and walking slowly toward Ellroy. She stopped at the body. Her throat still ached from his grip. She only had Ellroy's word that he was actually dead, and she was not going to take any chances. 'Get his mobile,' she ordered.

Ellroy did, nervously handing it to her. It was blank. Ramming the gun into the man's body so it would be impossible to miss if he arose from the dead, she pressed his finger against the screen and was rewarded by it lighting up. Maybe there was a pulse there after all, even if the brain was frozen. The message page came up immediately.

Having given them both one last look, Maggie made for the door of the orangery. The first set of hermetic sealed doors opened when she pressed the pad, the second opening as soon as the first closed behind her. She was out, and the warm night wrapped her, the air heavy with the smell of burning thatch and engine fuel. She shrank into the wall of the orangery, grateful for added shadows offered by the wisteria. Ahead of her were clumps of people around cars, some pointing to the village. Through the trees she saw headlights at the main gates. New arrivals. Nobody was near so she brought out the mobile and looked at the messages. They were in Cyrillic, the Russian alphabet. Slowly she deciphered them, working backwards, her lips working with the effort, her conscious brain telling her there were better things she could be doing.

'Why aren't you answering?'

'Tell us the best way in.'

'Close now.'

An outgoing one. 'All calm here. No problem.'

Vehicles were now on the driveway, having passed through the main gate. From their shapes they looked like top of the range, luxury four wheel drives of the type used for shooting parties, royalty and gangsters.

'Latest???????'

A word on the next line of an outgoing stopped her dead. 'The Bitch doesn't get it.'

Above it, a question. 'Does she suspect anything?'

She scrolled up the stream of messages until she came to a picture. It was one of her inside the control room, taken from the security man's console. She deciphered the caption. Roughly translated it was Russian for 'look what the cat brought in'.

The four by fours had stopped, and men were getting out of each. They were cookie cutter copies of the men and women mounting security around the Hall, some of whom greeted the new arrivals in ways that suggested they knew each other. The whole crew were fit, sinewy or muscled, with statement haircuts, some close cropped and a couple with hair pulled back into small pony tails. The backs of the cars opened and weapons came out, the carbines being handled and slung with an easy familiarity.

A hand came over mouth and locked her tight. She jumped, tried to kick back, her heart giving a massive kick of adrenalin.

'Maggie'. A whisper in her ear. It was Ash. Only then did he relax his arm and have a finger over his lips as she turned, her eyes widening at the state of him. His face was filthy, covered in black smears and speckled with blood spots. He pulled her further back into the wisteria.

'Those men,' he said quietly. 'They're here for you.'

@@@@@@@@@@@@@@@@@@@@@@@@@

As soon as Maggie left Norman Ellroy lapsed into a stream of expletives. 'I want her dead,' he managed eventually. 'You see what she did to me?', and he waved his hand vaguely around below his waist.

It was an invitation Eric chose to ignore.

'Lock this place down. And follow her. I want eyes on.'

'Ok, let me just get into the security side.' Eric was tip tapping.

'And put the race back on for the punters.'

The two super cars were nearing the end of the race, going neck and neck. Not that the global audience seemed interested. Many of the faces were obviously doing other things, a few were off camera. In the control room the screen went blank. 'Uh, ho,' said Eric.

'What's that?'

It was clear what it was as there was a caption on the blank screen saying "Control Room Entrance."

'I'll get the history.' Up it came. The entrance and then the camera being knocked sideways, the lens cracking before it jolted sideways went blank.

'She couldn't have done that.'

'No.' Look at the time code. It happened before she came out.'

'So there is someone else out there, and we have no idea whether she went right or left.' Ellroy breathed hard, clicking his fingers. 'We have a hunt,' and the thought seemed to give him pleasure. He indicated his dwindling audience watching the end of the race. 'That will keep the interest of those bastards, and show them what we can do. Launch more drones, including the killers. Find her, or them. We have Ash's DNA don't we?'

'Yes, Safedeen took some hair from his house.'

'Well programme that into the drones, along with his image and vital stats. Shoot on sight. We'll do that when we have everyone back watching. Make it all part of the show. Same for Safedeen.'

Eric raised an eyebrow.

'Don't question me. The only person likely to have messed with that camera is Ash. And if he survived then Safedeen failed, and I have no use for losers. When we get sights on her, I want her for myself when it comes to pushing the button.'

On screen Eric punched up a camera showing the four by fours and the men around them. 'Our guests won't like that,' he said pointedly. 'They're on a promise, as far as she's concerned.'

'Call them,' snarled Ellroy. 'She's mine now.'

At the keyboard Eric shrugged. It was not the time, he felt, to tell Norman Ellroy, his computer was acting strangely.

Chapter 40

Maggie activated the security man's mobile to show Ash the picture of her inside Ellroy's control room. 'The bastard was telling them where I was,' she said.

'Well,' he said, 'At least you put him out. Now send the picture to his social media. And take one of those goons over there. Give the location. Thorswick Hall. Tag it for Russia and security. Also, Laughing Gnome.'

'In Russian or English?'

'English.' Ash was tense. 'And we don't have long.'

'Just as well,' she muttered. 'I've no idea what gnome is in Russian,' She signed off adding an image of a black cat. As soon as she was finished he took out the battery and broke the phone card in half. 'The security services will be across that almost as quickly as them,' said Ash as he nodded toward Hall. 'Now we vanish.'

'Trust me Ash, they have cameras everywhere. I messed with the computer a bit, but that may not hold them for long. They'll soon be abler to set the drones on us. We won't get far.'

The area at the back of the Hall seemed to be filling with more people, the visitors proving to be a popular draw. Six people had got out the cars and there were about a dozen others from the Hall contingent. Groups and individuals were chatting around the super cars and looking up at the lift system that was about to be put into motion to hoist an Aston Martin up into the mansion. On the circuit the race was reaching its climax as the two super cars whipped through the finish, and started to slow. Nobody seemed to be under any time pressure.

'So we go to Plan B.'

'Which is?' Her voice was barely audible. At the Hall everyone suddenly stopped. She could see the screens of multiple mobiles lighting up, and then a rising hubbub with people showing those without a phone to hand. Her message must be on the net. Someone was shouting now, the voice commanding and angry.

Ash grabbed a gnarled trunk and gave it a pull. 'Plan B is that we climb, and hope to God this takes our weight.'

She went first, a leg up from him enabling her to a grab a branch above her head with one hand while the other gripped the wooden trellis behind it. As she moved she heard rustling as Ash began to follow. The trellis supporting the plant was like a giant's ladder with the rungs a half metre apart. Not that it went all the way up. It stopped two thirds up the wall leaving the Wisteria to continue on its way for the last eight feet unsupported. Steadying herself with those branches Maggie pulled herself onto the top of the trellis, the old wood creaking as she did so.

Behind her Ash whispered. 'Problem?'

'No more trellis. Just a plant gripping mortar on dodgy brickwork.' Maggie was sweating heavily, feeling vulnerable. As she climbed her silver metal watch caught the light. At any moment someone could catch a flash and see their exposed and vulnerable bodies hanging on the wall.

'Ok.' Ash resumed his climb. She could hear the trellis protesting while mortar powdered and fell earthwards. He stopped when his head was above her waist, arms gripping the top of the wooden structure. 'Climb up me and get to the parapet.'

She did so, her foot on his shoulder drawing an unexpected grunt of pain. The next obvious step was his head, which got her high enough to get her hands to the parapet. Taking a deep breath she gripped and started to pull herself up, feet scrabbling as she went. Below Ash had to close his eyes from the falling dust and debris. He was not optimistic about making it himself. His shoulder was weak and he was going to have to rely for grip on the plant and places where mortar had gone between the bricks. Slowly, carefully he spread his hands up and got a foot onto the top of the trellis. Gripping a stem he brought up the other.

He had just got his foot there when the old wood of the trellis snapped with a sharp retort. He almost fell. As it was he was hanging for a moment, his wounded shoulder feeling as if it were being wrenched from its socket. A shout came from somewhere around the cars. Shots would be next. Lifting his right knee his foot lodged on a centimetre sized ledge in the brickwork. Up came the left as a shot missed his head, dashing him with brick splinters and ricocheting song into the night with a high pitched song.

His hands were on the ledge now. From its shelter Maggie was shooting. Ash's shoulder delivered another level of pain as he pulled himself up and over like a snake to fall where Maggie crouched, her fist gripping the pistol above her head as she fired blindly toward the Hall. Carbine shots were now beating the brickwork, sending up puff balls of dust and starting to take chunks from their cover. Suddenly from amongst the cars there was the crack of an explosion. The shooting stalled. The sound was followed quickly by a different one. The second was a deeper and came with a fireball that rose into the sky.

Almost as one Ash and Maggie rose to risk a look. In front of the car lift a wreck was burning in a spreading pool of flame, a wheel arch badly mangled and fire spreading toward two other brightly coloured cars. Close by two people were smothering someone on the ground with coats.

'A grenade,' Ash said. He lifted one from his rucksack and twirled it in the eerie light coming from the floodlights and fire. 'From your loft. I pulled the pin on one and put it under a tyre of the Aston while everyone was watching the race. I guess someone moved it.'

'You've got more?'

'Three altogether.'

Their space was lit by light from the glass prism shape above the control room. In a corner hummed a wardrobe sized air conditioning unit, its double beside it. Keeping close to the ground Maggie made her way over to the glass and looked down. Ash joined to see a thin young man furiously working at a keyboard and Norman Ellroy leaning over, the back of his neck inflamed and bulging as he gesticulated.

'I changed one of Eric's password when I was down there,' breathed Maggie. 'He operates on several different levels at once, and I don't know what he was logged into when I got the keyboard. But he's good, and whatever I messed up he will sort it out quickly.'

As if to underline her words, Eric suddenly seemed to give a start of excitement and turned to look at Ellroy with a look of triumph. Ash took in the room. The blinking computers around the room and how the only stain on Ellroy was around his groin and not under his armpits. 'Cold in there was it?' he asked.

She nodded.

'Ok, let's take it out. Keep your head down.' Ash moved away, heading for the air conditioning units. They were both solid things, built to withstand weather with downward facing slatted panels, and dampened bases to limit vibrations. One was humming, and the orange metal handle on the front opened easily. Reaching into the rucksack Ash brought out a grenade, pulled the pin and placed it on the floor at the back of the unit. Swiftly closing the door, he rolled away coming to rest by Maggie as they covered their heads in their hands.

It went off with a crump, blowing out the slats and sending the twisted debris flying, with one piece now shaped like a boomerang thumping against the brickwork beside them. There was a short period of silence and then the second machine started up. Back up, thought Ash. Maggie and Ash uncurled and looked down to see the faces of Norman Ellroy and Eric upturned to the glass. Ellroy's face was suffused with anger, while Eric movement's seem to aimed at being reassuring, his hands temporarily off the keyboard. Around them both were clouds of dust.

'Better get the other one,' said Ash. At least no more shots were being fired. It must have occurred to someone that the woman they wanted should not be harmed. Even so they were trapped and needed to find a way off the roof. Squeezing between the now misshapen air conditioning unit with its puffed out sides and the other, Ash looked down the side of the building and saw a metal ladder fixed into the wall.

'Ash!' Maggie was signalling. Her hand chopped the air toward the wisteria route and then higher back to the Hall. Up above the lift shaft were figures, one with a very long rifle. In seconds that sniper would have anyone on the roof in their sights. Trying to get over the short distance from the air con units to Maggie would be suicide for him.

'Get over here.' Before moving Maggie again chopped a hand toward the rampart before squirming across the floor using her elbows. Out came another grenade. He pulled the pin, holding the safety level down for the few steps to the second unit, watching the people on the roof of the Hall. They were crouching now as a huddle, and he could imagine a sharpshooter squinting down the sights. He pulled at the door of the unit. It was locked. Or stuck. He tried the handle again. No joy. His grip on the live grenade tightened. Maggie was on her knees beside him now, looking back.

'Get cover behind the other one,' he hissed. Picking up the strip of metal blown off the other unit he put it between the slats and yanked it up and down. They flexed into a hole. Not big enough. He must be well within the sights of the sniper now. There was no choice but to stand to get leverage as he used his palm to force a slat upwards. Still not enough. He smacked at it again and then gripped and wrenched down, before pushing the grenade into the hole. It stuck, but the safety arm flicked free with a decisive click. With a backward sweep of his fist he smashed the grenade through, the movement powering a vault for the shelter of the destroyed air con. Rounding the corner he fell over Maggie as the hammer blow of a heavy round hit the housing.

Over the wall a head disfigured by the frog eye lenses of night vision goggles appeared along with a hand clutching a pistol. Another similar figure came over the rampart, the movement made awkward by a bullet proof vest. Sitting astride he heaved up his colleague, their weapons ready.

The grenade exploded.

This time with an unmuffled crack. It had fallen to the front of the unit, the bulk of the motor directing the force across the roof space, catching the two men in a spray of metal shards from the shutters and housing. One fell over the wall immediately. The other swayed, blinded by the blast in his goggles and dashed by fragments. He might have recovered, and was still holding his weapon. Even preparing to fire blind. Deafened and stunned himself by the blast, Ash was down, hands empty. It was Maggie who took the shot. The bullet hit the plate of the body armour, driving the man back. His foot caught the rampant, bowling him over the edge. He fell with a howl, while another shot from the sniper hit the machinery wreckage like a sledgehammer. As if in an echo, another petrol tank went up near the hall, a black fringed fireball rising majestically over the scene.

'Let's go.' Where they were it was only going to be a matter of time before they were picked off or caught. Another bullet tore a hole in the twisted housing. Ash guided Maggie to the ladder, which she slid down with hands and foot on the outside, not troubling the rungs. That was a trick he did not trust himself to do. Adrenalin was dulling pain, but his shoulder was stiff and wrenched, his back felt as it were made up of rubble and the hand he smacked against the grenade was swelling and useless.

'What do we do now?'

Honestly now, Ash really had no idea. But any answer he might have given pre-empted by a sound from the other side. It was the swish of the air tight doors opening.

251

Chapter 41

Carefully Ash and Maggie moved around the sides of the building, reaching the corner as Norman Ellroy stormed out and ran as best he could for a few yards toward his burning mansion.

'You idiots!', he shouted. 'Fools. Mindless lunatics. You are destroying beautiful things.' Looking up to the roof, his widespread arms embraced the tarmac full of cars and people. Including everything, and everybody, on his estate. Still with a throat mike, his words were echoing off loud speakers.

'Stop it I tell you. This must stop.'

He sounded quite mad. The lower floor of the Hall around the lift was burning across several of the glass panels, while a column of flame leapt up the shaft. There was no way out for his collection of super cars, and that, Ash was sure, is what had unhinged Norman Ellroy. What he needed was a good proportion of the region's fire services and, even if they turned up, they would be working amongst bodies, and a Russian hit squad.

'It stops now! Everyone must down their weapons. My drones have been programmed to kill anyone carrying a weapon.'

'My God,' breathed Maggie. 'Look.'

Small objects were rising up from various points around the grounds. Bigger ones with four rotors were flying and staying above, travelling through black smoke to create mesmerising, cylindrical whorls. Ash counted. There were a dozen or so, and then more rose. A score, and with more coming. 'Clever boy that Eric,' mused Maggie.

'We need to save the cars. And if you don't work at it you will die.'

On the roof of the Hall a sparkle of light, like a small firework throwing out a couple of star shells. 'It looks,' proclaimed Ellroy, 'as if someone didn't get the memo. Well too bad for anyone up there who thought it a good idea to defy me.'

A team near the wing of the Hall nearest the control centre were shedding their weapons, looking at each other at first and then dropping them to the ground. Above their heads was one of the bigger drones, a light flashing. From somewhere nearer the cars there was a burst of automatic fire. Like aliens aware that one of their number was being attacked, drones started for the spot, going arrow straight before they heard a crackle of sharp retorts.

Ash leaned against the wall and pulled out the last grenade. He needed time. And chaos. Human confusion to allow their escape. 'Oh shit,' said Maggie. A thrashing noise was climbing in volume ahead of them. Coming round a piece of topiary shaped like a peacock was a drone of a type they both recognised. It was the same as the one in Whistledown's cottage. Quickly Maggie got to her feet and stood in front of Ash. 'Get behind me.'

'You don't...'

'Don't be stupid. You knew up there on the roof the sniper would kill you, but not me. I'm just hoping the same applies for these things.'

Ash did as he was told, getting behind her, his back to the wall and his arm holding the grenade around her neck. Gripping the safety spoon he edged them both around the corner, the drone following them with quick changes of direction, nose down like a great, angry hornet. Maggie moved as if they were in a dance in which her partner was the machine. As it edged sideways she sashayed, a foot brushing up against the other as she glided them both to keep her facing the threat. Ellroy turned as they appeared and took in the two of them.

'I suppose,' he said disparagingly, 'that prehistoric thing is real?'

'The grenade, yes. And if I let go it will do for us all. So call off that drone.'

'Not going to do that.'

'In fact call them all off.'

'You're obviously bluffing. You want her to survive, in fact those are your orders, and like any puppet you can do nothing else but obey. Rather like these drones, you are programmed and there is really nothing I can do.' Ellroy's face was confident, his expression slipping only when Ash threw the pin onto the ground between them.

'It's a lottery isn't it, Norman? At any moment that drone could get a good enough on me to shoot. If that happens this thing goes live. You will hear the spoon click and then, whatever you think I want, whatever argument you have, whatever power you have, will not matter a damn. Because it will go off. And if you are hoping that you might be too far away, think again. You will be caught, and you should think about what these things do. Pieces of jagged, hot metal will bury into you. Perhaps into your brain. Other perforations may be to your arteries or gut. There will also be slashes, almost certainly enough to put your body into shock. You may even bleed out from multiple wounds.'

'I could run, whereas you two would not get far as a four legged partnership. And by the way, the drones have been given your scent.'

'You've killed here Norman. And those left would garrotte you with that throat mike if they got a chance. The drones may be programmed to attack anyone with a gun. But not a grenade. Or bare hands. And they will hover with their all seeing eye as someone cuts that wire through your breathing tube, or kicks out your brains. So put the drones down, and I, or we, will make sure they don't get to you because we don't like them much either.'

From the way the billionaires eyes flicked left and right, Ash knew he was getting through. His hand moved to his throat and the microphone, the slump in his shoulders suggesting resignation if not defeat.

'Can you smell that?' It was Maggie, still moving against him as she matched the drone. On the air was an odour fast becoming a noxious reek. It was a momentary distraction and Ellroy jumped for the door. The hand to the microphone was a bluff, and he was making a bid for sanctuary in the bunker of his control room. There was nothing Ash could do without being nailed by the drone. For a man unused to physical activity Ellroy was moving fast, his face turning to smirk at Ash as he neared the doorway. Which meant he did not see the figure coming out at an even faster speed.

Eric cannoned into Norman Ellroy, sending him back so hard his feet came off the ground and he fell backwards onto the ground with the computer geek landing on top. Eyes open, his mouth working like a goldfish, the billionaire was completely winded. He hands went to his throat, accidently switching on the mike, which broadcasted his gurgles across the estate.

'Fire.' Eric too was struggling with his breath. 'It's over heated.'

That was it. The smell. An electrical fire giving off the smell of fish as plastic coating burned. From within came another sound. A whoosh, clearly audible because the two men struggling for breath on the ground were preventing the doors from closing. In a moment they were all enveloped in an impenetrable cloud of silvery gas from the fire systems. They were all struggling for breath as extinguisher gases robbed them, and the fire, of oxygen

'Run,' gasped Ash. And they did. The drone was lost in the miasma, but he heard a crash as something hit it in the gas cloud. He followed the sound of Maggie, his mouth sealed and the arm still holding the grenade across his nose. Only when they were well clear and on a lawn with open country behind them did they stop to gasp in air. As she bent over Maggie dropped a length of misshapen slat from the air conditioning units.

'I took a wild swing at where I last saw the drone,' she managed between sucks of air. 'Got lucky.'

That was a result, thought Ash dully, but it would not be much of a respite. Other drones were still in the air, and there was now no chance of reprogramming them. Even if computer systems currently being doused and smoked were saved, Eric and Ellroy, might be dead or unconscious.

Fire was making a proper banquet of the Hall, the odd burp coming as a fuel tank erupted. Beyond the gate there was still a glow and thick smoke rising from the cricket pavilion. Thorswick's prized emblems, so redolent of tradition, class and entitlement, were being laid waste.

'Ash. You've still got that live grenade.'

It was true, in a way. His arm ached from gripping if for so long. Holding it up in front of her he released his palm. The pin was still in place.

'You were bluffing!'

'Had to. I wasn't going to be the one that kills you Maggie.' His eyes stayed on her for a bit longer than necessary.

'And the one you threw on the ground?' This was really just to say something, Maggie already knew the answer.

'One of the older ones. And my hand has cramp from holding it so he didn't see the pin.'

She nodded and looked away. 'Looks like help is on the way.' She nodded over to the gates, and just visible through the smoke, milling people and burning cars were blue flashing lights. He looked behind to see more coming on the cross country road. Overhead there were aircraft. And not just the helicopters.

'There's a drone!'

Flying toward them backlit by the flames was a shape. In fact two. 'How many bullets do you have?'

'We can't use the guns, Maggie. Remember? Your best chance now is to step away from me.' For the second time in his life Ash knew he was going to die. At least this time it would be quick and no slipping away in a morass of pain wanting a last sight of his mother's face, sweeping away her sari as she bent to kiss him. Instead there was an infinite sadness. Not least because he now knew he wanted more time to spend with the woman beside him. Now these things with the spinning rotors were going to stop him even putting that into words, and to hold her as he said it.

'Go away,' he said hoarsely, and turned toward the oncoming killers.

'I'll stay.' And he felt her hand take his.

Chapter 42

The adrenalin coursing through Maggie punctured, to be replaced by a soul sucking horror. She would be allowed to live. Of that she was sure. The man beside her however had only seconds left. A single breath away from execution. She ought to say something. To tell him how grateful she was. Grateful? Christ, was that all? What on earth is the last thing a man wants to hear? Her hand reached out. No time left. Their touch created a flash of unbearable, heart breaking intensity.

She counted five machines in the air. There could be more. One was in the lead racing toward them, swooping smoothly down to head height for the last metres. A brief squeeze of her hand. Involuntary, perhaps. Her eyes were wide with the horror, staring into the nose of the robot killer. And it dipped.

The crash was not loud. Thrashing plastic diving into the ankle length grass. Down too were the other drones. Dropping like stones. She had not taken a breath for what felt like an age. Taking one now, but with eyes as wide as the moon, she looked nervously behind. There were no drones, but the sky was suddenly full. Helicopters were landing some way off with people leaping out and running as if in a Vietnam movie. Overhead, noisily, but out of sight, were other aircraft.

Ash was still looking ahead. Three people, their silhouettes black against the flames, were emerging from the wild light of the conflagration and walking steadily toward them. His hand still gripped Maggie's, and he was going to need it to use the last grenade. He was reluctant though, not wanting to let go, his brain stupefied and breaths coming in shallow draughts.

'Ash! It's me!' Adrian Holesworthy knew better than to get close without making clear he was a friendly. Peering at him, Ash made out the features of his boss. He let go of her hand, and put a finger through the ring pull. The two men with Holesworthy were eccentric additions to the party. They were dressed like estate gamekeepers with tweedy caps and waxed jackets but, even in that light, Ash could see their shotguns were pump action and magazine fed. Without a word they divided to take up positions behind and to the side, as Holsworthy came forward his foot crunching onto a downed drone. He looked at it curiously. 'That was a close one,' he managed finally. Before him were two people who looked as if the power of speech was, for the moment, beyond them.

'I suppose we have to thank the Americans,' sighed Holesworthy, waving a hand vaguely up to the aircraft above them. 'They have been working with the Europeans on new drone suppression kit. They were watching ever since they heard Ellroy was organising something. When their monitoring took in what was going on they thought they would try it out. As much as anything, I think personally, to test it against Ellroy Industries' latest gadgets. I'm sure they will eventually share it with us.'

'This was a bit more than a technical exercise as far as we were concerned.'

Holesworthy nodded his head thoughtfully, as if to empathise with Ash's barely masked anger. 'Of course, and Norman Ellroy has suffered some personal humiliation. Although we understand that those watching tonight's events were impressed by what his prediction software accomplished.'

Behind him came the dull boom of another car fuel tank going up. At the Hall jets of water were playing on the front of the building, and the light from the fire caught tableaus of people having guns pointed at them. There was also the occasional sound of a shot.

'It doesn't look much like an advert.'

'On the contrary. Well beforehand his prediction system said you, Ash, would indeed take part in his competition, that you could win if there were an equal competition. Which it was never going to be. It also predicted a violent incident a third of the way into the race. We were running this race through our own systems, and frankly Ellroy's did better. Neither though came up with the disruption the two of you were able to cause with what we thought would be the limited options at your disposal. And no doubt the developers will be making software more reflexive as a result.'

'Norman Ellroy is a criminal. A traitor at least.' This from Maggie, and Ash saw how Holesworthy's mouth twitched slightly at the mention of something as old fashioned as treachery.

'Indeed. And he will pay a cost.'

'How?'

'These gentlemen,' and here Holesworthy indicated the two men dressed in country jackets, 'are from a place very near here where usual rules do not apply. A sort of legal free zone, if you will. All sanctioned by Parliament. So nothing untoward. There he will be encouraged to overcome his own ruthless self-interest and help stop the Chinese taking us down. Unfortunately, at the moment we are losing an undeclared war and the country is becoming ungovernable. Because of his contacts, and the way they use his systems gear and information, we believe he will be able to cut us a deal.'

'Because we've lost.'

'Yes. On every level. But the two of you unbundled Norman Ellroy to a considerable degree. He was untouchable. Wrapped in a protective cocoon. Beyond the reach of the laws everywhere he went. It was like dealing with an avatar. One that simply erased everything we ever had on him. Tonight, you punctured the armour and delivered the naked man. Him being here with several bodies and a wet patch on his trousers means we have something we can work with. We also have his talented sidekick Eric, who no doubt will be a mine of information. It will all help to get us back onto the table with the Americans as they develop their own tools. So very well done.'

Ash was tired, but knew this would his only chance to get answers. 'If I understand this right, our country's one hope rests on an unscrupulous billionaire. What happens if he chooses to call up some friends and use a get out of jail free card?'

'We think he will cooperate. What happens in that place is clever. He will be faced, with the ultimate sanction, which is to be made digitally dead. That involves having your entire life expunged and dumped somewhere ghastly. Believe me there are one time masters of the universe in towns where the only choice is which drug dealer to beg from. In the meantime his programmes and data will have us punching well above our weight at last, with Norman Ellroy dancing to our tune. That's what I mean when I say, all in all, this is a result and the party is delighted.'

'Our Minister Carrick-Rhodes is corrupt. Bought and paid for by Ellroy.'

Holesworthy shrugged. 'Of course he is.' He sounded impatient. 'As for corruption, "special interests" have always been represented in government. The fossil fuel companies owned governments all over the place for decades as they fixed energy policies.'

'And look how well that turned out,' said Ash.

That was not a conversational line Holesworthy seemed keen to progress. 'You both must be very tired and you should get some rest,' he offered. 'There will be no need for statements from either of you on all this. And, as for the RAF Ms. Johnson, they have been told to fuck off and behave themselves as far as you are concerned. There's probably even a promotion.'

'Thanks but I think those days for me are over.'

'A pity. I gather it would be a Squadron Leader position, one suddenly having become vacant. But, a woman of your talents, I'm sure, will find something else to occupy yourself should you choose. And, by the by, you were never here. Nor you for that matter,' he added to Ash.

'Safedeen Khan of Pakistan intelligence and all points around is injured in the woods over there.'

'No he's not. He's gone. Disappeared. He called us as he was grateful you did not take the opportunity to kill one of the more dangerous people on the planet, and even got him away from the flames. He seemed particularly pissed off that Ellroy had one of those drone cars driven at him rather than you. What he told us should make Ellroy very afraid and willing to help us with the Chinese. But if you ever get near him again, I wouldn't rely on any remaining feelings from that individual.'

Maggie heard, but felt no desire to lay claim to what she had done in the control room. A nasty thought meanwhile was forming in Ash's mind. 'Ellroy said I had been programmed,' he started, feeling suddenly foolish. 'It was an odd term to use. And I wonder why I ended up here. Because it seems to me there were a lot of connections, and I was set up like a tethered goat in a tiger trap. And that phrase. Programmed.'

Somewhere in the deeper reaches of the Zapata moustache, something twitched. I could have been anything, but he did not meet Ash's eye. 'I can't think what you are suggesting,' he said eventually. 'Nobody expected you to do all this, but then, it all happened when the mobiles were down. So I suppose....', and he suddenly stopped as if realising that whatever thought must not be said. With a small nod of finality, he took several steps slowly backwards, giving them both a hard stare as if he never expected to see them again before striding away.

Maggie blew out her cheeks. 'Unbelievable'. She was looking at Ash curiously, and not quite as before. 'I would keep away from your work mobile if I were you', she added quietly.

He nodded, trying to make sense of what he had just heard. How Holesworthy spoke. The familiar tone, used when lies are being peddled. 'My reading is that nothing will happen to Ellroy as long as he delivers for our ruling party. And we will never be safe knowing what we do, and having done all this.'

'And those men. The ones in the tweeds. It was a threat wasn't it? And not about Ellroy at all.'

Together they walked slowly back toward the Hall. Gas and smoke were clearing from the entrance to the control room, and from somewhere deep inside came a flickering light. 'I've still got one grenade left,' Ash said reflectively.

'Are you thinking of lobbing it in there to foil their dastardly plans for a digital dictatorship?' Her words might have suggested humour, but she sounded depressed. 'The data is out there. Equally assisting the good and the evil. Working for whoever asks.' The two of them gazed into the control room entrance as if it were the birth channel of a despotic future.

'Ellroy knows how to hate,' said Ash, 'and he'll be after us. At the very least it will be our records wiped and us begging on the pavement.'

'Thanks for suggesting that rather than having me as something else making a living from the street.' Despite herself, Maggie managed a smile. 'He would have gutted me personally in there.'

'We're never going to be safe,' Ash repeated. He looked at her before taking in the scene at the back of the Hall. The fire had the place firmly in its grip, the orange light playing far beyond the gutted structure. Groups of people were being divided up. The Russians were in a seated huddle together under the guns of four soldiers. A kneeling paramedic was amongst them giving treatment to one who was leaning back against the walls of the grand house. Ambulance blankets covered two shapes each with boots protruding.

Ellroy was striding about, with Eric a few steps behind as Adrian Holesworthy joined them. An odd assortment of people were emerging from around the topiary decorated corner of the Hall. Young women and men, barely dressed interspersed with some older men, amongst whom, in a dressing gown, was Minister Vavascour Carrick-Rhodes. As one Ellroy and Holesworthy hurried over, while waving over some kind of police higher up. Without bothering with a handshake Ellroy started haranguing the Minister, gesticulating back to Ash and Maggie and sweeping around to include the hit squad. A man wronged, speaking to an underling.

Intently watching were the Russians. One in particular. Ash sensed the hatred. Saw his shoulders flexing against the binding on wrists as he sat straight legged on the ground. His attention was that of a cobra, a raised hood loaded with poison feeding on the violence as Ellroy smacked a fist repeatedly into his palm. A killer tuned to attack a threat.

Ash breathed as he did at the wicket. What he saw was an arena suspended in a perfect moment of drama. A game poised. Hinged on the last ball. An ensemble of emotion, framed in a hellish firelight, that deserved to be recorded by the brush of Rembrandt. In a moment the composition would disperse, the inherent tension and aggression dissipating into the night. A tipping point lost. And power relationships restored.

Ping. Ash pulled the pin. Leaning back he flung the grenade as far as possible into the darkest part of the night. A place where there was no one to hurt. As one, he and Maggie dived for the ground. It was still in the air as Ellroy turned toward them with a pointed figure of accusation. Ash was counting, the numbers barely audible as they pressed into the grass. Beside him Maggie sucked in a sharp breath. At four the explosion cracked through the night.

Faces swung toward it, but it was the Russians who smashed the frieze. One scissor gripped his legs around the nearest guard, causing the man's arms to windmill as he fell, his weapon flying and coming to his attacker's hand. Another Russian, the one with the stare loaded with hatred, was on his feet, hands free. He barrelled into a soldier, knocking him down, and grabbing his rifle. Another shot sounded and the Russian spun, falling away to the side but now with the weapon. And he was firing, joining his companion who, contorted, was managing to fire even with both hands bound. Up too was the one who was being treated, his helper comatose.

Their spray of bullets caught the group around Norman Ellroy. Billionaire, minister, policeman and security chief were hit. More shooting and the Russians was also now jerking under the impacts, the magazines emptying into the ground, the air, and finally, Eric.

Only when shouting replaced the sound of firing did Ash and Maggie come up to kneeling. Figures were running. Even at that distance it was obvious that Ellroy and the two with him were beyond saving. Holesworthy was on the ground an arm twitching as if he were trying to summon help.

'Blimey,' said Maggie flatly.

'I think its best if we head off home, before anyone starts to wonder about that last bang', said Ash eventually. Striding into the inferno were the two men in tweeds, their shotguns working. 'Particularly as they're now getting rid of witnesses.'

For a long while they walked in silence, taking the long way round to avoid the green and the crowd starring at the embers of the pavilion. 'I needed to know,' said Ash suddenly, and went no further as if he dared not sound his fear. That he been turned into some kind of automaton, set to do things, and the only way to find out if that were true was to do the unexpected.

'Understood.' Maggie took his arm, uncertain about how she felt. They walked a bit longer before she continued. 'You were holding something dangerous that needed to be defused. You did what was needed to prevent harm.'

It could have been words from one of her drone pilot training manuals. But they both knew she was not justifying disposal of a live grenade.

Skirting the far side of the green they avoided the crowd of villagers still milling around the ashes of their clubhouse. 'You know, he wanted to be God', she said. 'Everything back there, was because of the world he created. He thought he would always be in control, and the master. And yet he wanted even more power, while never imagining his creation could eat him as well.'

They turned toward their cottages. Another decision needed. 'Better be your place,' she added. 'I haven't even got a bed made up in mine.'

The Author

Martin Dawes is a former BBC Correspondent who reported on the conflicts in Bosnia and Chechnya before being based in Nairobi to cover East Africa. He then joined UNICEF and worked on humanitarian operations in south Sudan during the civil war. Later he was based in South Asia and West Africa, living in Nepal and Senegal. He is married with two grown children and lives in the South West of England.

'Deadly Inception' is his first work of fiction, having self-published two other books. 'Ebola's Fertile Breeding Ground' about the roots of the 2013 pandemic, and 'Covid-19 and the Aid Business; a Survival Guide.'

Martin_Dawes@twitter.com

Printed in Great Britain
by Amazon